Texas Men

Texas Men

Delilah Devlin

APHRODISIA

KENSINGTON PUBLISHING CORP.

http://www.kensingtonbooks.com

APHRODISIA BOOKS are published by

Kensington Publishing Corp.
850 Third Avenue
New York, NY 10022

Copyright © 2009 by Delilah Devlin

All Kensington Titles, Imprints, and Distributed Lines are available at special quantity discounts for bulk purchases for sales promotions, premiums, fund-raising, and educational or institutional use.

Special book excerpts or customized printings can also be created to fit specific needs. For details, write or phone the office of the Kensington special sales manager: Kensington Publishing Corp., 850 Third Avenue, New York, NY 10022, attn: Special Sales Department, Phone: 1-800-221-2647.

Aphrodisia and the A logo Reg. U.S. Pat & TM Off.

ISBN-13: 978-0-7582-2873-4
ISBN-10: 0-7582-2873-2

First Trade Paperback Printing: March 2009

10 9 8 7 6 5 4 3 2 1

Printed in the United States of America

For Sasha, who is her own "White" knight

Acknowledgments

Special thanks to the ladies who attended the charity bachelor's auction with me in Hot Springs, Arkansas! You know who you are, but I won't "out" you here . . . Cyndi, Shayla, EC!

Thanks to my critique partners and dear friends for putting the polish on this "plum": Shada Royce, Shayla Kersten, and Kaye Chambers

Contents

Bound and Determined

1

When the deejay's speaker set crashed to the floor as the first women to arrive rushed the tables nearest the stage, Tara Toomey scrambled for a replacement and chalked the mishap up to high spirits.

When one of the volunteers carrying a tray of Jell-O shots tripped, and cherry and lime gelatin slid in glistening trails down his face and naked chest, she laughed as eager women offered to lick him clean.

However, it wasn't until one of her staff whispered in her ear that she knew she was in for a long night. The main attraction had yet to arrive.

She crushed her dog-eared copy of the "Hook-Up" program in her fist and headed toward the old-fashioned, double swinging doors, ready to stomp all the way to Redbone Ranch to drag his butt to town.

As she passed excited, tittering women, her smile felt strained, and her nerves stretched taut. The "Annual Honkytonk Hook-Up" had always been a good time, but this year she wished she hadn't been so quick to volunteer her bar again. Sure, it was good for business, and many of the "blow-ins" from Houston, San Antonio, and San Angelo returned throughout the year because they enjoyed the event and Honkytonk's authentic Western ambience.

But Tara wished she could return home, crawl into bed, and pull the covers over her head. The last thing she felt ready to do was watch one particular cowboy strut his stuff across the stage and land in some other woman's clutches—even if it was just one night, completely innocent—*right*—and for a really good cause. The fact he might blow off the auction pissed her off almost as much as the thought of the spectacle he'd cause if he did finally make an entrance.

If anyone thought splintered speaker casings or a little spilled Jell-O were trouble, they hadn't seen a roomful of women erupt in the wake of one seriously sexy cowboy.

The thought soured her stomach. Still, she had a part to play in tonight's festivities. Everyone seemed to think it was her job to make sure that cowboy showed up because she was one of the few true friends he had. And after all, his picture in the auction advertisement had been the big pull.

Too many gussied-up women crowded the entrance to the bar, and the line wrapped twice around the narrow foyer. Not that anyone complained about the wait as bare-chested men wearing tight jeans, cowboy hats, and wicked smiles carried more trays laden with drinks down the long line.

Rather than wade through the cloud of perfume when all her "polite" was gone, Tara swept past the sign-in tables where volunteers busily took the women's cash and handed out programs, shiny Mardi Gras beads, and wooden bidding paddles.

The combined scent of expensive perfumes made Tara's nose twitch, so she pivoted on her heel and stomped toward the side entrance, reminded again about the cause of her agitation.

Perfume was like doe piss to this horned buck—*irresistible bait.* So where the hell was he?

"He's late!" a high-pitched voice squeaked behind her.

Tara didn't even bother trying to pretend she didn't know who "he" was, or that she didn't know he hadn't shown. Any woman with an ounce of estrogen in her veins would feel the tingle the moment the cowboy sauntered into the room.

"Tell me something I don't already know," Tara muttered, pausing at the door to shoot a glance over her shoulder.

Meaghan Garrity, the event's "man wrangler," trotted toward her, her anxious gaze rising over the top of the clipboard she clutched to her chest. Spots of hectic color glazed each pale cheek. Her long red hair escaped the untidy knot at the top of her head in long, curling tendrils. "Didn't you tell him he was second on the program? We can't start until he gets here."

"He'll be here," Tara bit out and then forced a smile. No use getting Meaghan more nervous than she already was. He wouldn't stand them all up, would he?

Even as she said it, her stomach churned. There was only one thing that would keep the cowboy from his adoring fans— an easier fish to land—one he didn't even have to bother moving his adorable tail to find.

Tara wondered what her name was, and the image of a beauty with her head snatched bald flashed through her mind. But she pasted on a smile to reassure her friend, while inside her anger began a slow, hot boil.

Leave it to Cody Westhofen to keep three hundred intoxicated women waitin' on his sweet ass. Does the man think his sex appeal will forgive all sins?

Tara carefully ignored the little voice inside her that screamed an emphatic "Yes!" Instead she murmured, "Think that man would miss a chance at addin' a hundred more numbers to his little black book?" Although she began the statement as a joke, anger scraped a sharper edge toward the end.

Tara caught herself before she began a rant, afraid Meaghan, whom she'd known since kindergarten, would wonder why one slow-as-molasses cowboy could get under her skin. After all, Tara was known for her ready smile and even temper, but especially her cowboy-proof armor.

She shoved her crumpled program into Meaghan's hand. "Um . . . I'll check outside and see what's keepin' him."

"Or who! Better check backseats!" Meaghan whispered loudly. "That man can't take a step without trippin' over a droolin' woman."

With a wry twist of her lips, Tara pushed open the glass door to step out into the parking lot.

Outside, stars twinkled above the spotlight that illuminated the gravel lot overflowing with cars, SUVs, and pickup trucks. More vehicles lined the road leading to the bar for as far as she could see. Luckily the southerly wind that had whipped up the stink from the stockyards earlier had changed course. Although a little humid, the air was sweet and cool.

Muffled music and laughter sounded from the building behind her, but for a moment, a peaceful calm surrounded her. Tara closed her eyes and dragged in a deep breath, sure this would be the last time she'd get a chance to relax tonight.

Gravel crunched behind her, and her eyes shot open. Thick, corded arms encircled her waist, a cowboy hat held in one hand. The crisp scent of spicy cologne tickled her nose. "Hey, darlin', afraid I wouldn't show?"

Even if he hadn't spoken first, she'd have known it was him. That telltale tingle raised goose bumps all over her body. Tara stiffened, and her eyes slid open, but she didn't push the arms away. The snug pressure provided a moment's reassurance, however empty the promise.

She slid her hands over the tops of his and squeezed. "Cuttin' it a little close, aren't ya, cowboy?" she said, hoping she didn't sound as breathless as she felt. "The natives are gettin' restless."

"Been waitin' on you, sweetheart. Thought I'd let you get mad enough to wrestle me inside. You know how much I love to get you riled." Cody's arms withdrew, but before she had a chance to light into him good for being late, his hands gripped her hips and twirled her around.

And although she knew peeking up into his face would spell the end of her self-possession, her gaze rose to lock with his for a long, charged moment.

Even in the shadows, shards of pale electric blue pierced the night. Whoever didn't think there was a God had never looked into Cody's bluer-than-blue eyes. Their gazes had never lingered over the width of his shoulders, the masculine curve of his jaw, the strong jut of his square chin and straight nose.

With a body made for loving and hair so pale and silky it captured light like a halo around his head, a woman could be fooled into thinking he just might be an angel incarnate.

Until they saw the wicked curl of his lips—a smile so seductive, so sensually ripe, it triggered a primal response an octogenarian nun couldn't deny.

Trapped against his naked chest, Tara dug deep for any frayed fragments of pride she still possessed and scowled. "What do you think you're doin'? Anyone could look outside and see us."

"What do you care?"

"I'm not your girlfriend," Tara growled. "And I don't want to be mistaken for one of your good-time squeezes. I'd just as soon keep it on the down low that I've succumbed a time or two to your charms."

Cody's brows drew together, deepening the shadows engulfing his eyes, making his appearance seem a tad sinister.

"Ashamed of me?" he asked softly. "Or are you ashamed you want me?"

Tara shivered—whether from the cooling tension in his voice or her own tightly wound anger, she couldn't have said.

Her last speck of self-respect kept her frowning, denying his overpowering attraction. "No, I'm not ashamed of you, and I'm woman enough not to be ashamed all my parts seem to function just fine when you're around, but I do have a reputation to uphold. If anyone found out I've been sleeping with the biggest womanizer in Texas, it would be ripped to shreds."

"Sure sounds like shame to me."

The easy, sexy slide of his voice told her she'd amused him. Cody always said he knew when she was lying because she talked too much without saying anything at all.

She took another deep breath to calm her racing heart. "I just don't want everyone knowin' my business. And because there isn't really anything for them to know—I mean, it's not like we're a couple, right?—I'd just as soon not ask for trouble."

"What kinda trouble you expectin'?"

Tara rolled her eyes. "You're kidding, right? Trouble follows you everywhere you go! That wasn't you Brandon Tynan took a couple of swings at for gettin' fresh with Lyss? Sarah Michelson didn't almost get arrested for indecent exposure when she cornered you in the bathroom?"

"No man's gonna punch me out for messin' with you. They'd probably pin a medal on my chest for havin' the guts. And I didn't ask Sarah to follow me inside the bathroom."

"No, you didn't, but she did. And she wasn't the first to throw herself at you. Do you think I'd have a business left if half my customers, *the female half*, decided to boycott me?"

Cody snorted. Then his lips stretched again into a smile. "You're not makin' any sense at all. Tonight got you rattled, sugar?" His hands slid up and down her back in an attempt to soothe her.

Her irritation spiked like oil breaching a wellhead. "Cody, we don't have time for you to play with me. Besides, would you want any of those women you're trolling for tonight to think you're already taken? They don't know you like the rest of Honkytonk does. They might think you actually do have a loyal bone in your body."

Cody's lips tightened for a second and then relaxed, slowly sliding into his trademark smirk. "Gimme a kiss for good luck?"

"Do you promise you'll get your butt inside if I do?"

"Lady, don't you know all you have to do is ask? Your pleasure's all mine."

She stifled the sigh sifting between her lips. If only that were true. "Well, I'm askin'."

"For a kiss?"

She wrinkled her nose at him and forced a lighthearted laugh. "You're impossible."

His grin stretched. "And you're beautiful."

His head bent toward hers, and Tara forced herself to turn her head to the side. "This isn't part of our agreement," she whispered.

"It's just a goddamn kiss," he growled.

"Any time you want to change the rules . . ."

His hands tightened on her waist. "Maybe those rules should be up for renegotiation. All I want's a kiss. Not anything I'm not gonna give a dozen women tonight."

"You're wasting time."

"You wanna explain what kept me in the parking lot?"

Tara tightened her lips and turned her head toward him. "Be quick."

"Stubborn woman," he said softly as he bent toward her.

A smile tugged at her lips as he bent over her again. No way was he gonna let a woman have the last word.

All her arguments bled away as he closed in. She pushed aside her concern that anyone might see. She'd waited all night for this kiss. Not that she'd let him know it. And, lordy, he didn't disappoint. Never did.

Never mind his mouth would be kissing dozens of lips before the night ended. For this moment, he was all hers.

His firm mouth captured hers and began a sexy, circling glide that sent an electric jolt of awareness straight through her. Her pulse began a delicious throb, her nipples beaded, and moist little tugs of arousal stirred between her legs.

She gasped against his mouth, and his tongue swept inside to ravish. A low, throaty growl rumbled from his chest into her mouth, and he jerked back his head. "Damn. Do we really have to go inside now?"

"It's that or risk having three hundred women descending upon us midstroke in the parking lot."

He settled his forehead against hers. "I love when you talk dirty. You should do it more often."

"It's a sad fact it doesn't take more than 'hello' for you to get horny. Better get inside. Meaghan's gonna have a coronary. And you forgot your shirt."

"No, I didn't. Just didn't want it disappearing like the rest of my clothes did last year."

"Women takin' souvenirs?"

His grin stretched wide. "Will you fight them off if they manage to get my pants this year?"

Her glance fell to the blue jeans lovingly curved over the bulge at the front of his pants and the leather chaps that encased both his thick, muscled thighs. "Why on Earth would you think I'd care?"

His eyes narrowed, falling to her mouth.

She fought to keep her lips from thinning, or Cody would know she was lying. Another little "tell" she'd never known she gave away—until he'd mentioned it.

His chest expanded around a deep sigh. "You sure know how to sink a dent in a man's ego."

"Someone has to give it a prick every now and then, or you'd be a complete jerk."

"Why do you put up with me if I'm such a pain?"

Tara felt her face and chest warm. "I live in hope of seeing you hog-tied to one woman some day and lovin' it."

His snort jerked back his head. "Better plan on livin' a long, long time, sweetheart."

She lifted an eyebrow. "You had your kiss. . . ."

His hands dropped from her hips. "Guess Meaghan's havin' kittens right about now."

"*Kittens?* I'm havin' goddamn orange tabbies and alley cats!" Meaghan shouted from the side door. "Get your butt inside before they start a riot!"

Cody set his cowboy hat on his head, strolled to the door, and gave Meaghan a once-over that had the happily married lady fanning her face with her clipboard.

Tara stepped past her, tapping Meaghan's chin to close her dropped jaw. "I found him."

"But you lost your lipstick," Meaghan said, her voice syrupy sweet.

"Maybe I wasn't wearin' any."

"Cody Westhofen kissed you in the parking lot!"

Deciding denials would only make her look guiltier, Tara shrugged. "He was only warmin' up. Keep out of his path, or you might be next."

Meaghan's eyelids dipped closed, and she sighed. "I wouldn't survive. One kiss, and I'd forget my own name and never get through tonight."

11

"Well, the last cowboy's in the corral. Let's get to work."

Twenty minutes later, the last of the women had made their way to their tables, shifting chairs closer to the stage. Many abandoned their pizza-sized tables to scoot closer still. The moderator gave the introductions, thanking the sponsors of the event. Then the auction began in earnest.

As she watched from behind the bar where she mixed pitchers of drinks, Tara fidgeted, not sure why she was in such a restless, grumpy mood. The stage was set for a rowdy good time.

Yet she couldn't let go of the blue mood that settled around her as pernicious as the cloud of perfume hovering in the room.

While Cody had made his way through his adoring throng, Tara had had a moment of perfect clarity in the midst of mayhem. A "come to Jesus" moment—if she'd been the religious sort, which she wasn't.

As it was, the raucous noise coming from the crowd of rowdy women crammed inside her bar faded. The Christmas lights that had been hung around the raised dais of the stage ceased to flicker. The scents of sickly sweet margaritas and sour beer, served by the pitcher, of perfume and hair spray, spicy cologne and musty cattle all coalesced for one sharp, unforgiving moment.

In her early forties, Tara sat squarely at the upper end of the age scale of all the women in the room. Older than the majority of the young hunks up for auction.

Hell, she was older than most everyone except Oscar Fuentes, who was tending bar beside her, whose loud guffaws jerked the T-shirt stretched tight around his round belly.

For five years she'd played host to the town's annual "Hook-Up." Five years she'd watched young women flood the little town from all parts of south Texas for the chance at one of the county's unattached cowboys.

For a good cause and the ultimate fantasy, women showed up dressed in their polished, unbroken boots, designer blue jeans that wouldn't hold up to a day's real work in a saddle, and wallets overflowing with greenbacks.

For one night, they forgot the reality of what hooking up with a dusty cowboy really meant. They bought into the image—the mythical man astride a powerful beast who just might be as untamed between the sheets.

So had she.

And look what it had gotten her.

"Ladies, meet Casper Coolidge from Texas Game & Fisheries. Yeah, he's a park ranger. Casper's favorite movie is *The Notebook*, and his idea of the perfect date is a picnic on a blanket under the stars."

Tara rolled her eyes at that bit of fiction from the moderator of the event. *The Notebook*? A picnic on a blanket?

A snort sounded next to her. "That man's perfect date is a gal who can put her own worm on a hook. He's just hopin' to get laid."

Tara shot Oscar an amused glare. "Be nice, now. Maybe Casper's been hidin' his sensitive side all this time."

"All for a good cause. Yeah," he said, the curl of his lips just visible under the thick brush of his handlebar mustache, "I heard you the first time."

As Marvin Gaye's "Sexual Healing" began to play on the loudspeakers, Casper entered from the left, rolling his hips as he made his way up the steps of the stage. Casper didn't have an ounce of rhythm in his bony, long-limbed frame, but that didn't curb this crowd's enthusiasm one iota. Whistles, catcalls, and the heavy stomp of booted heels accompanied each bump and grind he attempted as he rotated his skinny hips.

"Boy's gonna hurt himself."

Tara shook her head. "Only thing's gonna take a poundin' is some woman's bank account, and most of 'em are too fired up to care whether or not he can dance a lick."

Which was true. With the raising of half a dozen ping-pong paddles, the bidding started briskly at a hundred dollars.

Tara sighed and wiped the counter with her bar towel, reminding herself that she'd agreed to host this all in the name of new playground equipment and a good time.

"Oh, hell, now what's that knucklehead doin'?"

Tara's gaze whipped back to the stage to watch as Casper slowly stripped off his chambray shirt to reveal a chest so milky white the stage lighting made him appear as pale as his namesake.

"Boy's gonna blind us all." Oscar's mouth twisted in a grimace. "How does a man who works all day in the sun manage to look like that?"

Casper twirled his shirt in the air and released it into the crowd.

Smiling, Tara leaned a hip against the counter. "Why don't you relax, *mijo*? The women came to see a little cowboy beefcake. Casper's just makin' sure the rest of the guys have to up the ante, too."

"You put 'im up to that?"

Tara placed her hands on her hips and arched one eyebrow. "Now, I'm not gonna say yay or nay."

"Damnit, Tara," Oscar said, his voice grinding in disgust. "If it's not bad enough we get overrun every weekend by desk jockeys in cowboy gear, now you've got our own boys makin' asses out of themselves."

"*All for a good cause*," she repeated, slinging her arm around his well-padded shoulders. "And don't think our boys aren't enjoyin' every minute of the attention."

"We have four hundred dollars from the lady in red," the auctioneer said. "Do we have four fifty?"

Oscar's mouth dropped open. "Four hundred for Casper? Don't they know that boy's so bashful he's never been out with a girl who wasn't his sister?"

Tara didn't even try to hold back her laughter. It rolled out of her, turning a few heads. "Say it a little louder and watch what happens," she murmured.

Tara enjoyed the banter but kept only part of her attention on what new chestnut Oscar would drop. Laughter right about now was a welcome relief. Her body was tense, her stomach knotting. A plan began to form in her mind, gathering strength like circling clouds on a hot summer's day.

What she planned to do tonight was either the dumbest thing she'd ever done or the most inspired.

"Sold! To number two thirteen."

Tara tossed her towel on the bar and lifted the bar ledge to step through it.

"Now, where do you think you're goin'?" Oscar asked, raising one brow, suspicion darkening his black eyes.

With a defiant tilt of her chin, she said, "To get my paddle."

"Wait a second! You plannin' on buyin' yerself a date?"

"Cody's comin' up next. Someone has to keep him from startin' a riot."

"*Cody?*" Oscar's snort ruffled the bristles lying like a caterpillar atop his lip. "I think that boy could manage this crowd all by himself. Just let 'em take numbers."

Tara didn't bother acknowledging his statement. It was a well-known fact in these parts that Cody had a way with women. Young and old. One look from his sleepy blue eyes made wet puddles of them all.

But handsome is as handsome does, and Cody Westhofen

was nothing more than a man whore when it came to women. With a crook of one long, calloused finger, he could have almost any unattached woman he wanted, and he'd made it all too clear he'd never be satisfied with just one.

Damn, if she hadn't fallen like all the rest. Since the day he'd brushed up next to her and settled his startling blue gaze on her, she'd been his willing doormat—his go-to girl when he was between lovers.

Maybe he thought her safe because she'd been down that track a time or two. Surely she'd have no expectations that he'd stick around long enough to leave behind a toothbrush, let alone his heart.

So, over the months of their arrangement, he'd become complacent, taking for granted the fact she'd always leave the door open when he came to call.

Only, she hadn't been exactly truthful with him about their open-ended relationship when she'd smiled as he swept other girls into his arms and led them toward the dance floor and eventually his bed. Her expression might have said she didn't care, but inside she'd harbored a hurt and disappointment that no amount of stern self-admonishment could relieve.

She'd gone and fallen in love with the bastard.

Tonight she'd get him out of her system once and for all. Give him a time he'd never forget. Burn the experience into her soul because she knew no matter who might replace him in her bed, she'd never get over him.

So even if she did have to lay down some serious cash, it was all for a damn good cause.

2

Cody Westhofen sucked on a cold beer while he waited in the lounge beside the main bar along with the rest of the night's "offerings."

He sat alone. Not that he minded. Not that the fact even registered for more than a second. Men tended to want to fight him, not befriend him.

Fact was, he liked his own company—unless one of the fairer sex was in the vicinity. Sparking on women was a hormonal imperative, and what caused most of the disagreements with competing bucks—something Cody understood on an elemental level far better than any of his competition.

Since he'd reached puberty, he'd understood he had a gift. It was more than his handsome face—he'd also been blessed with a natural sexual appeal he wasn't in the least ashamed to use to his advantage.

Women understood it. Some even drew on it for more than just their own pleasure. Tonight's gratuitous display was one such example.

Cody didn't mind that Meaghan and her crew were pimping

him out. The auction was always good fun. And for the money one woman would plunk down for the pleasure of his company, he'd do his best to please her.

Cody never left a woman wanting. He took pride in that fact. And usually pride, and the promise of a sexy ride between the sheets, was enough to still the restlessness inside him.

However, tonight he felt off his game.

One look into Tara's blue eyes while he'd made his way through the crowd to the lounge, and his pleasure in the event had spoiled like tomatoes left too long on the vine.

So he'd had a little fun. He'd stopped to twirl a woman under his arm and bend her over for a kiss. Then he'd had to kiss her friend so she wouldn't be jealous. Ten kisses later, and he'd finally been able to slide into the room where the rest of the bachelors waited their turn on the stage.

All those kisses were in good fun. The crowd had hooted, the women around him had eagerly pressed closer—but then he'd caught Tara's stare.

The woman had a way of looking right through him, seeing straight inside him, that scared the shit out of him while completely arousing him.

Her ready smile hadn't slipped, but he'd seen the way one brow had lifted in derision, and suddenly the fun had been sucked right out of the night.

Somehow he'd disappointed her. Which shouldn't have mattered. He'd had prettier. Younger. More *athletic* lovers.

But with Tara, he could be himself. Didn't have to make promises he knew he couldn't keep. She was old enough, secure enough that she didn't need sweet, romantic lies to dress up what they had.

They'd bandy words back and forth in public that would flay the skin off more sensitive people. Alone, they abandoned conversation for an honest, naked, no-holds-barred fucking.

No one had ever made him feel more like a man or a naughty boy all at the same time.

At the beginning of their relationship, he'd been content knowing her door would always be open. He even admitted he'd become complacent. She was his best friend, a confidant who always told him the truth even when it hurt, a sister when he needed advice about where to point his dick, the only person he could be completely natural with—no games, no lies.

But lately he'd sensed a change in her.

Or maybe something had changed inside him.

Tonight he'd seen the militant lift of her chin as she'd stared him down, a challenge that left him feeling naked and exposed for the whore he really was.

Which left him feeling off his game and growing quietly angrier by the minute.

Tara knew what tonight was all about. Sure, most of the women here only expected a good time with their girlfriends while they laughed and hollered at men they didn't know, tossing away money on drinks and trinkets—all for a good cause. They didn't care that most of the men on display weren't perfect, but they appreciated a real man over an unapproachable Chippendale poser.

A few might get lucky. The woman who bought his company knew she was the most likely to score. The ones who were regulars of the event knew that and came prepared to pay big bucks for the "privilege."

Cody didn't mind obliging, because giving a woman a great time was as close to a real relationship as he'd ever allow himself to have.

Until Tara.

Still, for all their honesty about their mutual needs, he'd held back the part of himself he could never share with another human being. The part that painted him ugly, the core of him that kept him a loner who sought companionship only when his needs grew too strong for a little one-fisted rub to assuage.

She'd gotten under his skin. Made him wish for things he could never have. The closer he'd been drawn, the harder he pushed back, acting like a horned toad on Viagra whenever she was watching.

Tonight he'd answer the challenge in her eyes with a reminder of what he really was. He'd give the lucky winner a ride she'd never forget and then make sure Tara knew all about it. Just to put their tenuous relationship back on track.

The empty chair beside him scraped as it was jerked back, pulling Cody from his thoughts.

Joe Chavez slid into the seat. Joe's buddy, Logan Ross, took the empty seat opposite them both.

Cody narrowed his eyes, wondering whether he had any outstanding tickets because he sure hadn't a clue why two deputies would be ponying up to his table. "Tables all filled up?" he muttered and then took another sip of his beer.

Both wore their deputy's tan uniform shirts, black pants, and cream-colored cowboy hats, but they'd left behind their holsters. Both were dark haired, dark eyed, and deeply tanned, Joe's skin having a slightly darker cast due to his Mexican blood.

Cody had to admit the ladies were going to go wild with these two. Good thing he was coming up next. Still didn't explain what they were doing at his table.

Logan's lips pressed together as though he was trying not to laugh.

Joe gave Logan a withering glare and then eased his expression as he turned back to Cody. "We've got a question for you."

"*He* has a question for you," Logan said, sitting back with his arms crossed over her chest. "I'm just riding shotgun."

Cody narrowed his eyes further. "What do you wanna know?"

Joe cleared his throat. "Sarah Michelson. You got anything goin' on with her?"

"Sarah?" Cody's lips twitched. That was twice tonight that "Sweet" Sarah's name had come up. "No. Why do you ask?"

"Just wondering. She did follow you into the men's room."

"Sarah was a little toasted and lost her way," he drawled, noting the way Joe's shoulders tensed and wondering if he was about to be asked to step outside.

"I heard Oscar had to chase you both out of the same stall."

Cody shrugged. "Okay, you've got me. I didn't ask her to leave when she followed me inside. Gonna arrest me for something?"

"Just wanted to know if she was taken," Joe said, his voice deepening, tightening.

Oh, she'd been taken, all right, but probably not in the context Joe was trying to clarify.

Cody leaned back in his seat, relaxing his posture and hoping the other man would lighten up as well. Tonight wasn't the night to start something. "You thinkin' about askin' her out? She's not too keen on cops."

"Heard that. I haven't been around these parts long, so I thought I'd ask you why."

Was he really here just to get a little information about a girl? "You know her daddy's the judge, right?"

"Yeah, heard that, too."

"Well, the judge is pretty evenhanded. No special privileges, even for his own blood. Sarah gets a little wild now and then, but she doesn't like her daddy knowin' everything she does. She can get a little huffy when she's threatened with being hauled into his court."

"She follow many men into the bathroom?"

"Can't say as I've ever heard her pull that one before." Cody canted his head to the side. "Is that all you wanted to know?"

Joe shrugged. "What are you doing in the morning?"

Cody's eyebrows shot up. "Why, you askin' me out?"

Logan snorted and barely hid a smile behind the beer he lifted to his mouth.

"No," Joe said, aiming another killing glare at his friend, "but we figure you've been around here a while. We just hired into the department. Figured because you know your way around these parts, you might take us hunting."

Cody narrowed his eyes on the deputies, wondering what they were up to. As long as he'd hung his hat in these parts, he'd never had a single male friend. Never been hunting with anyone other than fellow ranch hands when work was done for the day, never even been asked to grab a beer.

Still, their expressions didn't seem to harbor any kind of trap. "Sounds fine."

"We'll meet up here in the morning."

Cody nodded.

Logan lowered his beer to the table. "So, why'd they put you second on the program? You seem kinda popular. Shouldn't you have been the last one up?"

Cody gave them a wide smile. "Meaghan wanted to make sure the ladies didn't hold on to their money all night waitin' for me."

Logan snorted. "Think a lot of yourself, don't you?"

With the arch of one eyebrow and a slow, stretching grin, Cody said, "This is my fifth year. Some of the women are regulars. They come every year to bid on me."

Logan snorted. "Must be some date they win."

"I always aim to please," he drawled.

"You're up, Cody!" Meaghan shouted out.

"Gentlemen." He set his beer down and straightened, forcing a smirk on his lips as he headed toward the door.

Meaghan handed him a bottle of baby oil as he approached

her. "Might want to use a little of this before you go out there, or you won't make it to the stage. The women'll slide right off."

He leaned close to Meaghan, noted the sharp intake of breath with satisfaction, and whispered, "Now, darlin', what would be the point of that?"

Cody reached the door just as the strains to "Wild Thing" blasted from the speakers. He shook his head, a wry grin tugging at his lips.

"Ladies, get your money ready! Up next is that cowboy you all know and love, *Cody Westhofen . . .*"

The rest of the introduction was lost in the surging roar.

Feeling a little like a rock star in a very tiny venue, Cody pushed through the door and into the crowd.

The women were on their feet, chanting, "Cod-ee! Cod-ee!" He snuck a hand around the neck of the woman nearest him and bent to press a quick kiss to her smiling lips; then he lifted his cowboy hat high in the air to prevent it being snatched and strode through the bodies, pressing ever closer.

Walking through so many grasping women wasn't any stroll in the park as hands reached out to stroke, pinch, and fondle him. By the time he'd reached the steps to the stage, he regretted turning down Meaghan's slippery oil.

His smile firmly in place, he strode to the center of the stage to stand under the hot spotlight. He didn't give them any sexy bump 'n' grind, didn't court their bidding with any "come 'n' get me" flutters of his fingers.

Cody already had them in the palm of his hand. Any encouragement would be overkill. Instead he tucked his thumbs into his pockets and slowly scanned the crowd.

Tara ground her teeth, watching Cody standing in the center of the stage, not moving a muscle, confidence oozing from every pore.

As the bidding rose, fast and furious, his smile crimped into a smirk that only encouraged them further.

His self-assurance rankled. Did he think he was God's gift to women?

By the excited squeals and whistles piercing the air, she thought maybe he had a right to his high opinion of himself. His upper body gleamed with a light sheen of sweat, the stage lights emphasizing the swell of powerful muscles and deepening the shadows beneath them. His broad chest and ripped abs drew every feminine eye. The sharp edge of his square jaw flexed, and she felt a sigh blow between her own lips as her gaze snagged on the wry, sexy curve of his mouth.

Without moving any of his amazing muscles, the man was inciting a crest of orgiastic bliss among the women eager to win him.

Did she really want to pluck him out of their grasp? What did she really hope to gain? It wasn't like he wouldn't show up on her door a few days from now with a lopsided smile and a teasing glint in his eyes.

With the handle of her bidding paddle stuffed into her back pocket, she had second and third thoughts about what she intended to do, not wanting to become a part of the spectacle surrounding the furious bidding war erupting around the room.

"Oh. My. God!" came an excited whisper beside her. "Do you think they'd let us pool our money to buy him?"

Tara sent a glare to the women beside her. *Shit.* Maybe she didn't even have a hope in hell of outbidding this determined crowd.

She began to back her way out of the room when Cody's roaming glance landed on her.

His gaze held hers, challenge ripening in his narrowed eyes. Then he puckered his lips and blew her a kiss before letting his glance slide away to find another mark.

In an instant, Tara knew spontaneous combustion wasn't any urban legend. Like a noxious solar flare, heat exploded in her face, seeping down her neck to her chest. She sucked in a deep, furious gasp and reached for the paddle in her pocket, whipping it high into the air.

"We have five thousand from the lady who owns this bar! Do we have fifty-five hundred?"

Several paddles darted into the air, but Tara didn't care, she kept hers held high, never letting it dip as bidding continued. She no longer heard the amounts, ignored the stinging glares pointing her way, and lifted her chin in defiance when Cody's gaze slammed into hers.

In the end, no one stood a chance against her fury.

"Sold! To Tara Toomey!"

Tara blinked as the noise from the crowd died down around her. Curious gazes slid from her to Cody.

"Well, what are you waitin' for?" the moderator drawled. "Come claim your cowboy!"

Tara's eyes widened, sliding to Oscar, who shook his head in disgust. Then she caught Meaghan's openmouthed dismay. What the hell had she just done? She'd spent a small fortune on a man who didn't give a damn about her. Worse, she'd exposed her lust for him to people who respected her.

"Seems Tara's in shock," the moderator said, chuckling. "Cody, you better go get your woman."

Cody lifted his hat off his head and bowed to the crowd as soft laughter began to filter through the crowd. He stepped down the wooden stage steps and strode toward her, his expression set.

When he stood in front of her, he lifted her chin with his crooked finger and planted a kiss on her lips that left her even more stunned and embarrassed when she didn't demur.

Slowly she shook herself free of his spell and stepped back.

"Darlin'," he whispered, "what are you doin'?"

Tara licked her lips and locked her gaze with his, unable to give him an answer because she didn't have a clue.

His palm cupped her cheek, and he bent so close the rim of his cowboy hat slid across the top of her head. "Well, pretty lady, looks like I've got my work cut out to give you your money's worth."

3

Cody followed in the wake of "Hurricane Tara" while she finalized her purchase, still shaking his head over the fact the woman had plunked down seven thousand dollars for a date with him.

Oscar brought her purse from behind the bar, his glance sliding warily between them.

Cody's chin came up, daring the older man to say a word.

Oscar's stiffening posture and black scowl blared a silent warning that Cody better not mess with his boss.

As if he'd ever do a thing to hurt her. Then again, tonight was shaping up a whole lot different than he'd envisioned when he'd showered off trail dirt before hustling to town.

Never in a hundred years would he have guessed what Tara would do. He still didn't have a clue what was running through the stubborn woman's mind right now. With short, savage strokes of her pen, she filled out her check, crossing a *t* with a sharp stab.

Even the ladies with the perpetual smiles manning the payment table looked on wide-eyed as the Tara thrust her check at them. No doubt, tongues would be wagging tonight.

Cody couldn't believe she'd outted their relationship in such a public way. Tara was a private woman. She might be everyone's best friend, the life of any party, but her private life had always been just that—*intensely private.*

Why she'd gone and done something as crazy as this was beyond his comprehension. He didn't think she'd bid on him for the sake of a good cause, because some other woman would have happily snatched him right up. He wasn't even sure she'd done it for the promise of pleasure—because she sure didn't look happy at the moment.

"Don't worry about a thing, Tara," Oscar said, eyeing Cody with displeasure. "I've got everything handled here."

Tara slipped the strap of her purse over one shoulder, nodded at Oscar, and finally turned to face Cody. "We better go."

"Not staying for the bachelor dinner?" Meaghan chirped, her eyebrows raised high.

Oscar gave a short shake of his head, and Meaghan pressed her lips into a thin-lipped line.

Cody touched Tara's elbow to escort her from the bar, but she rushed ahead of him, leaving him to stroll nonchalantly out while a dozen disapproving stares caused a slow burn of anger to creep down the back of his neck.

Outside he caught up with her as she opened her vehicle door. "Want me to follow you?" he asked, knowing everyone would note how late his pickup remained parked in front of the Honkytonk.

She shook her head. "Just get in."

Once inside her silver SUV, the tension grew thick enough to cut with a butter knife. Sensing she wasn't in the mood for conversation, he settled against the soft leather and stretched an arm out along the back of the bench seat, turning to study her.

Dressed in a "Honkytonk Hook-Up" T-shirt and bottom-hugging blue jeans, Tara's mature figure was still trim and lithe, her breasts ripe and stretching the thin cotton. In profile, her features were striking. Not truly beautiful, definitely not cute, but strong and feminine. Her chin was a little too square, her nose a tad short and blunt, but—balanced by her big blue eyes—pleasing to a man.

Any other man would consider himself lucky to call her his. He wondered why she'd never married. Why she'd taken up with him. Maybe she prized her independence, which made sense. She had a good life. Great friends. Several honorary "nieces" and "nephews." Maybe she'd never felt the need to change a thing. Maybe she had her own ghosts that held her back from ever wanting to share her life or expose her inner self completely to another.

Maybe they had more in common than he'd ever know.

While his fingers plucked at wavy locks of blond hair, he tried to think of ways to break the silence. Clever, sexy asides that might put a smile back on her face.

However, the frown furrowing her brows was off-putting, to say the least, so he sat silently beside her until minutes later she pulled into the drive of her one-story, white limestone ranch house.

Tara flung open her door and slid down onto the gravel drive, never once looking back to see if he followed her inside the house.

Pursing his lips, he blew a long, silent whistle, wondering what the hell had happened to get her so worked up.

Inside, warm yellow walls, Mexican art and pottery, deep leather couches, red Saltillo tiles—all blended into a warm welcome.

Tara dumped her purse onto a dark oak end table and turned

her back to him, her hands settling on her hips. She inhaled deeply and then glanced over her shoulder.

Her expression arrested him. The frown bisecting her brows was still deep, but something a little wild and desperate shimmered in her eyes.

The desperate part he could certainly understand. His own body had been primed from the moment she'd raised her paddle high in the air. Something about her willingness to claim him publicly had sent a wave of heat zinging straight below his belt buckle.

Knowing he'd only court an argument if he tried to find out what burr had worked its way beneath her saddle, he strode straight for her, halting inches from the toes of her boots.

Her glance fell to his naked chest, and she sucked one corner of her bottom lip between her teeth. Her chest rose sharply, pressing her full breasts outward.

That was all the invitation he needed. He lifted his hands and cupped her soft mounds through the tee, squeezing gently, and then bent to aim a kiss at her lips.

But she turned her face away and tilted it down.

He held himself still, confused by her mixed signals. With her nipples stiffening beneath his palms, he stifled the urge to press again, waiting for her to make up her mind about what she wanted of him. "What gives?"

Her face came up to his, her gaze skimming his features and then tangling with his gaze. She shrugged, her mouth settling into a straight line. "Why are you still dressed?"

Cody tilted his head, trying to read her expression but coming up with nothing. Her gaze was steady. Her features set. So she didn't want to talk about what was eating her. Why should he care? At least she was ready to get down to what they did best together.

He stepped back and bent to yank off his boots, unhitched his chaps, and drew them off his legs. Then he unbuckled his belt, unbuttoned his blue jeans, and lowered them.

She hadn't moved, but her gaze raked his body, pausing on his thickening cock before sweeping upward. A swallow worked the muscles of her throat, but she didn't betray what she thought in her face. Instead she turned on her heels and walked straight down the hallway leading off the living room to her bedroom.

Cody bit back a curse, feeling foolish, but scooped his clothing off the floor and walked barefoot behind her. He was starting to get a little annoyed with her mood. Maybe she was suffering "buyer's remorse" now that she'd had time to think about how much money she'd parted with. Although why she'd be angry with him, he didn't know. No one had twisted her arm to bid on him.

Tara flipped the light switch inside her bedroom. Cody dumped his clothes on top of the chest at the foot of her bed and began to pull down the covers, preparing to slip inside the cool sheets and wait for her.

With a fistful of white cotton in his hand, he paused as she picked up his blue jeans from the jumble of his clothing and began searching his pockets.

"What are you doing?"

Her gaze locked with his as her hand came out of one back pocket with a business card pinched between two fingers. "Camille says call her anytime."

"I don't know Camille. She must have slipped it in when I was makin' my way to the stage."

She dropped the card on the floor and shoved her hand into one of his front pockets, drawing out three more cards. "I suppose you didn't know they were slipping their hands into your front pockets either?"

Cody narrowed his eyes. "Kinda hard to miss when they

were slidin' up close to my dick," he said, keeping his voice even.

"Yeah, impossible, I'd say. Did you like it?"

"Guess so, since I didn't stop them. Seemed like it'd be a little rude."

Her snort was accompanied by a derisive curl of her lips.

Cody raked a hand through his hair. "Why are you acting this way? It never bothered you before, the way women come on to me."

"I expect them to. What disappoints me is that you accept it."

His stomach tightened. He felt exposed in a way that didn't have a thing to do with the fact he stood entirely naked before her. "Do you want me to leave?"

Tara's dark blue eyes glittered, and her chin raised a nudge higher. "I want you to give me what you would have given to any other woman who won you tonight."

"If you'd wanted exactly the same treatment, we'd have gone on to Steers 'n' Steaks for the dinner first."

She shook her head. "Where you and your date would have disappeared somewhere between the appetizer and the meal, I know. Thought I'd save you some moves, cowboy."

Cody sucked in a slow, deep breath. He'd rarely made it through the after-auction dinner before his date was primed but didn't like the fact she knew it. "Are you mad because I expected to end up in the winner's bed?"

"No, Cody," she said, her features tightening, "I'm disappointed you're willing to be with any woman who pays."

"Tara . . ." Cody was at a loss as to what to say, and a tremor of dread worked its way through him. Tara had never judged him before. At least, never out loud. They'd had an understanding, a convenient arrangement. Something they'd never talked about but had eased into over the past few months.

In public, they remained casual friends, sniping occasionally because they enjoyed the friction it built. In private, they rarely made it to the bed before their bodies were sweetly fused.

The thought that their relationship might be faltering chilled him to the bone. His whole body tensed, but then he forced himself to relax, holding still until his racing heart calmed. She was angry now. She'd been pissed at him before and gotten over it.

When he'd flirted with Lyssa McDonough on the dance floor of the Honkytonk, which had precipitated a fist fight with her beau, Brandon Tynan, it had taken a while for him to work his way back into Tara's good graces. The best way he knew to soothe a woman's ruffled feathers called for a little sensual finesse. Something he possessed in bucket loads. He still had a chance to make it right between them.

Only, he felt awkward, unbalanced. With any other woman, he'd have her backed up to the bed and have figured out what would please her by the way she sighed or moaned as he felt his way around her body.

He knew Tara's preferences and would happily accommodate them, but he'd never made love to her the way he had other women. Never taken his time.

With Tara he let himself go. Sought his own pleasure while providing hers with equal enthusiasm. With another woman, he'd seek her praise, want to be the best she'd ever had. He'd *perform*.

What brought him back to Tara time and time again was how natural they were together. If he did as she asked, he might lose what he prized most. She'd become just another conquest.

Not his only lover.

"What would you do first once you got her inside a motel room?" she asked, her chin lifting higher.

Was she really asking him to make love to her like she was a stranger? Usually so good at reading women, he faltered, wondering if he wasn't walking into some kind of feminine trap.

Feeling a little ashamed because he really did have a routine he followed with women, he couldn't quite meet her gaze.

He tightened his jaw and then shrugged like he didn't care that she asked such an intimate thing. "I'd soften the lighting. Most women prefer some shadows to hide their flaws." Having said it, he lifted his own chin to pin her with a glare, daring her to make him continue.

She nodded her head toward the bedside lamp.

Cody swore under his breath, taking her slight action as a command, and turned on the small lamp beside the bed and then shut off the overhead lamp.

Bathed in the golden glow of the shaded lamp, Tara's blunt features were softened. The fine wrinkles that bracketed her mouth and fanned from the corners of her large eyes faded. Her golden hair took on the hue of warm honey.

Naked, her body would be a blend of shadow and light, agelessly beautiful. If he could manage to get her out of her clothes without a fight.

Approaching her warily, he cleared his throat. "Most times, I strip a woman first. But seeing as how I got a little ahead of myself . . ." He reached for the bottom edge of her T-shirt, hesitating for a second, hoping for a clue that she didn't really want to play this game. What he did with other women wasn't something he wanted to color their relationship.

However, Tara merely lifted her arms. Her gaze locked with his as she let him peel the shirt over her head. When her head was clear, she shook out her curls. "Is this how you act with them? 'Cause I'm wondering how you manage to get their pants off, you're so slow."

As heat seared his cheeks, Cody bit his tongue to keep from snapping back. He tossed her shirt into a corner and slid his hands around her rib cage to bring her closer; then he jammed his hips against hers so she could feel his hardening desire for her.

Her gasp opened her lips, and he swept down, covering her mouth with his and thrusting his tongue inside—one sure way to get her to shut up.

Her tongue slid deep into his mouth, and he sucked on it before opening his mouth wider and drawing on her lips, opening and closing as he ate her mouth. Their kisses had always been passionate, but they'd also been playful, sometimes sweet. Over quickly because they never had the patience to linger.

This time he unleashed a bitter heat that had him rolling his hips to grind hard against her, his hand rising to pull her hair and angle her head so he could deepen the pressure of the kiss.

Only when they were both gasping hard did he ease off, tugging her bottom lip between his teeth before lifting his head.

One brow arched high. Her deep blue eyes glinted beneath her half-open lids as if to say, "That all you got?"

Before she could put to words whatever grating comment she was about to make, he reached behind her, unclasped her bra, and then slid his hands around her to cup her full breasts, rubbing his calloused thumbs over the distended nipples.

Another gasp, this one more agonized, gusted against his face. He ducked his head and hid his smile against her neck as he glided his lips along her silky skin and pulled the bra down her arms. "While I'm feeling them up a bit, I slide my hands right down their bodies, just to see how far they'll let me go. If I meet the least resistance, I move right back up to their breasts and play a little while longer."

Feeling surer of himself, he squeezed her breasts and then slid a hand down her taut belly and slipped his fingers just inside the waistband of her low-riding jeans.

Soft curls tangled around his fingertips, and he dragged at

them, sliding deeper until his middle finger entered her moist slit, reaching just far enough to slide over the top of her sex.

"I don't open their pants right away," he whispered. "I wait until they beg me to."

With one hand cupping her firm ass, he rubbed her clitoris up and down until she sucked in a deep breath to give him greater access.

This was what he gave those other women. Temptation by increments. Teasing thrusts and caresses that swept away any inhibitions or reluctance to let him lead them anywhere he wanted. So Tara hadn't said out loud what she wanted, but her jagged sighs and trembling belly told him everything he needed to know.

He pressed his body closer, forcing her to shuffle backward until her knees met the edge of the mattress. Pulling his hand from inside her pants, he shoved her gently, forcing her to fall to the bed, and climbed on top of her.

Holding her gaze while her cheeks flushed red, he clasped her hands and lifted them above her head while he leaned down and fluttered his tongue against the rigid tip of one nipple. Then he changed breasts and did the same again.

When his head came up, he caught her gaze. "Seeing as how your belly is already shivering, I might forgo playing with your tits a little longer and just slide on down."

Tara's slitted gaze blinked once. "Whatever it is you usually do . . . I want it."

He pressed her hands into the mattress. "You can't touch me. Keep them here or grab a fistful of your comforter, but don't touch me."

He climbed backward off the bed and turned around to straddle one leg as he lifted it and pulled her boot off her foot and slid down her thin sock. Then he stepped forward until the curve of the top of her foot was snuggled against his balls. "I like how soft a woman is, even her feet." His hands wrapped around her slender foot and massaged, kneading the bottom of her foot and heel, tugging at her toes and then sliding her foot against his groin again.

When her ankle gave a sharp tug, and he felt a quiver work its way up her calf, he dropped her foot and straddled the other leg. He made quick work of stripping her foot and then turned and knelt, caressing her all the while, pulling, kneading, separating the toes, and then leaning forward to suck her big toe into his mouth.

She jerked her foot back, but he didn't let her go.

"Stop that," she said, inhaling sharply.

He licked the pad of her big toe. "Why? Does it tickle?" he asked innocently.

"No, but it's weird. And I've been in those boots a while."

He lapped at her curved instep. "You have pretty feet."

Her nose wrinkled. "Feet aren't an erogenous zone unless you have some weird fetish."

"No fetish. But a woman should have every part of her body explored. That way, a man doesn't miss something special."

"You do this with every woman?" she asked, her tone as disbelieving as her raised brows.

"You wonderin' why I never sucked your toes?"

She didn't answer, but her stillness told him she wanted one. He sighed and dropped her foot, reaching immediately for the button at the waistband of her jeans—just so he'd have an excuse not to meet her gaze. "Because I figure I'll never be anyone's one and only, I'll settle for being the best she's ever had. I like finding the kinks she never knew could set her off."

Tara's eyes darkened. "That's the sum total of what you expect when you make love to a woman? That she remember you?"

He shrugged and plucked at the tab of her zipper at the top of her jeans, scraping it down slowly, one tooth at a time.

Her belly jumped, and her thighs tightened around his hips. "You still haven't said why you never did that . . . with me," she said, her voice growing strained.

"Didn't think I had to," he growled. "We pleasure each other. I've never had to strategize. It just happens. Makes it special."

As her pants eased open, he bent to kiss the soft white skin he exposed. He wrapped his fingers around her waistband and tugged.

She lifted her hips to help him, and he pulled them and her underwear slowly down her long legs, sliding kisses all the way to her curled toes.

When he had them off, he tossed the jeans over his shoulder and grasped her thighs, easing them open. One glance, and he could tell she was deeply aroused. Moisture glazed her plump outer folds.

A satisfied smile stretched his lips. His fingers tightened on her as he fought the urge to dive between her legs and end the torture now. His glance flicked up to her face.

Another swallow worked her straining throat as she lifted her head to watch him. "While you're pleasuring these women," she said softly, "what do you feel? Don't you get frustrated?"

"Are you asking if I get hard?" At her nod, he shrugged and caressed the back of her knee. " 'Course I do. But not so bad I can't make myself wait. I'm not a boy."

"When you're with me," she said, pausing to take a shallow, rasping gulp of air, "it feels like you can't wait to take another breath before you're inside me."

Cody's body tightened, anger once again fueling rebellion inside him. "Like I said, you're special. Didn't think I had to play these games. Didn't think I had to hold a thing back."

"Damnit, Cody." Her eyes slid closed. "Is it too late for me to change my mind?"

4

Cody smoothed his hands up the insides of Tara's thighs, and his thumbs glided right over her outer folds, rubbing them and then opening the sparsely furred lips. His head lowered toward her cunt, her spicy aroma working on his cock, creating an urgency he'd pay hell to hide if he had to pretend he could be patient with her a second longer.

Her hand slid down to cover herself, denying him access. "I said I've changed my mind. I'd just as soon get down to business."

Cody stroked her fingers with his tongue, sliding between them to touch her slippery, wet sex. "Who says you're in charge here?"

Her legs clasped him tighter as she tried to close them. Both her hands tucked between her legs, and her back arched as she tried to escape him. "Uncle, already," she said with a short, forced laugh.

Cody wasn't having any of it. She'd tried to change things between them. She'd tipped her chin skyward and led him around like she had a right to be angry with his behavior. She didn't own him. He hadn't made any promises, but maybe it was time to lay down a few rules now.

He sank his hands beneath her and cupped her ass, sliding fingers along her crevice—just to make sure he had her *undivided* attention. "Tell me, Tara. What were you thinking when you laid down all that money?"

"I wasn't thinkin' at all," she gasped.

"Were you pissed because I kissed a few women?" he asked silkily, one finger sliding over her small, puckered hole.

Her body jerked. " 'Course not, cowboy," she bit out. "Never even raised an eyebrow. A kiss is just your way of sayin' hello."

"Did your blood pressure rise when all those women swarmed me like honeybees around a hive?"

"They didn't have any better sense."

"Did you think I should have pushed them away?"

"Not my business what you do."

Cody dipped the end of his index finger into her ass, ignoring her sharp gasp. "Was it the kiss I blew at you? Seemed like your face screwed up into a scowl when I did that."

Tara's whole body shuddered, and her legs came over his shoulders, her heels digging into his back as she arched. "What the hell were you thinking?" she replied in an angry rush. "Kissing at me when all you were tryin' to do was get the crowd goin'? Why'd you have to bring me into it? First that kiss in the parking lot and then you singling me out like that—did you want everyone I know to think we have something goin' on?"

His finger thrust deeper, and her buttocks tensed and then began to undulate in shallow waves as he twisted inside her. "I asked before, are you ashamed of wanting me? Ashamed of fucking me?"

Her breaths gusted, edged by soft, shattered moans as she ground her heels harder to move her buttocks up and down. "I'm old enough... been around long enough... I should know better than to expect anything at all from you."

Her hands fell away from her pussy, and Cody accepted her

invitation, diving to slide his tongue between her folds and lap at silky flesh coated with salty cream.

His cock jerked, and a groan rumbled through his throat. Tara's taste and texture, the simple act of surrender, were all it took to steal his mind.

"Everyone knows you're not the stayin' kind," Tara whispered. "I don't want them shakin' their heads . . . and thinkin' I'm so lonely . . . so pathetic that I have to resort to sleeping with you to fill the void."

Cody's body grew still. *He was a last resort?*

Hot, fierce anger singed his veins, bulking out the muscles flexing across his shoulders and down his arms while he did his best to control the urge to fly at her, to cover her and thrust his cock so deep she couldn't deny to a single soul that his cock belonged inside her.

That sharp need caught him by surprise, sucking the air right out of his lungs. He didn't belong inside her. He'd never have a place in her life. And she didn't have a single claim on him.

The last thing she'd want was him hanging his hat on the rack beside the door. She didn't need him. That chilling certainty doused the arousal that pumped through his body.

And because he'd always played fair, and because he'd never given more than he could stand to lose, he drew back and pulled away his hands, lowering her ass to the bed.

Her eyes flew open.

"Guess you're not happy with our little arrangement anymore. I'll see your money's returned."

Tara lay with her legs splayed, her hands outswept to clutch the bedding, too shocked for a few seconds to react.

While Cody walked jerkily to the end of the bed and slowly began to pull on his clothes, she blinked, her eyes slowly filling. Which never happened.

She wasn't a crybaby. Had never resorted to tears to hold on to a man. Had never even attempted to keep someone hell-bent on leaving.

Truth was, she'd never felt deeply enough about anyone to care when a relationship fizzled. Which cost her long moments while she searched inside herself to wonder why she cared now.

Cody wasn't a keeper. She'd known that from the start. She'd even planned on telling him things were over after they'd enjoyed themselves one last time.

She hadn't thought he'd care, other than losing the convenience of a willing body. But something in his expression told her there was more going on here than she understood.

By the deep flex of his jaw, he wasn't gonna talk about it but expected her to complain. Something told her that would be the wrong thing to do—act like she cared he'd left her on the edge. Let him know he'd hurt her by withdrawing so abruptly.

Instead she slowly sat up and combed her hair back with a casual swipe of her hand. "I'll have to take you back to town," she said, her tone carefully devoid of emotion.

"I can make my own way back."

"That's silly. Why don't you take a shower? I'll feed you and then take you back in my truck."

His hands paused as he buckled his belt. His gaze came up, his brows lowered, pausing on her for a long moment as if trying to read her mind.

She forced a slight smile. "We're missing that dinner. Least you can do is keep me company while I rustle up something from the fridge."

His nod was slow in coming, but she let out the breath she'd been holding and then got up off the bed and went into the bathroom.

One glance at her own reflection, and she wondered how she'd ever fooled him. Her face was unusually pale. Lines bracketed her mouth from the tension gripping her. Her haunted eyes gave away the deep emotions swirling inside. Hurt made them shimmer.

She twisted the taps, splashed cool water on her face, and then reached for the yellow robe hanging from a hook at the back of the door before easing out of the bathroom. "It's all yours," she said. "Don't be long."

As he passed her, his gaze not meeting hers, her heart thudded dully inside her. What was it about him that made her care? Sure, he was the best-looking man she'd ever seen. The best lover she'd ever known. But he was promiscuous, flirting with every woman he met regardless of her age or looks. The fact he'd added her to his conquests should have been an insult because it wasn't a measure of her attractiveness—just her willingness to be used.

So what the hell had just happened? She'd dared to call him to accounts, and he'd felt what? Smothered? Was she all of a sudden no longer convenient because she'd dared to question him?

She tightened the tie around her waist with a vicious jerk and stomped toward the kitchen, her Irish temper rising so hot and swift she felt suffocated.

She slammed open the refrigerator door and stared at the contents, not really ready to weigh whether she should quickly defrost a couple steaks or fry some eggs. Who the hell did he think he was, anyway?

Her gaze went to the darkened backyard, a delightfully sinful thought forming in her mind. It was a fenced backyard, where she'd kept her best friend until he'd passed away. The heavy chain she'd used to hold the rottweiler while workers swarmed her roof last year still sat in a coiled pile beside his doghouse.

Cody seemed mighty determined not to talk about what ate

him. Seemed ready to throw her over because she'd pricked his easy, shallow charm.

She deserved answers before she cut him loose, and she damn sure deserved some pleasure for the inconvenient lust he'd stirred in her tonight.

Cody Westhofen might be the best she'd ever had, but by the time this night was over, he'd know she was a goddamn sex goddess. She'd leave him reeling, wondering what lust train had hit him!

Cody stepped out of the shower, unsatisfied with the quick wash he'd given his skin. He still felt dirty, ashamed of how callously he'd handled Tara.

He'd taken a cold shower, needing to ease his lust and his anger. Not until his thoughts had slowed did he admit he'd made a mistake. Self-preservation had made him turn like a cornered animal to strike out.

He'd left her confused, helplessly aroused. He'd pulled away because he'd felt afraid of the feelings she stirred inside him. She didn't deserve any of this.

A sound like a dull clink came from the bedroom, pulling his attention from his depressing thoughts, and he wondered if she waited for him there.

He didn't want to face her and instead dug into her drawers for the package of feminine razors he'd used before, filled the sink with steaming water, and used a bar of sweetly scented soap to work up a lather. He took his time shaving, hoping she'd be gone from the room by the time he'd finished, that she'd be dressed and ready to kick his ass to the door.

The last thing he wanted to do was sit across a table from her and hold a conversation like nothing had ever happened. What the hell could he say? Sorry I hurt you? Sorry I'm such a coward I can't make love to you because I'm afraid I won't have the strength to walk away afterward?

The razor nipped his neck, and he winced as the cut filled with stinging soap.

Done, he swiped at his face with a towel and then pressed toilet paper to the cut until the bleeding slowed. He dressed wishing he'd thought to bring a shirt along. Standing half dressed in front of a whole room of women hadn't made him feel as naked as facing Tara without a little cotton armor.

After several more seconds standing at the door while he girded his loins, he slowly opened it. The bedroom was darkened. Music, Tejano happy, filtered through the door leading down the hallway. Just like every other time they'd finished a night of lovemaking. Some of his tension eased.

"Cody?"

He jerked, his gaze whipping toward the bed. She stood in the shadows on the far side of the bed. "I dropped something behind the headboard. Could you help me reach it?"

"Sure," he muttered and strode toward her. "Why don't you get the light?"

"All right," she said softly, standing aside as he eased to his knees and reached down to slide the mattress back toward the foot of the bed so he could fit his hand inside the narrow space.

Only, she didn't move away. Her body pressed closer to his back, and he dragged in a deep breath, loving the way her scent surrounded him and her warm skin heated his own.

He closed his eyes briefly. "That light?" he ground out.

"Sure," she said, straightening . . . but only slightly. Something cold encircled his wrist, followed by a metallic click.

He tugged back his arm but could bring it back only a few inches. He felt with his free hand to confirm she'd manacled his wrist. "Tara," he said softly, "what the hell do you think you're doing?"

45

"Starting a conversation." She turned on the bedside lamp, and he looked down at his wrist.

Steel handcuffs bound him, one cuff linked around his wrist, and the other clamped around the rung of a long steel chain, which in turn was wrapped around the solid oak bedpost.

Cody pulled his arm, rattling the chain. There was enough slack for him to rise but not enough for him to step closer to her because she hugged the wall three feet away.

His gaze narrowed on her. "Tara, get the key," he said softly.

She cleared her throat and eased along the wall, keeping well out of his reach. "You may as well have a seat on the bed. You aren't going anywhere. I hid the key."

"I have to pee."

"No, you don't. But if you did, I still wouldn't unlock those cuffs."

He raised on eyebrow. "Plan on giving me a jar?"

She shrugged. "Maybe we won't be here all that long. Depends on you."

Cody looked at the cuff, fisted his hand beneath it, and tugged hard, but the solid oak post didn't budge, didn't even creak. When his gaze came back up to meet hers, he saw her lips crimp at the corners as though she was trying not to smile.

He still couldn't believe she'd done something like this just to keep him here to talk. Cuffing him seemed a little drastic, if that's all she wanted. Maybe conversation wasn't her true motive at all. Maybe she wanted him to finish what he'd started.

So, she wanted to play another sort of sexy game with him . . . . Cody had never left a woman unfulfilled. Even if she was the one holding the key, he could still be in charge.

Tara wouldn't know until it was too late.

5

Tara felt pretty pleased with herself, knowing that she'd taken the lead, until she noted the way his body relaxed, shoulders falling, his hands unfisting to settle on his hips. His gaze was still narrowed, but she doubted he was angry—one side of his mouth started a sexy upward slide.

Just looking at him, trussed up for her pleasure, she stifled a sigh.

Lord, he took a woman's breath away with that silver bracelet glinting against crisp hairs and a tanned wrist, his bare chest gleaming, every bulge and indentation emphasizing his masculine appeal. A glimpse of his body would make any woman salivate, but add his blond hair, drying in short, soft curls around his head, and his hard-edged, handsome face . . . It was all a girl could do not to pant like a bitch in heat.

"I don't think I can manage my boots with one hand," he growled. "You're gonna have to slide them off."

"You don't need them off," she said, her voice equally gruff as she tried not to give him a clue she lied.

"Because we may be talkin' a long time," he said, his voice

oozing sensual appeal, "I want to get comfortable. I wouldn't like to get dirt on your covers."

"I don't have the key on me," she said quickly, "if you're just waitin' for me to get close enough to wrestle me for it."

One dark blond brow arched. "Who says I wanna be freed?"

She tilted her head, not trusting his slick tone. He used the same sexy rumble when he was sliding deep inside her. Her gaze dropped to the front of his jeans. His arousal jutted outward in a long, thick bulge behind his zipper.

Moisture pooled in her mouth at the thought of what she wanted to do first. She swallowed hard. "We're going to play a little game."

His lips curled, his eyelids dipped as his gaze swept her body. "Your last resort's not the only game in town," he said softly. "Woman like you shouldn't have any trouble finding someone more . . . suitable."

Tara grew still, understanding his reaction now. "That upset you? My saying that?"

"A man doesn't like to know he's last on a woman's list."

"That's not what I meant."

"Well, maybe you should explain what you did mean."

She lifted her chin. "Mind if I do it while we play?"

Tension melted away as they shared rueful smiles.

Relieved he wasn't truly angry, Tara unbelted her robe and shrugged out of it, leaving it behind on the floor while she sauntered closer, hips swaying. When she reached him, she placed both hands on his chest and shoved hard.

He fell, bouncing slightly, the manacled arm stretched to one side. He chuckled while she climbed over him the same way he had earlier. She spread her knees over his hips and settled her sex against his clothed cock.

Bending over him, she leaned low until her lips hovered just above his. "You're not in charge here, Cody."

White teeth flashed briefly. "Anything you say, sweetheart, but you can't have your wicked way with me until you drag down that zipper."

"Who says that's where I'm heading?"

"It'd be a goddamn waste not to let me finish what I started."

She raised her brows and smiled. "You had your chance."

"I'd hate to leave a lady wanting."

Her eyes narrowed on him. "This lady doesn't like being lumped in with the rest of the population."

"I don't like leaving *you* wanting, Tara," he whispered against her lips. "Let me make it up to you."

"A question first. Then a reward."

"I don't like games," he growled again.

"At least not ones where you can't rig the outcome. Am I right?"

"I'm a man. Can't talk when my cock's about to drill a hole through denim."

She ground down on him, rubbing her pussy along his thick column. "I could get off just like this. Couldn't you?"

"*Fuck*, Tara," he groaned. "Just open my pants. We'll get this over quick. Then you can play your game."

She scooted higher up his body until she straddled his waist. She leaned slightly away, cupped one breast, and aimed the spiked nipple at his lips. "Make it good, baby."

His head came off the mattress, and he burrowed lips and nose against her soft breast, rooting until his mouth clamped around the tip.

Tara closed her eyes, squeezing her thighs hard around his taut middle as his tongue lashed and lips tugged. When his teeth bit gently, she shuddered and slipped a hand beneath his head to bring him closer.

"So good. . . ." she moaned.

His lips opened, releasing the tip, and then he licked around the areola and nuzzled the tender underside of her breast. "Gimme the other."

She ignored the fact he commanded her and slipped to the side to let him devour her opposite breast. When his free hand smoothed down her back, she began to rock against him, letting her moist center dampen his belly.

His hand slipped between their bodies as he continued to lavish her breast with soft swirls of his tongue. Fingers combed through her short curls. One calloused tip scraped the rounded knot at the top of her folds.

Tara's breath caught. Her hips undulated, dragging on his fingertip. She pushed off his belly just enough to give him access, moaning as he slid between her folds and plunged into her pussy.

Her body quivering, she pumped softly, up and down, until soon it wasn't enough. She pulled her breast away from his suctioning mouth, straightened, and began to bounce. Heat curled deep in her womb. Moisture spilled from her channel to soak his hand. Another finger joined the two he'd stuffed inside her.

"That's it. Ride me, Tara."

Tara opened her eyes to find his gaze on her face, his jaw sawing shut. She thrust onto his hand twice more and then came up on her knees. She pushed his hand away and backed off the bed.

Boots, socks, jeans—all flew off in a flurry despite her shaking hands. She urged him to stretch the length of the bed, and then she lay down beside him.

His hand combed her hair back from her face, and he pressed

a quick, hot kiss against her lips. "Unlock the cuff. Let me come over you."

"Lift up. I'll slide under you."

They managed between his sharp, fierce curses and her raspy commands. In the end, his cuffed hand stretched above them, his elbow digging into the mattress beside her shoulder. Their bodies lay at a slant, stretched across the bed, but now they lay aligned, her legs parted, her thighs cradling his hips.

Cody's head sagged against her shoulder as he slowly thrust his cock inside her.

They both moaned, and then their mingled breaths hitched. Choked laughter gusted.

"God, this feels so good," she sighed as he drove deeper with each shallow thrust, wedging his cock inside her narrow channel.

"Wish I could get some leverage. I'd buck like a bronc."

A smile tugged the edges of her mouth. "Guess you'll have to keep this horse at a slow gait."

"Woo-ee," he whispered.

"Ride me, cowboy." Her arms came around his waist, and she dug her heels into the bed to tilt her hips upward, searching for just the right angle. . . .

His cock drove straight up her pussy in quick short strokes. When he nudged the bundled nerves deep inside her, air hissed between her teeth. "That get it?"

"Uh-huh."

"Hold on."

The bed creaked as he pounded into her, forcing air from her lungs as he angled his hips side to side with each lunge.

His knees came up beneath him, and she raised her legs higher, tilting to cup his groin, giving him an unimpeded target to pummel her pussy with delicious jolts of his thick, hard cock.

Tara scraped his back with her nails, trying to wrap herself around him, trying to climb her legs around his hips and take him deeper. Cody grunted, widened his knees, and pounded harder.

This was what she loved about him. Stamina, and then some. Thick, corded muscle that could deliver powerful thrusts. A long, thick cock that rammed through soft tissue, friction burning, swelling her passage until only the natural lubricant of her arousal eased his harsh thrusts.

He filled her body, her heart. One of those facts he knew well; the other she'd have to guard against him ever discovering, or he'd be gone.

When the sweet tension tightening her belly reached critical mass, she arched beneath him, keening, her head slamming the mattress as lightning heat engulfed her.

When she slowly came down, she opened her eyes.

Cody had stopped rocking between her thighs. His chest heaved with exertion, and sweat bathed his face, arms and torso. Stretched over her, he pinned her to the mattress with his massive cock deeply embedded inside her. Soft aftershocks caressed his length, but still he didn't move.

Tara struggled to catch her breath, winning the battle gradually. Trying to gather her shattered thoughts was a different story. The tension radiating from his body telegraphed the fact he was very far from done with her.

"You okay?" he asked softly.

"I'm . . . fantastic." She really was, but she'd just thrown in the towel, hadn't she? Wasn't this supposed to be her turn to blow his mind?

"What did you mean when you said I was a last resort?"

From the frown furrowing his forehead, she knew he didn't like asking the question. He didn't want to care what she thought.

She concentrated on that need and drew one more ragged inhalation before answering. "Cody. I'm forty-two years old. And I don't buy that shit about forty being the new thirty. I'm beyond my prime. Finding lovers isn't that easy anymore. Finding someone special . . . well, that's proven even more elusive."

"You think you're too old? But you have so much to offer a man."

"What? A business? A home of my own? I suppose if I was looking for someone who wanted me to play sugar mama, I'd have no problems at all. But look where I live. Cowboy country. No good cowboy wants a woman just because she can take care of him. And I wouldn't respect him if he did."

Cody's gaze slid away. "You sell yourself short if you think you can't offer a man anything more than money."

"Well, I'm glad you think so, but I know there are some pretty important things I just can't do."

"Like what?"

"Well, one thing a man hooking up with a woman might expect is kids. I'm a little old to start poppin' out babies."

"Why'd you stay single so long?"

She shrugged, knowing her answer would seem ridiculous. "I never found someone I wanted for more than sex."

His eyebrows jagged up and down. "I hear you there."

"I mean, I've had lovers who were friends, but I never felt anything more than slight regret when they were gone. Maybe I don't know how to love a man."

Cody grunted. "That's plain foolish. Anyone who knows how to be a friend can love."

Uncomfortable now that she'd revealed so much, she snorted. "Yeah, well, that's my story, and I'm stickin' to it. Now it's your turn. Tell me something. . . ."

He didn't bother trying to hide a grimace.

"Fair's fair," she said, arching one brow. "I answered your questions."

His lips tightened into a straight line, and then he rolled his eyes. "All right. Ask away."

"You said what we have is special. I don't get that. Is it special because you don't have to try with me? 'Cause I can tell you, I wasn't flattered one bit."

Cody let out a deep sigh. "Guess it doesn't sound so special put that way, but I don't usually come back for seconds. I sure as hell don't stay when I think a woman wants more from me than what I have to give."

"I still don't get it. So all you like is the sex?"

He paused, his glance sliding away. "I like you," he said softly.

"Oh." That wasn't so bad. Like was better than nothing.

"I don't feel like I have to be a certain way. It's straight-up sex, sure. But I like talking to you, too. I'm not in a rush to get back into my clothes and back on down the road."

She snorted. "Now I feel so much better."

"Tara . . ."

She wrinkled her nose. "No, don't worry. I'm not asking for declarations here. I just needed to know where I stand. I'm good enough to fuck. Good enough to share a meal and a laugh. That's something, I guess."

His face turned into an anxious frown. "Tara, stop. I can't give a woman any more than that. I've never given so much."

"But why?"

He shook his head. "That was one question. Don't I deserve a little something in return?"

She forced a smile, knowing she'd been close to getting a deeper revelation, but that door had slammed shut. "Fair's fair. But you have to get off me first. I can't breathe."

His head dipped. His forehead rolled on her shoulder. "Jesus, don't ask me to pull out."

Tara grinned as she shoved aside her curiosity, determined to burrow a little deeper the next time she got the chance. But for now, she had a man chained to her bed, and her body was once again beginning the slow build to full-blown arousal.

"Cody," she purred, "I swear you'll have something else warm to sink inside."

His head came up, his gaze locking with hers. Blue eyes darkened, but he grimaced again as he withdrew, groaning as the last luscious inch slipped from inside her. He rolled away, covering his eyes with his manacled arm.

His cock, slick with her honeyed arousal, was reddened, pulsing. Tara came to her knees, stepping between his legs and sinking over him, first rubbing her hair along his wet flesh and then her cheek, inhaling the combined scents of their arousal and musk. She cupped his balls in her palm and rolled them, squeezing gently and tugging.

His arm moved, and he jerked his head up to watch her. "Easy there."

"Not gentle enough?"

"Man gets a little nervous."

She slid farther down his body and opened her mouth, stroking out her tongue to lave one ball, swirling on it, and then she opened her mouth again and sucked it inside, gobbling at him playfully until his head fell back again on a long groan.

His free hand smoothed over the top of her head, and fingers sank into her hair to pull her closer.

She swallowed the other ball into her mouth, tongue and lips working on him, suctioning and then soothing with gentle laps until his hips began to pulse.

Only then did she release his balls and lick her way up his

cock, following his long shaft upward, curving her tongue around him to glide up the outside and then giving him little doggy laps down the sensitive top of his shaft.

His knees came up on either side of her, his ass lifting from the bed to stroke upward, pressing against her cheek and mouth, begging silently for her to capture the tip and swallow him down.

Tara gave him a smug smile and wrapped her fingers around his shaft, pointing his cock toward her mouth. She gave the tip a wet swipe of her tongue and then opened wide. She swallowed the soft, broad cap and suctioned on it, sliding her tongue into the narrow slit at the center and then scooping under the ridge.

Cody stroked upward again, trying to thrust deep into her mouth, but she backed away, not letting him sink inside her. Instead she continued to lick the cap and began to softly chew with her teeth buffered by her lips.

"Jesus, Tara," he moaned.

She liked the edge of desperation in his tone and the deep growl that followed. But she wasn't nearly done.

She cupped his velvet sac, tugging once, and glided the tip of one finger beneath it, tracing a path downward that had his breath catching.

"Tara . . ." he said, his voice rising in warning.

She came off his cock. Her fingertip continued to circle the tender flesh just beneath his balls. "What do you want? Me sucking you dry? Or shall I stop?" she asked silkily.

"Careful there," he bit out.

"Really want me to stop here?" she asked, scraping her nail lower, nearing the crevice he seemed so concerned she'd explore.

His hot glare could have blistered paint, but he laid his head back and stared stoically at the ceiling.

"That's better," she murmured and then removed her finger,

bringing it to her mouth to wet it. Then she bent over his cock, opened wide, and sank down his shaft while sliding her finger between his buttocks.

When she glided over his back entrance, he jerked, drew a deep breath, and then relented, opening his knees wider, giving his silent assent for her to explore. She entered his ass on a gentle glide.

With age came experience, something Tara had in spades. She crooked her finger and stroked deeper, rubbing over the little gland that gave her complete command over Cody's arousal.

6

Cody gritted his teeth, torn between embarrassment and arousal so sharp it hurt.

No one had ever dared touch him like that. He'd fucked his fingers and his cock into Tara's ass a time or two, just to watch her climb the wall, but he'd never been on the receiving end.

How had she ever stood it? The pressure against the tight little ring from the thrust of one slender finger burned. When she curled it and stroked a place only a doctor had ever touched during a physical, he nearly came unglued.

"Easy," he ground out again.

Maybe she didn't hear him. She seemed a little busy. Her head bobbed up and down his cock, surrounding him in moist heat, her tongue swirling up and down his shaft.

Her finger poked deeper and then pulled away, but before he could even groan with relief, two pushed inside. Together they stroked his prostate, circling on it, while his thighs trembled and his belly leaped.

He curved his palm over the back of her head and pressed down, urging her to take him deeper down her throat.

A soft, choked laugh was followed by a sexy murmur that vibrated around him, and Cody couldn't help it. His thighs tensed, his buttocks hardened like steel, and he punched his hips upward.

She took the forceful jab, widening her jaws and opening the back of her throat to accommodate his thrusts.

Surrounded by wet, silky heat above, prodded with wicked, hot thrusts and rubs below, he couldn't resist her double-pronged assault.

He pumped upward, helpless against the pressure building in his balls. Jerking up, driving past the back of her throat, he erupted with a shout that echoed against the walls while cum spurted in thick, scalding bursts.

Her throat clasped him as she swallowed it down, a snug, spasming caress that kept him driving upward well past the point his balls were wrung dry.

When at last he lowered himself to the bed, his chest billowed with choppy gasps to fill his starved lungs. His fingers threaded through her hair and pulled hard, dragging her off his cock and upward, her head tilted toward his hand, her mouth open as she scrambled up his body.

He forced her mouth to his, mashed his lips against hers, and then drew back. "Don't ever do that again."

"'Again' assumes I'll let you come back to my bed."

Still breathing hard, he lifted his head, pressing his lips to hers, forcing his tongue between her lips—just to stop her from talking. *Not let him come back?*

Made sense, he guessed. He'd had seconds, thirds, fourths . . . *Fuck, what was she doing now?*

Tara climbed over him, straddling his hips. Her hands reached between them to stuff his wilted cock inside her.

She was drenched, inside and out. Her swollen tissues engulfed him, fine ripples working along her inner walls, urging him inward.

Tara leaned over him, placing her face just above him. Then she began to slowly roll her hips, dragging on his semihard cock with an upward roll, relaxing her muscles to allow him to slide back inside with a downward curve of her hips.

"This working for you?" he said softly.

The expression on her reddening face betrayed her frustration.

"Might have to wait a bit. I'll give it to you the way you need, baby."

"Shut up, Cody," she said, giving him another sensual, snake-like roll. Her pussy ground against his pubic bone as she tried to increase the friction.

"Baby, come over my mouth. Put that sweet cunt right over my face."

A shattered sob broke, moist air gusting over his face.

"Let me eat you out," he whispered. "Same as you did for me."

"I'm in charge."

"I'm the one chained. Can't do a thing you don't want. Give me your pussy."

Her belly and legs trembled over and around him, and she fell against his chest. Skin to skin, their bodies combusted. A trickle of perspiration rolled from the edge of her hair; moisture pooled between their bodies.

"God, Tara. Take the fucking cuff off."

"No!" She jackknifed up. Her thighs tightened around him, jamming him deeper inside her. Then her features relaxed, and her breaths evened. A new look entered her eyes.

As close to begging as he'd ever seen her, her eyes filled, her lips trembled. Slowly she rose over him, dragging one last time off his cock until it fell against his belly.

She crawled up his body, placed both knees beside his shoulders, careful of the awkward angle of the tethered arm.

When the slick vee of her thighs edged over his chin, he turned his face and kissed her inner thigh. "Hold on to the headboard."

As Tara reached to grasp the headboard, her breaths rattled harshly inside her chest. Slowly she settled her pussy directly above his mouth and waited.

Lips latched on to the hot, furled inner folds and nibbled. She leaned her flaming face against the cool wood. "Christ, don't tease me, Cody. Not now."

Fingers parted her; his tongue swept inside her entrance, lapping in circles as if he licked melting ice cream. He burrowed his nose and tongue into her sex, newly shaved cheeks still adding a dash of surprising scrape until the gentle convulsions shimmering up her channel began again.

A finger toggled her clit, rubbing over it, pressing on it until it grew so hard she ached and jerked at each teasing caress.

"I'm close," she sobbed.

His lips glided upward, opening to suckle her clit. Fingers, three of them wedged up inside her pussy, delivered quick, insistent strokes that scraped knuckles and fingernails along her molten walls.

He sucked harder, and her head fell back. Her thighs stiffened, and her body jerked and then held perfectly still as her orgasm exploded, flowing outward from her cunt, rippling up her channel to her womb.

She gasped and bit her lip to hold back her cry. Quivering all over, she sagged against the headboard.

Cody released her clit and then dove into her cunt to gently lick the fluid her body had released. His hand clutched her buttock and squeezed. At last, he fell back, his face glistening.

Quietly, slowly she climbed off him, accepting the offer of his open arm to snuggle beside him.

He pressed a kiss against her forehead. "I really do have to piss now."

A short laugh nearly choked her, and she turned her face into his neck, slipping an arm across his chest to hold him. "I'll be sure to get that jar."

She nearly fell asleep, lying beside him like that. As she drifted away, she realized they'd never been like this. Quiet for so long. Holding each other.

She cleared her throat to warn him. "Is this so bad?"

His chest stilled. He'd heard her, but he remained silent so long, tears began to flood her eyes.

"I better find that key."

His arm tightened around her, his hand sliding up and down her back. "Don't go."

Tara tilted her face to watch his as he stared straight ahead.

"I was raised in foster care. My mother gave me up when I was ten. She drank too much."

A deep breath lifted her on his chest, but she kept silent, letting him tell whatever he felt she needed to know about why they shouldn't do this.

"I wasn't an easy kid. I started fights at school. My grades were bad. I went through four foster families until I landed in Rita Jenning's home. I was sixteen.

"Rita took one look at me and told me she knew I was trouble. Her husband worked at night, slept all day. She signed me up to work at a ranch just outside of Uvalde to keep me busy. I liked the work. It was hard, dirty work, but I was good with animals. I grew nearly half a foot in a year, and then Rita joined me in the shower one day."

Tara's hand soothed over his chest as bile burned the back of her throat. Still, she stayed silent.

"I thought the world of her. Thought she was the prettiest thing I'd ever seen. I thought what we had was love. But she regretted it. Was ashamed every time she snuck into my room at night, more so when she left early in the morning.

"One day, she had my bags packed beside the door, said she'd found work for me at a ranch where they'd see I finished school. And that was it. I never saw her again."

Tara didn't know what to say. Her throat closed tight.

"Now will you get that key?"

Tara started to move away and then hesitated. "Do you see me as Rita?" she asked, her throat tightening. "Another older woman taking advantage of a younger man?"

Cody's glance sliced her way. "Fuck no. I'm trying to tell you why I don't trust what I feel."

"Do you think all I want is this with you? That I'd have taken up with any handsome cowboy to scratch an itch?"

"How can it be anything more?" he asked, a ragged, aching quality to his voice. "We don't have a thing in common. I can't offer you anything you don't already have."

Tara wanted to shake him. "I don't have another man who wants me. Who can look past the lines on my face and still see me. Inside, I'm not a middle-aged woman. I'm just . . . a woman."

Cody's face turned toward her. His jaw flexed, and he hugged her close. "You can do better. You should expect better than me."

"You're an idiot, Cody Westhofen."

A bitter smile curled one corner of his mouth. "I'm just a cowboy. And a man whore. Everything you've been thinkin' all along."

Tara knew stubborn when she saw it. She looked it in the face every morning of her life. Cody cared, but it might be a long-haul kind of job to convince him he was worthy of love.

Patience wasn't something she'd ever been accused of having, but the warmth of the body stretched beside her, the shadows in those startling blue eyes, made her ache to prove him wrong. "I'll find that key. Both of us need showers."

"It's late. Why not just take me to my truck?"

Tara leaned over him and kissed him, giving him a small smile. "You haven't worked off that debt, cowboy. I promise. No more talk."

"My stomach's rattling."

"I'll grill steaks."

He pushed a lock of hair behind her ear. "Are you asking me to stay the night?"

She mustered up her brightest smile. "Just consider it the down payment."

Cody eyed her warily throughout dinner, looking for some clue of what she might be thinking about what he'd told her.

She didn't seem disgusted. Oddly she appeared happy, puttering around the kitchen as she fried steaks and eggs, adding fresh tomatoes and thick slices of bread to their plates.

They didn't talk much during dinner, but that might have been because he inhaled his meal while she looked on with amusement.

"I got something on my face?" he asked, catching her glance again.

She shook her head. "No. It's nice watching you eat. You really enjoy it."

"Have to keep up my strength."

"I'll let you sleep."

"Wouldn't want any complaints come morning."

"Cody, you're the man who says he never leaves a woman unsatisfied."

"Do have a rep to uphold. Any requests?"

"Gonna give me a menu? Let me choose my poison?"

"I'm feeling pretty generous. Lady's choice."

She chuckled softly. "I'll let you know."

He picked his napkin off his lap and laid it next to his plate. "What's for dessert?"

Tara laughed, throwing back her head. "Cowboy, you just polished off your steak and half of mine."

"And your point is?" He grinned, satisfied when he elicited another throaty laugh from her.

She sat across him in a fluffy yellow robe, her hair mussed and curling around her shoulders, looking warm as sunshine. A sweet ache settled in his chest.

He'd like to linger there a few more weeks, maybe months. Give it a try at being a one-woman man for as long as she could stand to have him underfoot.

He lunged from his chair, quickly stepped around the table, and shoved her chair to face him. Then, with a quick bend, he grabbed her arm and pulled her over his shoulder.

Rich, deep laughter followed him all the way down the hallway to her bedroom. He dropped her on the bed and followed her down, stretching over her, capturing her arms with his hands and wrapping them around his shoulders. "Hold tight."

With a little clumsy maneuvering, he opened her robe and his pants and plunged right inside, groaning at her wet welcome.

Even though he didn't give her a lick of practiced finesse, her face soon grew red, strained, her lips pursing as she blew hard.

Cody pounded inside her, shoving up her legs, sliding his arms under her knees, and moving her inexorably up the mattress with each concentrated thrust.

As quick as his arousal had spiked, his orgasm thundered through him, drenching her in his cum. Tara, game as ever, held on tight, the quickening of her own rise pulsing around him, caressing him with quivers that rode his shaft until she came, too.

When he'd spent the last of his strength, he lay over her, his head beside her on the bed. "Not so bad at all," he whispered, echoing her earlier comment.

Lips pressed soft kisses against his shoulder and cheek. Hands stroked over his damp skin.

"Don't go to sleep just yet. Better get out of your clothes, or you'll wake up tangled in those pants," she whispered.

Cody didn't bother opening his eyes—he just smiled.

7

Tara felt something cold encircle her wrist and came instantly awake, knowing exactly what the ornery cowboy had just done.

" 'Bout time you woke up," he said, smiling down at her. He sat next to her on the edge of the bed. Naked. "I've been playing with your pussy for ten minutes, and you snored all the way through it."

Tara turned her head toward the window. Sunlight peeked through the parting of the curtains. "It's morning? And I do not snore."

"How do you know?"

She yawned and reached to cover her mouth, only to come up short. "Cody . . ."

"Now, Tara, you had such a good time last night, I thought I'd give it a try."

Tara turned her head to find the metal cuff on one wrist and, on the other wrist, a length of material, neatly braided and tied. A deep cobalt-blue braid. "You cut up one of my nightgowns?"

"I'll get you another."

The spread of her legs was unnaturally wide, and she didn't

need to pull against the tethers to know he'd taken her idea and run wild with it.

"Now, how much fun can this be for you if I can't partici-pate?"

"The fun's in seeing how far you'll let me go before you start begging."

"I don't beg."

"Like you don't snore?" A wicked grin inched across his face.

Tara pretended irritation, wrinkling her nose at him, but she relaxed against her ties, eager to see what he had planned.

"You do know you're the only woman I don't wear a con-dom with, right?"

"You promised me that. I believe you."

"Just wanted you to know you never have to worry."

"Are you trying to make me nervous?"

Cody reached to the floor beside the bed and pulled up pil-lows they'd tossed because they'd gotten in the way. He held one between two hands. "I need a little cooperation."

"You're the one who tied me up. Can't backpedal now."

He snaked an arm beneath her hips and shoved the pillow under her butt and then scooted her feet upward until the make-shift ropes tightened. "Guess that's all the give they've got. I'll make do."

Make do? With her pussy in the air, her knees spread wide, she figured he had plenty of access for whatever wickedness he had up his invisible sleeve.

He'd bathed. His skin glittered with moisture he'd haphaz-ardly swiped with a towel. He smelled of her floral soap.

"I think I like this," he said softly, coming to the end of the bed and eyeing her open legs. He climbed onto the bed, his slow crawl and the predatory gleam in his eye awakening a heavy, pulsing throb at her center. "You're completely open. Vulnerable. Trust me still?" he murmured.

Tara swallowed hard, her breaths coming faster, shallower. Her thighs tensed as he skimmed knuckles along the top of one thigh.

He leaned over the bed again and picked up something else from the floor, which he cupped in his hand, hiding it from her.

"What do you have there, Cody?"

"Close your eyes."

"Aren't you tired of playing games?"

"You played. Now it's my turn. Close your eyes, or I'm going to go eat breakfast while you think a bit."

No way was he leaving her like this, aroused, her legs sprawled open with nothing sliding into the pussy he'd already primed for his pleasure. She shut her eyes, frowning so he'd know she wasn't completely in his thrall.

A low hum started, and she moaned. He'd found her stash of toys. The ones she used when he wasn't there to fill her.

Something cool was rubbed beneath her pussy, smoothed downward by the tip of a rough finger pressing until it glided over her sensitive back entrance.

A sharp inhalation was her only complaint. When the smooth, round tip of the vibrator hummed against her asshole, she forced herself to relax, knowing resistance wouldn't deter him and would only cause her discomfort.

The dildo slid inside, gliding in and out in gently shallow forays as he eased the tension in the muscles that clamped around the slender column.

Tara's belly quivered; her thighs moved restlessly, opening wider as she curved her bottom upward to beg for more. A flick of the switch increased the speed of the vibrations, and moisture trickled from her cunt, her lips spasming with wet little "kisses" as he thrust the toy deeper in her ass.

He held it there, increasing the speed again, his hand cupped against her entrance to keep her body from ejecting it.

"Ever wondered what it would be like to have two cocks coming in you hard?"

She shook her head, pressing her lips together so she wouldn't blurt the truth.

"Truth is, I don't like the idea of sharing you. Giving that to you. But we can pretend, can't we?"

His hands slipped under her ass and lifted her higher. His thighs snuggled closer to hers, and his cock fell heavy atop her mound. "Let's see how well you like it."

Tara grabbed the slender tethers and held on tight as Cody backed his hips up, sliding his cock slowly down her slit.

When the tip of his cock nudged her entrance, he pushed forward, sliding easily through moist tissue that rippled all along his thick shaft.

The first thrust pushed the dildo deeper inside, and Tara admitted to herself she felt relief. Christ, she was so full. The hum purred deep inside her body, and she knew he had to feel the vibrations, too.

He slipped away the braid binding one wrist. "Touch your clit."

She shook her head. She'd shoot off like a rocket if she did. "No. Too quick."

"Then play with your breasts. I want to watch you touch yourself."

Eyes still squeezed shut, she clutched a breast, plumping it up for his pleasure.

The pace of his steady thrusts increased. Burning heat and tension filled both her entrances, vibrating upward to curl tight inside her womb until her whole body quivered and shook with her escalating pleasure.

As he stroked harder, Cody's breaths grew labored. His fingers dug into her buttocks in a bruising grip that only heightened her excitement.

Not able to stand it a moment longer, she opened her eyes.

Cody's blazing gaze bored into hers, his lips drawn into thin lines against his teeth. His jaw was taut, his skin reddened and glistening now with a fine sheen of sweat.

And so goddamn beautiful he made her heart ache. He was any woman's wet dream. How the hell did she have any hope of holding on to him?

Cody slowed his thrusts and dropped his gaze.

She followed that heated look, watching as he drove between her folds, each inch disappearing between her reddened lips and then pulling out with thin threads of the creamy white arousal he churned up, coating his slick cock.

His gaze came back up, catching her watching his strokes. "Can't hold back any longer," he ground out.

"Never asked you to."

Pulling out until her pussy sucked only on the blunt crown, he powered forward, stabbing deep into her, so deep she felt the thud against her cervix. He drew out again and thrust hard at her center, repeating the motions, coming faster and faster, jolting against the dildo still tucked deep inside her.

Overwhelmed by the steady pounding, the vibrations deep inside her body, and the powerful picture he made as he hammered her, Tara's body jerked, her back arching, her head digging into the mattress. Her release washed over her, lifting her on an upward swell, setting her soaring higher. A thin, keening wail pierced the air.

Cody didn't slow. His thrusts grew more erratic, sharper, harder—until he flung back his head and groaned. "Ahhhhh . . ."

The little jiggles he made as he shook off the cum spurting inside her made her smile. When he grew still, his eyes opened, greeting her gaze with a rueful grin. "I won't be able to walk for a week."

"That's supposed to be my complaint. I'm the one who took the pounding."

"You did, didn't you?"

"Gonna untie me?"

He groaned again and raked her inner walls with short thrusts. "Can't let me savor it a minute longer?"

"Cody, I want to wrap myself around you."

His eyes darkened. "Need a cuddle after all that work?"

"I earned it." She pouted. "I let you have your wicked way."

With his cock still clutched deep inside her pulsating channel, he bent over her, giving her a long, hot kiss that had them both gasping when he lifted his head.

"Spend the day with me," she whispered, knowing she was clinging but unable to let go. Not yet.

"Still want me around?" he whispered, his lips sliding along the edge of her jaw.

"I have more nightgowns for you to shred up."

Mouths an inch apart, Tara savored the grin that wrinkled the sides of his blue eyes. She lifted her hand and combed her fingers through his damp hair and then gently tugged him closer.

Their kiss was a shimmer-soft caress of lips. Sweet, lingering.

"I have to confess, I love this part, too," he whispered.

"Not a very manly thing to admit. Most men are ready to roll off and sleep."

"I don't want to miss a thing."

At that moment, his spent cock slipped from her pussy.

Tara groaned and then gave a little laugh. "I really, really need that vibrator to go."

"Sorry." He came up quickly on his haunches and eased the vibrator from her ass.

Embarrassed, she turned her head aside. With a soft click, the hum stopped.

"Be right back," he said, climbing off the bed and heading to the bathroom, still clutching the dildo.

"I can manage that. . . ." she called after him, but the door was already shut.

Lying with her body still spread-eagle, fluid oozing from her pussy, Tara tugged at her remaining tethers and chain, hoping to free herself before he came back out, but to no avail. "Must have been a damn boy scout," she muttered, giving up.

The sound of running water lasted for endless minutes, and then the door opened. He strode inside, a washcloth in his hand.

"You can untie me now," she said, scowling.

"What would be the fun in that?" He washed her efficiently, careful not to abrade the tender, sensitized flesh between her legs. "Better?" he asked, his gaze lifting from her sex.

With her face flushed with embarrassment, she nodded.

"See? That wasn't so hard."

"I could have managed myself."

"But you would have deprived me of the pleasure. I'm the one who got you this way."

"Feeling pretty proud of yourself?"

"Yeah. I am." He traced a finger along the edge of one furled lip. "Did you like it?"

Again, emotion rose up to choke her. She nodded quickly.

Standing at the end of the bed, he bent and placed his hands on either side of her hips and stroked out his tongue to caress her swollen labia. He inhaled—taking a deep, slow breath. "Love that smell. It's like bread baking in the oven."

Tara couldn't help the snort of laughter that shook her body. "Do you use that line with every woman?"

" 'Course not," he said grinning up at her. "It's not exactly the smoothest line, is it?"

Tara rattled her remaining manacled hand. "The key?"

"Gettin' to it. Promise."

A sound like the rasp of footsteps on sand came from outside the window.

Cody's head canted, a frown drawing his brows together. "You expectin' company?" he whispered.

"Hell, no. Untie me now."

"Fuck, where'd I see that key?"

"I left it on the dresser."

The doorbell rang.

Cody and Tara shared an alarmed glance. He stripped the ties from her feet and then lunged at the dresser, swiping up the key before hurrying back to the bed.

A fist pounding on the front door echoed through the house.

"*Commiiinng!*" Tara shouted, jerking her hand away as soon as Cody unlocked the cuff.

He tossed her yellow robe at her, and she shrugged it on, already running for the front door.

She arrived breathless, ran her fingers through her hair, and pasted on a smile before opening the door.

Joe Chavez and Logan Ross stood on her stoop, their faces set in unyielding lines.

"Deputies? Is anything wrong?" she asked, eyeing them warily through the screen door. They were dressed in scruffy T-shirts and frayed jeans, cowboy hats shading their faces.

"Ma'am, we're here about a missing person," Joe said, his expression intimidatingly stern.

"A missing person? Who?" she asked, wondering why they'd be looking here.

Joe grabbed the edge of her screen door and opened it. "May we come in?" he asked, already stepping over her threshold.

Tara backed up, at a loss for words as they both charged inside. "But no one's here," she sputtered.

"Cody Westhofen missed an appointment this morning,"

Joe said over his shoulder as he peered into her kitchen and then headed directly down the hall, Logan at his back.

"Wait!" she said, following on their heels. "Why do you think he's missing?"

"His truck's still parked at the Honkytonk, and after the ruckus you two caused last night, we thought we'd better check it out."

"Ruckus? I'm telling you, he's not missing."

Joe didn't seem to hear her, reaching her door and swinging it open with a flourish. He halted in his tracks, a low whistle blowing through his lips.

Both men blocked the door, so Tara had to peer around them into the room. What she saw made her jaw drop and her face heat with mortification.

Cody lay spread-eagle on her mattress, still naked, his sex stirring between his legs, his feet bound by shiny blue braids and one hand secured by the silver cuff. He turned his head toward the men who stood chuckling softly in the doorway.

"Hey, Cody," Logan said. "Need rescuing?"

"Sorry I didn't make our date, boys. As you can see, I'm a little tied up at the moment."

Tara shot him a blistering glare and then elbowed her way past the men to throw a blanket over Cody's naked body. By the way the two deputy's eyes gleamed with amusement, there was no way in hell they'd keep this to themselves. "I'm going to kill you," Tara hissed at Cody.

"Sure everything's all right here?" Logan asked. "Meaghan seemed to think blood might have been spilled, the way Tara stomped off last night."

"No blood spilled," Cody drawled. "All my parts are still intact."

His parts were poking at the blanket, and Tara moved in

front of the bed to hide the fact. "If you two are satisfied . . ." she ground out between clenched teeth.

"Sorry to barge in, ma'am," Joe said, giving Cody one last glance and a wink.

Logan shook his head, his grin splitting his face. "Got a key for those handcuffs?"

" 'Fraid we lost it sometime last night," Cody drawled. "I'm sure we'll find it soon."

Joe and Logan tipped their hats and turned, soft, masculine laughter following them out of her house. When she'd finally gotten her anger in hand, she turned to Cody. "What the hell do you think you're doing? Those two are going to have this all over the county before noon."

"They won't tell a soul."

"Why would they do something like that?"

"They were just havin' some fun at my expense." His brows pulled closer, deepening the shadows in his eyes. "Tara, don't you think it's time we stopped sneakin' around?"

Tara blinked at the moisture welling in her eyes. "Where did you put that key?" she asked, her voice sounding ragged to her own ears.

He held it up between the thumb and forefinger of his free hand.

She held out her cupped palm, accepting the key, and then tossed it over her shoulder.

His eyes widened. "Why'd you do that?"

"Guess I'm not done having a little fun at your expense."

"Tara . . ."

She shook her head, sniffing to clear the tears clogging the back of her throat. "Because you don't seem to care that everyone and their mother's gonna know we've got something goin' on, why not give them something to really talk about?"

"What are you planning to do?"

Tara climbed onto the bed, still wearing her robe, and settled her spread legs around his hips. "I'm gonna keep you here until you admit I'm the only woman for you, cowboy."

Cody's lips twitched. His half-lidded gaze traced a path from her breasts to her pussy. "You're the only woman I want."

Tara wrinkled her nose. "You said that too quick to be convincing."

His gaze locked with hers. "I mean it."

Tara stilled, all anger bleeding away. A poignant glimpse of hope breaking through the angry cloud. "No other women?" she asked and then gruffly amended, "For as long as this lasts."

A muscle along his carved jaw flexed. "For as long as you'll have me."

"I'm serious, Cody."

"I love you, Tara Toomey."

Her lips trembled. The woman who never cried over dusty cowboys fell over his chest and snuggled her cheek against the corner of his shoulder, tears leaking from her eyes. "I love you, too."

"Is that why you raised that paddle last night? Were you tellin' the whole world how you felt?"

She nodded. "I thought it would get me in less trouble than tackling the woman who bought you."

His chest shook with soft laughter. "Might have been worth it to see." He kissed her hair. "Want me to find that key?"

Tara nuzzled his chest with her cheek. "I'm fine. Just like this. I want your arm around me."

The one arm he had free hugged her closer. "I've got you, baby."

"You really are going to have to work on a new nickname. I'm old enough to be your mo—"

"Not even. I'm thirty-two."

"Jesus. Now I feel much better," she said, wincing.

"Age is just a number."

"Says someone who's still in his prime."

"You really think you're old?"

She lifted her head. "Only when I look at you."

"I don't see it." His eyebrows drew together; his gaze was soft. "So you've got a few wrinkles. So do I."

"I might not be able to give you babies. And I know you'd miss that."

"You never know. Maybe you just need some young sperm swimming inside you."

"Elegantly put."

"I'm not a talker."

"No, you're a lover. *Mine,*" she said with a firmness he couldn't help but notice.

"Yours. Got it. Guess you'll have to keep that chain and lock me up every night."

"I kinda liked the way it felt on me," she admitted ruefully.

"I liked the way you looked," he growled. "Every part of you open to me. Helpless. So damn wet." His sex stirred against her, proving his words.

"Promise me something?" she said, raising her head.

Cody's gaze tangled with hers. "Anything."

She shook her head. "Not until you've heard me. Doesn't count if you don't know what I'm gonna ask."

"Ask."

Tara swallowed and then let him see everything she felt reflected in her expression: unconditional love and acceptance. "Don't stay any longer than you want. Not for me."

The muscles of his throat flexed around a swallow. "I promise, Tara." She gave him a soft smile and started to lay her head on his chest again, but he lifted her chin with his thumb. "My turn."

Tara read the shimmering tenderness in his gaze, and happiness unfurled like a budding rose.

"Marry me."

Breezy Ridin'

1

A hot breeze toyed with a strand of hair lying across her breast, but Sarah Michelson wasn't about to flick it away now. She was already in deep shit and wondering whether she should pour on the syrup and sweet-talk the two officers striding her way.

She'd been driving her bike without her headlight, following the pale gray thread of road she'd driven since she'd graduated to adulthood until she hit the winding canyon and had to flip it on. A quick drive-by of the bar, and she would have proven she was still the reigning bad girl of Honkytonk.

Then she'd seen the glint of metal at the side of the road and throttled down.

Damn, who knew she'd run into a speed trap on little ole Amman Road?

"Ma'am, I'll need to see your license and registration."

Sarah squinted against the spotlight aimed at her from the squad car parked beside the sawhorse barrier and shot a glare at the deputy who'd halted beside her. That glare was signature "Sarah" and would have had most men backing up half a dozen paces. To his credit, Joe Chavez didn't flinch, but neither did he crack a smile.

So that's the way he wanted to play it. She could pretend there wasn't a thing unusual about this particular traffic stop, too. "Officer, I seem to have misplaced it," she said, dropping her voice to a sultry purr.

"Forgot a few other things as well," the other deputy, Logan Ross, drawled, coming close enough she could make out his features in the bright light.

What were they—a tag team?

Two police cruisers, blue lights strobing, and a barricade with orange lights seemed overkill for a simple traffic stop. Of course, she'd probably given them fodder for sly jokes at the station house for months with this stunt.

While she might pretend nonchalance, a hint of where this was going would do a lot to quell her rising anxiety. But so far, they were letting her sweat. Where Deputy Chavez's face didn't betray an ounce of humor, Ross's lips were pressed together in a thin line as though he fought a smile.

Time to bait the trap.

"I was in a hurry when I left the house," she said, flipping her hair over her shoulder just to make sure Deputy Ross got an eyeful of what her hair had covered.

"Ma'am, you'll need to step away from the bike," Deputy Chavez broke in.

If Ross's slow perusal was a balm to her pride, Chavez's stony expression was the pinprick slowly deflating her confidence . . . which kind of turned her on.

However, if she moved off the bike, he'd see the wet spot on the leather—and how embarrassing would that be?

"Whenever you're ready," Deputy Chavez growled. "Refusing isn't an option."

"Why? You gonna frisk me?"

"I don't think I have to," he said with a sharpened edge to his voice. "I can tell you're not carrying."

"What gave it away, Deputy?" she said, flashing him a smile she hoped would thaw his icy reserve.

"I've got an eye for concealed weapons."

"Then you obviously missed a couple suspicious lumps," she said, drawing out her words in the sexiest whisper she could manage.

A muscle flexed along his strong, square jaw. "Do you want me to search you?"

"I wouldn't want you to give me any special favors on account of who my daddy is."

"Wouldn't think of it," he said silkily. "Wonder what the judge is going to say when we bring you in."

Up to that point, Sarah had thought the two men were just having a little fun at her expense, but Chavez's face didn't show a flicker of what was really going through his mind. For the first time, she wondered if she wasn't going to be able to talk her way out of this after all. "We don't have to wake Daddy up for something so minor, do we, boys? Can't we work something out?"

"What do you have in mind, kitten?" Deputy Ross murmured.

Her gaze swung from Chavez's impassive face to Ross's. His smile was appreciative, something she could work with. Maybe he'd be willing to convince his friend to let this incident slide right under the carpet.

"I don't know, Deputy Ross. Neither of you have been in Honkytonk long. You don't know how things really work in our little town."

"And you want to help us out? Hear that, Joe? Sarah here is worried about us. Sounds mighty neighborly of you, Sarah."

"Logan . . ." Deputy Chavez said, his deep voice rising in warning. "Go run her plates."

"Sure. This is your bust." His gaze flickered over Sarah's chest, and a grin split his face.

Sarah narrowed her eyes at him until he sauntered back to his squad car.

Alone with Chavez, she took a deep breath, looking at him from beneath the brush of her eyelashes to see if his gaze followed the movement of her chest.

Nope, his gaze was locked on her face. Deciding that maybe she should give him a little cooperation before she completely pissed him off, she kicked down the stand and climbed off her bike, knowing she was giving him an eyeful of her moist pussy— which, again, really turned her on. "Look, I know this looks bad."

"This looks like you're racking up multiple misdemeanor counts, Miss Michelson."

No hesitation. No clearing his throat because she'd shocked or pleased him. Damn, he was a tough nut to crack. "Honestly, it's just a little harmless hell raising."

The deputy shook his head, his expression turning downright grim. "Ever seen a person lay a bike down on pavement? Seen what road burn can do a person's skin?"

Was he worried about her skin? She shook her head and stepped closer until only a few measly inches separated his Kevlar-cloaked chest and her beaded nipples.

"Ever seen what can happen when a head hits the pavement without a helmet?" he continued.

"It's not against the law to ride without a helmet."

"It is against the law to ride buck naked in public."

She quirked one side of her mouth up. "But I'm not completely nude."

His chest rose, swift and hard. "Cowboy boots and chaps don't cover the important parts."

Sarah let her gaze sweep his body in a slow once-over. She lifted one brow when she locked with his dark brown eyes. "So you did notice my 'parts.' "

"I notice everything, Miss Michelson. This time you went too far."

She cocked her head to the side. "How'd you know about this ahead of time anyway? You had time to get a roadblock up."

"Do you think this is all about you?" he said evenly. "Maybe we were here stopping drunk drivers."

"On this little horse trail of a road? Come on, who ratted me out?"

Deputy Chavez's jaw flexed, but otherwise he didn't betray any emotion. The man had to be made of stone. "A concerned citizen phoned in."

She snorted. "Concerned—my ass. It was just someone who didn't want to lose a bet. Don't be a killjoy. Don't you ever do something just because it's fun?"

"Ma'am, pardon me for saying this, but your daddy should have spanked you more when you were a child."

"Daddy would never raise a hand against me."

"Well, he didn't do you any favors."

All this talk about spanking was getting her flustered. Her face grew warm; sweat beaded on her upper lip. She licked it away and tilted her head, widening her eyes to let him see a hint of worry. "Look, there's no reason for us to get into a fuss. There must be something I can do to make this right."

"You can. You can turn around and put your hands behind your back."

Her breath huffed. "You can't be serious."

"As a heart attack."

"No warrants on that bike, Joe!" Deputy Ross called out, approaching them again.

"Of course there's not," Sarah huffed. "It's my goddamn bike." Deputy Chavez's expression tightened, and she knew her attitude wasn't helping matters one bit, so she tried another tack, forcing her mouth into a tiny smile that never failed to make men melt. "Deputy, isn't there some way for us to work a trade? Something you want that will make you forget all about this?"

His gaze narrowed, landing on her lips. "What do you have in mind?"

She bit her lip to make sure his attention stayed there. "If you go easy on me . . . I'll be easy for you."

Deputy Ross's low, rumbling chuckle was encouraging.

"Let me get this straight," Deputy Chavez said. "Are you offering me sexual favors in exchange for me forgetting about the ticket I'm getting ready to write?"

She eyed him with suspicion. "Not if it means you're just gonna slap me with more charges."

"Sarah, Sarah, Sarah . . ." Something in Ross's softly stated words warned her she was pushing his buddy a little too far.

But she wasn't the patient sort, and Deputy Chavez was a challenge she couldn't back down from.

Why'd he have to be such a handsome man? If he'd been butt-ugly, she might have stood a chance at charming him. She'd like nothing better than to offer the deputy something he'd never have a hope of getting if he didn't already have a face that could make any woman wet.

Darker than Deputy Ross, with tawny skin, black hair, dark, hooded eyes, and a large, muscular frame that could sink a woman's body deep into a soft mattress when he covered her, she could barely withhold a deep, lustful sigh just looking at him.

Surely there was a way to cut through his starchy reserve.

Maybe she could try reasoning with him rather than seducing him. "Look, this doesn't have to be a big deal. How about you just let me turn my bike around, and I'll go on home? No harm, no foul."

"It's a little too late for that," Chavez said.

Sarah's hands fisted by her hips, and her chin tilted. "Please. I don't want to end up on my daddy's docket."

"Should have thought about that before you decided to take a ride on the wild side."

"You see there?" she said, again biting her lower lip to call his attention to everything he was passing up. "That's the problem. It's not like this was premeditated. I didn't decide. I didn't think about it ahead of time. Danny Dawg dared me and then had the gall to bet the bar I wouldn't have the nerve. . . ."

The slow shake of his head told her he wasn't swayed by her lame-ass argument.

"Argh!" she growled and stomped her foot.

"Turn around. Give me your hands."

Sarah rolled her eyes, pretending she wasn't growing concerned. Her dad would have a cow if he knew she'd planned to ride naked past the Honkytonk bar because of a bet. However, she couldn't think of another argument, because her breaths were quickening with her panic. She jerked around and put her hands behind her.

"Logan, why don't you move those barricades out of the way?"

Deputy Chavez clipped two manacles around her wrists but didn't step away immediately. A long, pregnant moment stretched her nerves tight as the heat radiating from his body warmed her backside.

"You change your mind?" she asked, her voice shaking, all bravado draining away.

"I'm going to do you a favor," he said quietly, his breath lifting the fine strands of her hair beside her ear.

"What kind of favor?" she whispered back, her heart starting to race because she sensed he was relenting . . . and because he stood so close his scent teased her senses. Coffee and musky man. *Yum.*

"I'm going to drive you back to your place and leave you with a warning."

"That sounds more than fair," she said softly.

"And you won't give me any more trouble from here on out on my watch, you hear?"

"You mean forever?" she said, unable to suppress the disbelief in her tone. Didn't he know he was asking the impossible?

"Yeah. As long as I'm here. No trouble."

"I can try, but I can't promise you a thing beyond tonight. Shit happens around me. I don't plan on getting into trouble, but somehow I end up on a highway in my birthday suit and a pair of boots. . . ."

"If you don't stay out of trouble, you can count on the fact I'm gonna know about it."

"You have people watching me?"

"You can bet on it."

Sarah swallowed hard. "Because I'm a troublemaker?"

"Because I'm staking a claim."

Goddamn, he did not just say that. Did he know he was waving a red flag right in front of her nose? "I'm not property. I won't be *staked.*"

"Funny, I thought that was what you were asking me to do when you were trying to bargain with me."

She swallowed again. Despite his arrogant claim, her body didn't seem the least bit offended. Fact was, pleasure slid right down her inner thighs. "Deputy?" she whispered.

"Yes, Miss Michelson?" he said just as softly.

"I have a confession to make."

"Confession's good for the soul. So I hear."

"Glad you think so. . . ." She paused and wet her lips, this time because her mouth was dry. "I'm carrying."

"You slide a weapon somewhere I can't see?"

"Uh-huh."

"Sarah . . ." A deep breath fluttered across her cheek. "I'm not playing games with you tonight. I'm on duty."

"I won't tell. I don't think your friend will either."

Footsteps crunched from the direction of the other squad car. "Man, you have to search her now," Logan said. "She says she's concealing a weapon. Um . . . I have to go gather up the flares."

A low groan sounded behind her. "Little witch! Spread 'em," he said, nudging apart her feet until her stance was wide. Cool air licked between her legs and carried the scent of the arousal gathering along the folds of her sex.

"Ah, God," she said and bit her lips because his large, warm hands landed on her shoulders, and she thought she might just melt into a puddle.

He started at her neck, lifting her long hair, thumbs skimming beneath the thick fall, pressing deep enough she sighed and tilted back her head. Then his hands glided over her shoulders, down her left arm and then her right. Hands skimmed her back and slid around her waist to smooth upward and check beneath her breasts.

Her breath caught, and his hands paused, thumbs nudging the tender undersides.

"Nothing hidden here," he murmured.

"Not curious about whether they're real?"

His breath deepened, and his hands cupped her breasts, lifting them to deliver a squeeze. "No foreign objects there."

Sarah smiled and then gasped as thumbs flicked her tightly beaded tips, but he didn't linger. His hands slid to her sides again and then to her hips, sinking lower to cup her buttocks.

89

When fingers glided between her legs and slid through the fluid smeared on her inner thighs, they slowed.

"Goddamn," he breathed.

Her thighs quivered, but he was already moving downward, smoothing down her black leather chaps to her boots and then up her outer thighs. He stepped backward. "You lied. You don't have any hidden weapons."

"Maybe you didn't check thoroughly enough," she said, her breaths ragged.

"Think you need a cavity search?"

She glanced over her shoulder and wrinkled her nose. "That sounds unappetizing. I was thinking more along the line of a thorough . . . probing."

His hands gripped the notches of her hips. "You don't make the rules, Sarah. I'm not playing your game."

She bit her tongue to keep from blurting out the fact she'd gotten him to let her off with a warning. And hadn't the pat down been her idea, too?

His breath stirred her hair again. "Think it was just a coincidence that Danny Dawg dared you to ride naked tonight?"

She stiffened against him. "Why would he do it on purpose? And why would he do it for you?"

"Danny got pulled over for a broken taillight last night. And wouldn't you know his license was expired?"

"Son of a bitch."

"That's me," he said, his grip tightening and then falling away. "And don't forget it. When I'm not wearing this badge, you can fight me all you like, but I know how hot you are right now." He slipped his fingers between her legs from behind and held them against her folds.

Sarah wished her pussy wasn't primed, but she couldn't help the little contraction that sucked at his fingertips. "It was the ride. Don't you know why girls like motorcycles?"

"It's a sad substitute." His fingers pulled away. "Wait for my call."

"When hell freezes over, Deputy," she bit out.

"Keep tellin' yourself that, if it helps your pride." He tugged the chain between her cuffs to shift her to the side and open the back door of the cruiser. "Now, slide on across that seat. I'll take you home."

Sarah bent and slid inside.

"Buddy, you need anything else?" Logan asked, closer than she'd known, her mind had been so filled with Deputy Chavez. "I got the bike off the road and hidden behind some bushes. She can come for it tomorrow."

Chavez slammed her door. Logan Ross winked as he passed, and then the tight-faced deputy slid into the driver's seat and pulled out onto the highway.

Sarah sat in stony silence. No way was she talking to the bastard. He'd set her up so he could do what? Get her attention to ask her on a date? How low was that?

While the cool air tightened her nipples, Sarah couldn't help the flush of pleasure that swept her cheeks and chest at the thought of the deliberate planning that'd gone into tonight's ingenious mousetrap.

He'd played her. Knew her hot buttons. He'd set the trap with sweet temptation and then baited her with a cool reserve that pricked her interest. How did he know her so well? Had he been watching her all along, talking to people she knew just to learn enough about her personality to strategize?

The thought was heady. Imagine what he'd be like once he got her into bed—not that she would give up the game so easily.

No, the next round would be hers.

2

"Not something you see every day," Logan said, humor lacing the staticky voice.

Joe was tempted to flip his cell phone closed. They'd used the phones instead of the radio during the stop to keep it off the radar. The last thing he'd wanted was more "help" arriving.

Sarah had been intimidated enough, at least in the first few minutes. The woman had recovered quickly. He'd remember that next time. She didn't have a lick of common sense, but she had guts.

"It's not something you'll see ever again," Joe growled.

"You think taming that wildcat's gonna be easy?"

"Of course not. The trick will be to stay one step ahead."

"We caught her off guard this time. You can bet she won't be as easy to trap the next time."

"Ever think the lady might want to be caught?" Joe asked, remembering the excitement simmering in her baby blues.

"Because she was creaming for you?"

"She's intrigued. Most of the boys around here think with their dicks."

"And you proved her wrong? I saw where those fingers were sliding."

"I didn't give her everything she wanted." But, damn, he'd wanted to. He'd been an inch from bending her over the hood of the cruiser.

"Did you ask her out?"

"Of course not. I told her to wait for my call."

A snort sounded from the phone.

Joe grinned.

"Betcha ten she's back at the Honkytonk tomorrow night," Logan drawled.

"I'm counting on it."

Soft chuckles filled the air. "How'd I do? Think she bought the good-cop, bad-cop act?"

"You were convincing. Imagine any woman thinking you'd be the easy one to manipulate."

"Couldn't have her turning those pretty blue eyes on me. Last thing she wants is a nice guy. You sure this is what you want? She's got quite a rep—most of it bad."

"She's acting out. She'll buck against anyone who tries to tie her down."

"Buddy, maybe it's not an act."

"You forget," Joe said slowly, raising his hand to his face and inhaling her pungent fragrance, "I had my fingers on her pulse. She's ready for this. I just have to redirect her rebellion. She wants to fight, but she's only fighting herself."

"Let me know what I can do to help."

"I will," he said, gritting his teeth. Much as he wanted to keep the woman all to himself, he admitted he wasn't the man to get her "softened" up. "Be there tomorrow night?"

"At the bar? Wouldn't miss it. Better get back out on the north road. Later."

Joe closed his phone and set it on the seat beside him and

then found the speed-trap blind he'd use until midnight. He sat in his squad car, the AC blasting in his face, the windows rolled all the way down. The better to hear the whine of a powerful engine screaming down the highway.

He turned off the cruiser's lights, not wanting to alert a driver heading his way of his presence until it was too late.

He'd been here earlier when Logan had called him to let him know Sarah had left her house in the buff ready to fly by the bar. Joe had cursed, which had elicited a deep rumble of laughter from Logan.

"Got those barriers up?" Joe had barked into the phone.

"Everything's set. Ready to rescue the lady from her own poor judgment?"

The single beam from a motorcycle had swept the curve of the road in a bright, blinding arc. Joe could tell the moment she spotted the cruiser hidden behind the tree.

The beam had wobbled as she'd applied the brakes, and Joe had cursed, afraid she'd lay the bike down on the pavement, but the engine revved, and she roared around the curve.

He'd turned on his headlights, flipped the switch to send the blue lights strobing, and pulled onto the deserted county road.

"I can't wait to hear what she has to say," Logan had said, his voice lazy and amused.

Joe had listened with only half his brain engaged. His bright twin beams reflected on creamy white skin and a head of pale blond curls that whipped around her shoulders.

The barricade with its orange lights and the patrol car parked beside it came into view beyond the motorcycle and its driver.

The bike hadn't slowed down. And for a second, Joe had wondered if she intended to make a run for it.

But "Sweet Sarah" had slowed, her tires spitting gravel as she'd turned the bike at the last moment and ground to a halt.

Joe had idled his engine, knowing better than to cut it with the wild-eyed glance she'd given him and then Logan. She'd still been considering her options.

He'd hit the speaker switch. "Sarah Michelson, cut your engine. You're under arrest."

Sarah's face had turned toward his, her full bottom lip pouting. She'd twisted the throttle, and the engine had growled.

"Don't even think about it, sweetheart," he'd said into the mic again.

Her chin had jutted upward. Her eyes narrowed. She hadn't liked being called sweetheart.

But she hadn't minded straddling a motorcycle buck naked.

"Sweet, sweet Sarah," he'd whispered to himself. "Don't you want to know what happens next?"

Joe's cock stirred at the thought of the warm, wet welcome her body had dripped all over his hand. He'd been tempted to take her up on her invitation and bend her over the hood. However, he wasn't in this for a quickie. He was in for the long haul. Everything he'd learned about her, everything he'd experienced in their short encounter told him she was the one for him.

He would never have thought a round baby-doll face, wild tangles of white-blond hair, and wide-set pale blue eyes would stop his heart. He'd always preferred brunettes. He'd always dated slender women with boyish hips. But Sarah's fleshy bottom had felt like heaven. Her large, round breasts had fit his palms just right.

Still, it wasn't her sweet body and face or even her tantalizing lemony scent that had convinced him in the end. It had been that hint of fear and spicy arousal, all wrapped up together to make her breaths shiver. The harder his expression had grown, the more aroused she'd become.

Sarah didn't know it, and would probably have denied it until the day she died, but she wanted a man to dominate her.

The boys she'd been with didn't have a clue. She'd walked all over them, tossing them away like candy wrappers once they'd been unwrapped and devoured.

Logan had guessed her proclivity first, as he should. As someone who lived the lifestyle, he had miles more experience recognizing potential submissiveness in a woman. Joe had only dabbled. Had never really considered himself a true dom, but something about Sarah told him he simply hadn't found the woman he wanted to be the softer half of him.

He'd watched her for weeks. Gathered all the intel he could from the gossips on the force, from Cody Westhofen over a beer while they'd sat in a deer stand. He thought he'd understood her until she'd slipped off her bike and stuck her chest out in front of him, her chin lifting in a challenge so blatant it rang completely false.

He'd taken one look at her, seen the excitement that stiffened her nipples into reddened buds, dragged his gaze to hers, and kept it locked there. If he'd dropped it once to study her attributes again, he would have missed it. The initial flare of excitement had dimmed, replaced by a hint of hopefulness. When he'd kept his tone hard, his will stalwart, her skin had flushed, and a thin sheen of sweat had made her skin dewy—she'd glowed.

He'd never felt more powerful, more deeply aroused or protective of a woman. Sarah had no choice in the matter now. She was going to be his.

Still, there was going to be a long battle ahead of him, but for now he'd settle for conquering her desire for her father's attention, no matter how inappropriate the means.

Had she been a man, her latest high jinks would have been waved off by her daddy with a slap on the shoulder and a wink to the good-ole boys. From what he'd heard, Daddy was exasperated with his little darling and would no longer try to protect her from her actions because he realized he'd spoiled her rotten.

Daddy wanted Sarah "settled." Joe didn't think he'd care too much about the method, which was a good thing because he wanted the judge's approval of the match on down the road—after he'd taught "Sweet Sarah" the merits of obedience.

Sarah tugged down the bottom edge of her short, black skirt and sauntered into the Honkytonk, satisfied when gazes swung her way and then stayed glued to the sway of her hips. She'd dressed to kill—or at least to get one deputy's undivided attention.

The spandex fabric hugged her ass, leaving no doubt to anyone observing that panties were an optional accessory this night. The black cropped top she wore above it dipped low between her breasts and had just enough stretch in the weave to support her tits without yet another "optional" accessory.

As she strolled past the bar, Danny Dawg's eyes lit up, and a low whistle blew between his pursed lips. Still dressed in his plumber's work shirt and blue jeans that lovingly clung to his nicely shaped body, Danny knew his common appeal and worked it. "Damn, girl. Don't suppose you're all wrapped up with a bow for me?"

The bow was the skinny red ribbon she'd tied around her neck. "I don't know, Danny. Depends on whether you were the one who ratted me out last night. The cops told me you did."

"Me?" he chirped, his eyes widening too innocently to be real. "You think I wasn't waitin' at the edge of the parking lot for a peek?"

She cupped his cheek with her palm and narrowed her eyes at him, but his gaze was far too appreciative, his expression hopeful. Maybe he hadn't been the one who'd passed the message to the deputies. "Just checkin'. They're probably just trying to make me think I can't trust my friends."

Danny slid off his stool, a wide grin splitting his face. "Does that mean you'll let me slide a hand up that skirt to check the plumbing?"

"My pipes are free and clear. 'Course, if you mean to keep those fingers attached to your hands, you might wanna give that plan a second thought."

Danny's eyelids dipped, and his head tilted back. "What are you up to tonight?"

"Just makin' a point. Someone thought they could corral me."

He shook his head. "Don't know you that well, do they?"

And Danny did. Back in high school she'd dated the star quarterback and rode the team's bus and Danny's cock to many a victory. "No, they don't. But you do, don't you?" she said, irony thick in her voice. Not that Danny was smart enough to figure out she was laughing at him.

"Speak of the devils. . . ." Danny cupped the top of her head and swiveled her face to a dark corner of the bar.

The deputies, looking like a matching pair of brindle pit bulls, sat in a booth watching her.

Had she been wearing any, her panties would have been soaked in seconds. Sarah grabbed Danny's hand and pulled him toward the dance floor. "Come on. Make it good for me, Danny."

"Always ready to oblige a lady," he said, amusement lacing his warm Texas drawl.

She slanted a gaze upward, wondering if she'd underestimated him, but his vacuous grin remained in place. "I won't mind a bit if one of your hands strays south, lover boy."

"So long as Deputy Chavez gets an eyeful of me feeling you up?"

She shot him another glance. So maybe he wasn't as stupid as she'd always thought. "Don't be shy."

"Not with you, darlin', although I have to warn you I don't think he's the kind to let you play your little games."

"Think so? Why's that? Did he say anything about me?"

"Something about trimming your wings."

Sarah snorted. "As though I'd ever let a man try to cage me."

"That's what I told him, too. But he didn't seem the least bit put off the challenge."

"I appreciate you tellin' him that, Danny."

"Thought you might."

He dropped her hand and smoothed both of his over her hips and around to her bottom.

Sarah snuggled next to his chest and sighed. "Ever wonder why we never got married?"

"Besides the fact your daddy doesn't think I'm good enough for you?"

"My daddy's not a snob."

"Nope, but he told me you were too much filly for me."

"I'm surprised you listened."

"I didn't, but the first time you opened my pants in the boy's locker room and had your wicked way scared the crap out of me. I just knew I was gonna blow my chance for a scholarship with you blowing my dick where anyone could walk in and see."

"That why you broke up with me?"

His arms tightened around her. "I didn't exactly break up with you," he grumbled.

"No, but you did go off to college without me." That she'd opted out of going to college even though her father had offered to pay for it, she didn't mention. Instead she'd stayed closer to home, accepting a job clerking at the courthouse—a job her daddy had arranged, reminding her that the courthouse was only ten steps from the jail in his best voice of doom.

"I told you I'd see you at Christmas break."

"But you didn't exactly stay true to me."

"None of those girls could light my torch the way you could. Besides, don't even try to tell me you waited."

"Not even a day, sweetheart." Sarah sighed again and then jerked when she felt the hem of her skirt inch upward. "What are you doing?"

"Hiking up your skirt to flash a little cheek. They're both watchin' real close."

"Trying to get us both arrested?"

"Nope, but one of 'em is headed this way. That's what you wanted, right?"

Sarah laughed against his chest. "Danny, I ever tell you I love you?"

"Nope. Would have been a lie. And that's not something you'd ever do."

"Excuse me," came a deep, hard-edged voice beside her.

Sarah didn't lift her head.

"I'm cutting in."

"Darlin'," Danny murmured. "That okay with you?"

Sarah glanced over her shoulder to meet Deputy Chavez's steel-eyed glare. "I suppose. Wouldn't want to make a fuss. Tara might ban me for another week like she did when I chased Cody into the bathroom."

Danny released her, tipped the rim of his baseball cap, and sauntered back to the bar. Sarah didn't have even a second to catch her breath before her wrist was manacled by hard fingers, and she was brought up against a solid chest.

Her nipples appreciated the pressure, spiking hard.

"I told you to wait for my call."

"Deputy Chavez, I don't follow orders very well. Ask anyone who knows me."

"I think you will. And call me Joe from now on."

"How you gonna make me, Joe? You and Logan gonna tie me down and take turns spanking me until I cry uncle?"

"Is that what it will take?"

Her tongue wet her lips. "I was just teasing."

"Sure you were. That's why you've got goose bumps rising on your skin?"

"Maybe I'm cold."

"Honey, want me to slip my fingers somewhere to see whether you're telling me the truth?"

Sarah lifted her chin. "Think my pussy's some kind of lie detector?"

"As a matter of fact . . ." He pressed her hand to his shoulder and angled her body toward the back booth and Logan Ross who sat at the end of the bench seat, one brow raised her way. Then Joe Chavez's hand slid over her rump, pulled up the edge of her skirt, and rubbed the globe of her ass.

Sarah drew in a deep breath and glanced around the dance floor, but no one could see what he was doing. His large body blocked their view. Fingers slid between her cheeks, arrowing downward, sliding deeper between her legs until they touched the moisture spilling from her body.

"Answer seems a very wet yes. Baby girl, you gonna let us take care of you tonight?"

Sarah wanted to deny him. To prove her will was strong. But he thrust a single digit inside her and swirled, and her knees nearly buckled beneath the wave of heat that suffused her body.

A thigh nudged between hers, supporting her weight. She clung weakly to his shoulders.

"Come with us. Now."

"I'll come this second if you'll just go a little deeper," she whispered.

A sexy chuckle shook the chest she cuddled closer to. "Don't you want to know how we plan to tame you, kitten?"

"Both of you?"

"At first. I think I need a little help getting the lessons across."

"I don't need any lessons. I know how to fuck."

"But you don't know how to obey, do you?"

"Who says I want to learn to obey a man?" she said, weakening, her body melting against his.

"You do," he said, swirling his fingers in the excitement spilling over his hand.

She knew she was going to come, but didn't like the fact her body telegraphed her decision. "I'm a little bored tonight," she said lazily. "Maybe I'm just curious."

"Whatever you want to call it. All I know is that when I challenge you, you melt like butter. The thought of a man taking charge of your body excites you. You want this."

Before she could voice a response, his fingers pulled away and clasped her wrist again, tugging her toward the booth and Logan.

Logan scooted toward the wall, and she found herself sandwiched between the two men, but not before Joe pulled up her skirt high enough that her bare bottom slid across cool vinyl. "Wouldn't want you to spoil your pretty skirt," he murmured.

As if he cared about her clothing. She snorted.

Logan lifted his beer with one hand; the other settled between her legs. "Relax. No one can see a thing. Let me take care of you."

Sarah stiffened. Relax? Her sex was drenched. Between Danny's "helpful" naughtiness, Joe's bossiness, and Logan's gentle but persistent pressure, she felt like all her defenses were slowly unraveling. Not a bad sensation, but she'd so wanted to be the one in charge tonight.

She settled her back against the squab and slowly parted her legs.

Fingers stroked her inner thighs in lazy circles. "Get your bike out of the bushes?" Logan asked, a grin tugging at the corners of his lips.

"Yes," she said breathlessly. "No problems."

"Can I get you folks something to drink?" Cody Westhofen sidled up next to the booth, his gaze dropping to where Logan's hand disappeared. "I take it you won't be staying long. Want me to get your tab?"

"What are you doing here anyway?" Sarah gasped, trying to close her legs, but Joe's wide palm slid down to cup her inner thigh, preventing the move.

Cody's crooked grin widened when she glared. "Tara's short-handed. And because she has to be here, I said I'd lend a hand."

"Glad things are working out between you two," Joe said. "She finally let you slip those knots?"

"Let's just say we take turns." His chin jutted toward Sarah. "Looks like you both have a handful."

"Appreciate the advice you gave me," Joe murmured.

Sarah narrowed her gaze on Joe and then lifted an embarrassed glance to meet Cody's smiling face. "Men are such gossips."

"Had to help out the deputy here. Can't let the fairer sex think they have the upper hand."

Joe lifted his beer in a rueful salute. "This one's gonna wear the proof on her sexy little ass."

"Wish I could be there to see it, but Tara would have my balls."

"I'll be sure to give you all the juicy details."

Cody walked away laughing, and Sarah dug her fingernails into two thick wrists. "Not funny, guys. I'm not some blow-up doll. You were discussing me like I didn't have a say in anything."

"You don't," Joe said, his words clipped. "That's what I'm trying to impress on you. From here on out, you're mine."

"Then why are you letting *him* finger me?" she said, jerking her head toward Logan.

"Because it's what I want. And you'll do whatever I ask."

"Cody's got our ticket ready," Logan interjected.

"You go pay," Joe said, sliding his hand away and standing beside the booth. "I'll hustle her to the truck."

"Maybe I've changed my mind," she gritted out.

"Do you want me to bend you over the table and let everyone here see how much you really want this?"

Sarah's jaw fell open. The thought that he might follow through on his threat was horrifying. So why was she sitting in a puddle of her own desire?

3

Joe walked briskly toward his truck, not slowing his steps despite the steady flow of cursing from the woman teetering on heels behind him.

His blood had been simmering slowly ever since he'd spotted her strolling into the bar, chatting up her old beau, Danny "Dawg" Denton.

Then she'd deliberately baited him, encouraging Danny to slide up her skirt to get a peek at her creamy cheeks. In her tight little skirt and next-to-nothing top, she should have looked slutty. Instead she seemed more like a little girl playing hard to be a grown-up. Like a woman trying to be bad.

Logan had laughed softly beside him. "Looks like she wasn't waitin' on your call for long. But the good news is you read her like a book."

With her soft bottom winking beneath her flirty skirt, Joe had been out of his seat so fast he'd nearly toppled the table.

"Slow down, will you?" Sarah griped behind him, tugging against his firm grip.

He reached his truck, opened the passenger door, and turned to grip her waist.

"I can manage on my own," she hissed.

"This is more fun, don't you think?" he said, lifting her up and sitting her sideways at the end of the bench seat. He reached for the bottom of her skirt and rolled it upward.

Her hands reached to tug it down as he continued shoving up. "We can wrestle over this scrap of fabric," he said, still seething inside, "but we both know you aren't shy."

"Maybe I don't want to flash my vajayjay to the entire parking lot."

"Who's gonna see? I want your skirt around your waist for the drive to Logan's."

Her face screwed into a fierce scowl, and then curiosity lent a gleam to her eyes. "Why Logan's house and not yours?"

"Logan has better toys."

Her blue eyes rounded. "Oh."

"Better hurry it up," Logan said, striding up behind him. "Dawg was making his way to the door."

Joe flashed her a determined look. "Pull it up or take the damn thing off. It wasn't covering anything anyway."

Sarah bit her lip and lifted her bottom as he slid up the skirt. Once again, her naked bottom settled onto a cool seat, this time leather.

"Get to the middle and straddle the stick."

He darted out of the doorway, and Logan stepped up, arching an eyebrow until she flounced to the center and clumsily swung a leg over the stick shift mounted on the floor of the cab.

Joe slid behind the wheel. "Wave at Danny so he knows you're all right. Don't want him breaking down Logan's door 'cause he thinks you might need rescuing."

Sarah glanced through the windshield and saw Danny pushing through the double swinging doors. She lifted a hand to wave, and he halted, his gaze narrowing on the two officers flanking her.

"Boyfriend?" Logan asked.

"Like you don't already know."

"Old boyfriend," Joe ammended. "But not the man for you, otherwise you wouldn't be here now, would you?"

Joe put the truck in reverse, which forced her to widen her legs as he shifted the gear. "Comfortable?" he asked as he pulled onto the road leading the opposite direction from the town.

"You're joking, right?"

"Logan . . ."

"Right," Logan murmured and then placed his hand between her legs again. Deft fingers trailed up her knee, tickling her inner thigh, and then pressed something cold between her folds.

She gasped and tried to wriggle away, but where could she go?

"Hold still," Logan said. "I'm just putting a little metal egg inside you. Something to keep your mind busy."

A low hum filled the cab as the egg vibrated.

"Jesus." Her inner muscles clasped around it, forcing it out, but Logan pressed against the end to hold it in place.

"One of your toys?" she said, clenching her teeth against the riot starting between her legs.

"This toy's for your pleasure."

The emphasis on the word *your* didn't pass her by. "This how you spend your nights off? Double-teaming some poor girl?"

Logan draped an arm around her shoulders while his fingers kept the egg lodged inside her. "No, tonight's special."

His thumb pushed the egg deeper, and the vibrations increased. Sarah couldn't help but lean back in his embrace to tilt her pussy higher. Hoping the darkness of the cab would cloak her action, she slid fingers toward the top of her cunt and rubbed her clitoris.

Logan curled his fingers around hers and placed her hand on her bare thigh. "Much as we love proof you're a horny little thing, you don't get to come until we say so."

"That was crude."

"You're sitting in a truck with two men you barely know, and you just fingered yourself. Tell me you didn't like it when I called you horny."

Joe cleared his throat. "Anything you want to know about us, Sarah? We have the advantage here, seeing as how everyone in Honkytonk has their own 'Sweet Sarah' tale to tell."

Logan's fingers smoothed down her thigh to cup her knee and pull it toward him, opening her wider.

Then Joe's hand settled on her leg and smoothed upward toward her pussy.

She tensed as his fingers strummed her as if pressing piano keys. Then he circled the end of the egg protruding between her folds and pushed it deeper, his fingers following it inside.

Sarah's hands came down on Logan's and Joe's thighs, and she dug her nails deep as she sank deeper in the seat. They were doing it again. Pretending there was nothing extraordinary happening here. Just a conversation. "You know each other well?" she panted. "Did you know each other before you came here?"

"We're both from San Antonio," Joe said evenly. "Worked at different substations, but we liked the same clubs."

His fingers filled her. Three of them—long and thick. "Bars?" she gasped.

"Private clubs," Logan said. "Some drinking involved, but that wasn't the draw."

"What was . . . the draw?" she bit out as the vibrations increased.

"The scene," Logan said, his hand slipping over her shoulder to palm her breast, his thumb starting a slow, wicked up-and-down glide that had her nipple beading hard. "I'm a dom, Sarah. Do you know what that is?"

"Whips . . . chains?"

"I've used them, but it's more than equipment."

"More . . ." she groaned.

"Need me to decrease the vibrations?" he whispered. "Wouldn't want you to lose your train of thought."

"No! The 'more' at the clubs . . . what did you mean?"

Logan bent closer to whisper in her ear. "I train submissives, sweetheart."

"But you came here," she gritted out. "Why? You're not going to find women like that here. Into the kinkier stuff."

"I find them everywhere I go. I was the one who first alerted Joe that you were a likely candidate."

Sarah froze. "Well, your kink radar needs adjusting. I don't want to be submissive to any man."

"Joe and I think otherwise. But I can understand you being a little scared to admit it to yourself."

"I'm not scared," she said, but her voice lacked conviction—only because Joe was flicking her clit with this thumb.

"Sure you are," Logan said, his voice soft and sexy as warm silk. "And incredibly aroused. You do know your whole body's quivering. That your pussy is pulsing, sucking on the egg now. I can hear the wet noises you're making."

"It's just the vibrations. I like dildos. Have a collection of my own."

"*Liar,*" he said, amusement in his rumbling whisper. "Maybe you have toys. But you like this. Like the little thrill of fear of the unknown. You're already wondering what it'll be like to feel the flick of a lash."

"Are you guys gonna make me crawl around on my knees and call you Master?"

"Only if you need it."

"How will you know . . . if I need that?"

"Our job is to figure out your needs. Introduce certain aspects of the life and see what works for you. Joe's not a dom. Not really. But he's willing to do whatever you need to make you happy. To free you."

Joe's fingers withdrew and made lazy circles around her opening.

Sarah took a deep, shuddering breath. "Anyone around here can tell you I'm already free. Free and easy."

"Sweetheart," Joe said, "you've been crying out for a man to take you in hand." He lifted his hand to change gears.

Sarah straightened in her seat to have a look around, grateful to have a moment free of frisky fingers to gather her scattered thoughts and shore up wilting defenses.

He turned into a rural subdivision outside of town where the lots were several acres large. Plenty of privacy. Plenty of live oak and mesquite to shut out curious gazes.

Joe brought the truck to a halt in front of a darkened house near the end of the street, only one light from a distant house blinking in the distance.

"I'm going to go inside and get set up," Logan said. "You and Joe can talk. Want me to take the egg, Sarah?"

She nodded wordlessly, and Logan slipped his fingers inside her to retrieve his toy.

Once the door closed behind him, she shifted her gaze to the stick shift between her legs.

"Tell me something, Sarah."

"I'm an open book. Obviously."

"If you don't want this, I'll take you home. If you want me to stay with you when we get there, I'll love you however you want it. Straight-up sex. But if you think you'd like to do a little exploring, see whether this is for you, we'll go inside now.

Thing is, if you walk through those doors, there won't be any going back."

Sarah swallowed. "Would you think me a coward if I chose to go home?"

"No. Your choice isn't part of the game."

"Will you be disappointed in me?"

"Do you really care what I think?"

She stayed silent for a long moment. "I think I might."

His lips twitched. "Never thought you were a girl who didn't know her own mind."

Her gaze slid away. "This is all new. I haven't ever . . ." She took another breath and tried again. "I haven't had two men. I haven't ever tried anything so extreme."

"Do you trust me?"

"Fuck, no."

"Do you at least trust the fact that we won't hurt you?"

"You can't be all that bad, or you never would've been hired. The town does pretty thorough background checks before they hire cops."

"That's right. There's nothing to find. No skeletons in the closet. No bound and gagged women lying in my bed either."

Sarah looked out the window toward Logan's front door. "He said this isn't your thing."

"I've always been curious. I've experimented some. I can take it or leave it, but I wouldn't be here now if I didn't think you needed this."

"What is it about me that makes you think I need this? Do I give off a freak vibe?"

"I'll explain it to you later. Come inside?"

She turned to tangle her gaze with his. "Do I have to act happy about everything?"

"I'd be disappointed if you didn't cuss me out at least once tonight."

"I can't back out? I don't get any 'safe' words?"

"You won't need them. If it's too much, it will be in a good way. If it gets too heavy, I'll make him stop."

"You're both going to have me? Fuck me? And you're all right with that?"

Joe's features grew taut. "I won't share you ever again. And you won't be flirting with other men either."

Sarah let her eyelashes dip. "But flirting's a biological thing—natural for me."

"You're going to learn some discipline because I'm a jealous man. You need to learn to restrain your natural inclinations except when you're with me. Ready?"

"Sweet fuck," she whispered.

"It will be. Promise."

Joe heard the string of curses from the playroom and met Logan's grin.

Joe grabbed his tackle box and strode through the playroom, not giving Sarah a single glance, and then sat at the table and opened his box.

Logan sauntered inside with two beers dangling from one hand and a leather flogger in the other.

Joe set out his tools, pliers, fishing line, feathers, and assorted hooks and began fashioning the first of several lures he intended to make while Sarah "settled."

From the corner of his eye, he caught a glimpse of her flushed face. Her neck craned upward to catch his eye.

Sarah knelt on a thickly padded step, her body draped forward over an upholstered bench that angled downward so her ass was raised high. Her wrists were buckled into restraints that were fastened with snap hooks to the side of the bench to hold her down.

Leather bands enclosing her upper thighs were also fastened

to the side of the bench so her knees were spread, her pussy open for anyone standing behind her to see. Only, he'd faced her toward the table so he could watch her changing expressions.

She'd made a show of reluctance, dragging her feet toward the bench. He'd seen the flicker of interest in her gaze when he'd called it a spanking bench, and he knew she'd assumed he'd get down to the business of spanking very quickly, followed by a wild fucking.

Patience wasn't one of Sweet Sarah's virtues. When he'd strapped her in and then left her, she'd squealed in frustration and then let loose a nonstop rant that questioned his masculinity, his sexual persuasion, and even his mother's species.

Logan tapped his foot under the table. Joe raised his gaze and followed it to the velvet pouch he'd deposited on the table along with other implements they'd use as the evening progressed.

Joe picked up the bag and poured the contents into his palm. Nipple clamps—tweezers, really. Joe shoved away from the table and walked toward Sarah.

Her gaze narrowed with deadly intent.

Joe dangled the clamps from the metal chain attached to both in front of her nose.

Her face screwed up in confusion, and then their function dawned on her. Her head reared back. "You are not putting those on my tits."

"Need I remind you that you left free will behind at the door?"

"That was before I knew you were just bringing me here to play with the furniture."

Joe knelt in front of her. The padded bench ended just beneath her breasts, so they swung free, the distended tips pointing toward the floor.

He pushed the metal circle at the bottom of one clamp down

113

to open it and held it to her nipple as he pushed the circle up to tighten it. "This too tight?" he asked softly.

Her lips trembled and then firmed into a straight line.

"I'll take that as a no." He slid the ring higher, listening to her erratic breaths. The higher he nudged the circle, the shorter her intakes of air—until a tiny whimper slipped between her lips.

He eased off slightly and then applied the second clamp to her other nipple.

When they were both in place, he tugged the chain suspended between them, straightened, and walked away.

Behind him, Sarah sighed.

Logan picked up an apple from the bowl of fruit he'd brought out. He polished it against his shirt and then dropped it back into the bowl, picking up a large plum next. Satisfaction gleamed in his eyes as his gaze met Joe's, and he stood.

Joe settled in his seat, peering over his shoulder as Logan walked toward Sarah and then circled behind her.

Although she tried, she couldn't quite crane her neck around to see what he was up to.

Logan knelt on the second kneeling pad behind her, causing the leather to squeak, and arched a wicked eyebrow at Joe. The plum disappeared.

From the opening and closing of her lips, Joe didn't have to guess where the plum went.

Logan bent over her, placed a kiss on the top of her hip. "Plums are made for dipping, don't you know?"

His face disappeared behind her. Sarah's eyes closed for a moment, her lips pursing around a quickly drawn breath and then easing as Logan came back up.

"Maybe a little too ripe for my taste. Joe, why don't you give it a try?"

Joe stood slowly, adjusting himself because he'd become too

aroused for his cock not to pass notice. Logan's smirk as he passed him on the way back to his table told him he understood his predicament, but didn't have an ounce of sympathy.

Sarah's face craned upward, color washing her cheeks beet red.

As he came around her backside, he couldn't resist sliding his open palm over one cheek. Soft, creamy skin, rounded buttocks—perfectly made to cushion a man when he came at her from behind.

Then his gaze fell on her open sex, where the purple plum was nestled between reddened labia, which were engorged and glistening with arousal.

His mouth watered even before he knelt on the padded bench and bent downward. He stroked his tongue over the fruit, touching the delicate lips gripping it.

Sarah's bottom quivered.

He stroked again, tasting the sweet plummy taste, and bit the flesh. Liquid dripped from the fruit, spilling over her hooded clit to land on the leather. "Juicy," he whispered just loud enough for her to hear. He smeared his finger in the juice and reached around to her face.

"Bite me and I promise you'll be here all night," he said softly.

Her lips opened, and her tongue swept out to take the sweet juice, licking his finger clean.

As a reward for her obedience, he licked the juices from around the fruit and then dipped lower and pulled her clitoris between his lips and suckled it.

Sarah's hips tilted higher, and he suckled harder, swirling his tongue across the hardening nub until her quivering came in waves, and her thighs tensed hard.

When she mewled, he pulled away, pressed his thumbs against each side of her opening, and popped out the plum.

As he walked back to the table, he ate the fruit, tossing the pit into the trash can without looking back to see her expression.

Logan's one-sided grin told him what he needed to know. Sarah wasn't happy. His chin lifted toward the lure Joe had just finished off with a snip of his pliers. "What kinda fish you gonna catch with that thing?"

Joe cocked one eyebrow. "What does it matter if it actually works—it's pretty." After all, the point wasn't at the end of the lure's hook.

His buddy stretched his arms above his head and feigned a yawn. Then he shoved away from the table and strode to the peg-board mounted on one wall. He plucked a red leather flogger from its mounting hooks and flicked the tail at the air, seeming satisfied with the crack it made.

Joe glanced at Sarah from the corner of his eye, noted her widening eyes, and grinned.

Her head ducked down to hide her expression.

He angled his chair to watch and then took a swig of his beer as Logan walked around Sarah, touching her shoulder, shifting her hair from one side to the other, tickling her back with the ends of the strands. Then he trailed the suede flanges of the flogger down her spine and over her buttocks.

The muscles of Sarah's arms flexed, and she tugged at her restraints. Her thighs tensed. Her breaths deepened.

"I'll be angry if you let me hurt you, Sarah," Logan said, his voice deepening from its usual drawl. "Don't be ashamed to tell me what you feel."

Logan glanced to the curtains covering a large picture window and lifted his chin to Joe.

Joe bit back a grin. He'd heard all about Logan's little Peeping Tomasina and walked to the window to open the curtains wide, making sure the house at the end of the little cul-de-sac had a good view into the playroom.

Logan was helping him out tonight. He didn't mind sharing Sarah's training with the woman who'd caught his buddy's attention. The house sitting on the neighboring property was completely dark, but Joe didn't doubt they'd be watched.

A glance over his shoulder at Sarah's shocked face said she wasn't nearly as open to the idea.

"Afraid someone's gonna call the cops?" he asked.

"Anyone could see us."

"It's just Amy Keating. She's probably already asleep."

"The schoolteacher? You trying to shock her into a heart attack?"

"Shock her into something," Logan muttered and then lifted the flogger and flicked it at one of Sarah's pale cheeks.

Sarah's breath hissed between clenched teeth. "That hurt."

"Glad you shared that," Logan said, raising it again to flick the opposite cheek.

"Thought you didn't want to hurt me."

"I'm not. You're ready to argue with me. Means you're not nearly there." Logan flicked the backs of her thighs, her buttocks, leaving red blotches all over her bottom.

Sarah's lips were held in a thin, mutinous line; her gaze aimed daggers at Joe. If not for the heady scent of arousal wafting through the room, he might have worried they'd taken this too far.

Logan stood directly behind her and draped the flanges along the crease of her buttocks; then he rubbed the suede into the moisture seeping between her legs.

When he lifted the handle again, the flicks had a sharper sound due to the moisture soaking the leather strands.

When her bottom was completely red, Logan walked back

to the table and opened his own plastic box. From inside he drew another pouch, which he tossed to Joe.

"Put this on her. Low buzz."

Joe came around behind Sarah, admiring her warmed flesh and the thickening of the labia framing her honey-slick entrance. He poured the contents of the pouch into his hand, grinning when he saw the pretty pink butterfly vibrator with matching straps.

He fit the gelled plastic to her entrance and slipped the straps around her thighs, hooking them in place to hold the vibrator snug against her clit.

The remote he palmed and walked back to the table, sitting with a wince. Chair still angled toward Sarah, he waited until her glance met his.

Uncertainty shone in her widened eyes, and he nearly relented. But her lips firmed slowly into a pinched, rebellious line.

He hit the first speed of the remote.

The hum seemed loud inside the quiet room. Sarah's eyes closed, her lips parted. He kept the speed low, just enough to add more tension to her body until she realized he didn't plan to let her come.

Her eyes opened, locked with his gaze, and narrowed to angry slits.

Joe reached over the top of Logan's box and pulled out a small tapered butt plug and a tube of gel.

"Sure she's ready for that?" Logan said softly.

"Of course not, but I am."

4

"Oh, hell, no," Sarah groaned, eyeing the butt plug he carried toward her. She'd had one stuck up her before by an adventurous boyfriend but hadn't enjoyed the experience very much. Shoving it up his ass had proven the greater thrill. "Did you hear me, Joe? I don't want that."

His steady stride never slowed as he walked behind her. "Ever had anal sex before?" he asked as calmly as if he'd asked a stranger whether they took cream in their coffee.

"Not really. Just one of those. It was enough to make me swear off."

The butterfly vibrating against her pussy revved up, and Sarah gasped. Fingers coated in gel smoothed down her crack, pausing to circle her sensitive hole. "That's not too bad," she offered as a token of consent. "Maybe you could just keep doing that?"

"Sarah, you have to learn to trust me. In all things. Whatever I do to your body will be pleasurable. Let me decide your limits."

"You shoving that thing in me will not get me off."

"It isn't intended to. In fact, it will be uncomfortable at first; it might burn as it stretches you. But it's necessary for what's coming inside you next. I'm not small, Sarah."

Her whole body vibrated.

Slippery fingers spread her cheeks; the cool, greasy tip of the plug pressed against her opening.

Sarah sucked in a breath, ready to let fly another round of curses, but she couldn't take a deep enough breath as the plug slid deeper.

At first it wasn't so bad. The slender part of it eased right in. The fullness was uncomfortable but bearable, however, the plug gradually broadened, and her thighs and buttocks tensed as her body tried to eject the plug.

"Take a deep breath," Logan said from his seat at the table.

"Easy for you to say," she gasped.

At the widest point, she mewled like the kitten they both called her just to annoy her.

"Easy, almost there."

When the plug narrowed again, she sobbed, sagging against the bench. Joe wiped his fingers on her ass and came around her. "Not so bad, was that?"

She raised her head and glared.

His low chuckle and the smirk that tipped one corner of his mouth set the fuse. She jerked against her restraints, bucking to free herself, but the leather restraints held.

"No use fighting. You'll injure yourself, baby."

"I'm not your baby."

"Not yet, but you'll be my playmate for the rest of tonight anyway. You agreed. You stepped across that threshold."

"I've changed my mind. I want it out now. And I'm gonna shove that goddamn plug up your ass, bastard."

"You're just a little scared, aren't you, kitten?" Logan said.

Sarah lifted her head and then held it erect as she watched Logan strip off his tee. His chest was massive, muscled slabs arranged in layers like sedimentary stone. Dark hair, thick and slightly wavy, furred his tanned chest nipple to nipple and then arrowed downward to disappear into his jeans.

"You want to see the rest?" he said, a grin sliding up one corner of his mouth.

"Make yourself comfortable," she choked out.

He opened his belt buckle and thumbed open the buttons down the placket of his jeans, exposing more tanned flesh. He shoved down his jeans, toed off his boots, and stepped out of his clothing.

His cock wasn't hard in the least. Wasn't he inspired with what he'd seen, what he'd done to her? Didn't he find her the least bit attractive?

He must have read the disappointment in her face because he chuckled. "I'm not a little boy. I have better control than that. I thought you might like the honor of getting him ready."

"Honor? Think highly of yourself?"

"I know I'm good," he said, sauntering toward her. "I know Joe and I are going to blow your mind tonight. But we have plenty of time to get to know each other. For now, I'd be satisfied to see that pretty pink mouth of yours busy doing something other than complaining."

He stepped closer, his cock inches from her nose.

Her eyes narrowed, wondering what he'd do if she took a great big bite.

"No teeth," he said, tapping her cheek with his finger. Then he pinched her chin and pulled it down to open her mouth. "Lips and tongue only."

Sarah couldn't help it. The hum strumming her pussy had her so wet her juices leaked down her thighs. Her ass was beginning to burn with a heat that wasn't all that unpleasant as her sphincter tightened and eased around the plug in tiny caresses. She stuck out her tongue and licked the tip of him.

"That's it. Open up and suck him right inside. He's soft enough you can cram all of him in there."

She opened wider, doing as he urged, sucking his soft cock into her mouth, warming his flesh with her moist heat. Without a conscious thought for what she ought to do, she began to suction, pulling at his dick, her head moving forward and back to encourage the blood to rush to his extremity and fill it.

Slowly he unfurled. Softness ripening, filling, hardening beneath her swirling tongue and suctioning mouth, until she couldn't breathe so much thick cock was stuffed inside. She drew back, pulling at him, rolling him out and then bobbing forward because she wanted more, wanted the fullness against the back of her throat.

Before she knew it she was groaning around him, salivating so well the long shaft glistened. The sounds she made, animalistic and wet, filled the room.

His hand cupped the back of her head. Fingers combed through her hair. He crooned, soft murmurs that grew more strained as she raked his length with her teeth—a tiny rebellion he allowed.

Suddenly he pulled back, his cock slipping from her lips, and she moaned.

"That was good. But I think Joe's a little jealous. Want to show him what he missed?"

"Give me yours again. He can jack himself off."

"I'm done for now, kitten. Want more cock to suck? Won't that make you happy? Your pussy must be sucking at that vibrator right about now. That plug has to be making you ache. Don't you want something else stuffing you?"

She liked the dirty talk, wanted it raw. From him.

She cast Joe a glance, shocked to see him naked, too, because she hadn't noted when he'd undressed.

His body was lean—thick, ropey muscles flexing along his arms, crunching across his stomach. His cock wasn't soft, wasn't waiting for her to unfurl it with her mouth.

His broad palm stroked up and down the bronze shaft. The tip was full, round, and her tongue rimmed her lips. She couldn't help it. She wanted that cock cramming somewhere—her pussy being her first preference—but maybe she could break them, make them crazy to fuck her if she did this right.

"Please," she said softly.

Joe's jaw sawed tight. His eyes narrowed. But he dragged his feet forward, pointing his cock at her mouth.

Logan strode back to the table, but she couldn't follow his movements for more than a second because Joe was pushing that fat crown between her lips, and she had to swallow.

Her lips surrounded him, sucking on the soft, spongy head. Her tongue lovingly delved into his narrow slit and fluttered against the edges until she heard his breath release in a rasping moan.

"Take it down, baby. Open wide." His hands cupped her ears, and he centered himself in front of her and pulsed inward, stabbing past her tongue, bumping the back of her throat. "Swallow. Give me a kiss with that deep throat of yours."

She obeyed, quelling the urge to gag, and swallowed around him, loving the way the muscles in her throat caressed and squeezed around him.

Then he was pulling back, and she couldn't have that. She sucked hard, trying to follow him, but he laughed and plunged back inside.

The wet choking sounds she made earned her praise. His hands gripped her hair hard, pulling, but she didn't care; he couldn't be gentle, and that was what she wanted, him letting go, him stroking deep, his thighs thickening, trembling with the effort to control the strength and depth of his strokes.

A stinging flick touched her buttocks, and her teeth bit into her lips, closing hard around Joe's cock.

"Logan! Fuck!" Joe said and drew his cock slowly from her mouth.

Sarah twisted her jaw side to side to ease the ache and then lifted her head.

Joe's gaze was thoughtful, his grin a little rueful as he fisted himself and slowly stroked his fist toward his groin.

She couldn't help smiling as he soothed himself.

The straps holding the butterfly in place loosened, and the device fell away. Fingers slipped inside her, and she tightened her inner muscles around them, gripping them as hard as she could.

"I know. You've been very good," Logan purred. "Joe, do you mind?"

Joe's face tightened, but he nodded sharply, and the kneeler creaked as Logan lowered himself behind her and snuggled his thighs up behind hers. His cock prodded her opening, and she sucked air between her teeth.

A tap to her cheek, and she opened her eyes to meet Joe's gaze. "Don't come until I say so, or you'll only get this once."

Once would be enough. She licked her lips and looked at the fierce erection he still stroked within his fist.

God, she wanted Logan's and then Joe's cocks. As many times as they'd give it to her. She held that thought as Logan chuckled behind her and then thrust sharply inside her body.

Her back bowed, and her arms pulled hard against the restraints, but again they wouldn't give. She took his firm strokes, wishing she could sink to the floor and let him rock her world as she ground her nipples in the carpet.

Which brought her back to the tweezers still clasping hers tightly. Joe tugged the chain between them; then he reached to one set of tweezers and increased the pinch and then did the same to the other. Painful throbbing in her breasts and ass was almost enough to slow the rise of her orgasm that cramped her belly it was so strong.

"Joe, please," she begged. "I can't . . . it's too much . . . please, please."

He bent, and his mouth covered hers. She nearly wept at having her mouth filled with his tongue while both her ass and pussy burned.

Logan's thrusts quickened; his hands gripped her stinging buttocks. Then he pulled all the way out, leaving her on the edge.

Joe's mouth lapped hers, his tongue sweetly stroking hers and withdrawing. When he leaned back, she felt abandoned. "No," she said and tried to follow.

He knelt beside her, undid the buckles at one wrist and then the other and then unsnapped the hooks that held her thighs open.

He helped her up, and she slumped against his body.

"Get the doors," he said to Logan and then bent and swept her into his arms.

They trailed Logan through the house, down a darkened corridor, and into a bedroom. Low-wattage lamps flanked the king-size bed. A soft, satiny comforter in deep brown met her back as Joe lowered her to the mattress.

Joe followed her down, wrapping his arms around her as he lay beside her. The bed dipped behind her, but she didn't care what Logan was doing because Joe was kissing her again, and she was starved for the taste of him.

Her thigh was lifted and draped over Joe's hip.

A hand slid over her ass and tugged at the plug, still lodged firmly inside her. She moaned into Joe's mouth as it was removed.

Something warm and wet smoothed over her. A light floral scent accompanying efficient wipes as she was cleaned. Then another cloth stroked deeper between her legs, scrubbing between her legs to cleanse her labia, and she knew what was coming next and moaned again.

Joe broke the kiss. His forehead touched hers. "I want you to straddle Logan's face."

Sarah sucked his bottom lip between hers, bit him gently, and let go. "No. Fuck me, just like this," she said, rutting her belly against his hard cock.

"I want your pussy on his lips," he said slowly. "I want you to suck his cock until he comes."

"And Eskimos want an excuse to use Coppertone. I want this," she said, sliding her hand between them and down his belly to his dick, which she clasped inside her fist. At his unyielding stare, she frowned. "What about you?"

Joe's smile stretched slowly, wickedly across his lips. "I think you know."

"But you're huge!" she said, measuring him with her fingers.

"Not huge. But it will be tight, so you have to hold steady above Logan."

She pushed against his chest, but he held her easily against him. His fingers bit into her waist.

Her fingers curled, digging into his chest. "I ache, Joe. No more goddamn games. I can't do this. Just please fuck me . . . one at a time, if you like."

"Sweetheart, we'll get to that . . . eventually. You don't think we'll be done with you after this, do you?" His cheek rubbed hers. "We have time. With two of us pleasuring your sweet body, we have plenty of stamina to give you what you need."

"Jesus," she whispered, rubbing her face against him and then sighing as he blew into her ear.

"You'll be praying to the whole trinity before we're through," he whispered. "So hold that thought. Or do you want us to take the choice of compliance away from you? Do you need the leather and the buckles?"

She shook her head. "I want to move."

"Thought so. Do it now, Sarah. Give Logan your cunt."

Sarah pressed her forehead against his shoulder, and his arms squeezed her to give her a reassuring hug. She could do this without shattering like glass. *Sure, she could.*

She raised to her knees, waiting while Logan rearranged himself, his head toward the foot of the bed, his legs splayed.

When she checked his expression, his eyes seemed slumberous, his features relaxed. If his cock wasn't perpendicular to his body she would have thought he wasn't that into her.

He patted her thigh. "Come over me."

"This is embarrassing."

"Really? How can it be worse than being tied to the kneeler with your ass in the air and a plum peeking from your pussy?"

She growled low in her throat. "Not helping. . . ."

His smile was pure, wicked sin. "You have a pretty ass and an even prettier pussy. Plum becomes you."

A gust of laughter caught her by surprise. "Damnit, are you always such an asshole?"

"Only when I meet someone worthy of the effort."

"Will you let me come this time?"

"Only when Joe says so. I know he's not too happy about my mouth and cock being anywhere near you at the moment, and he's getting more territorial by the minute."

"Shut up, Logan," Joe snarled.

Sarah's body nearly melted at his angry growl. "But this was his idea, right?"

Logan snorted. "We conspired."

"You just helping out a buddy?"

He nodded. "What are friends for?"

"Do this often?"

"Only when needed."

"Ever do it with him before?"

Logan's glance met Joe's, and Joe's eyes narrowed to fierce slits. "Best not to talk about the old days. It might give you ideas. And we both know how impulsive you can be."

Sarah wrinkled her nose. "You make me sound like an unruly child."

"You're no child. I can tell," he said, sliding a hand between her legs and fondling her sex.

"Every girl's got one of those."

"Not every girl gets wet when her ass is stung with a whip. Not every girl creams when her man instructs her."

Sarah glared. "I haven't exactly been obedient yet."

"But you creamed at the tone of his voice, didn't you?"

Sarah didn't answer. She didn't have to—his fingers were swirling in the proof.

"You cream because you know the fight's just begun, and that turns you on. You see, Joe likes your rebellious nature. He likes to see how far he can push—how much you're willing to take before your sensual nature forces you to surrender. Surrender's sweet, *chica*."

Sarah pushed his hand from her pussy. "What do you get out of this? Besides the sex?"

His eyes got sleepier looking, his smile softer. "You're stalling. Slide that sweet pussy over my face."

"Need a pillow?" Joe asked, his voice sounding garbled.

"Yeah." Logan grabbed the one Joe slung his way and then settled his head on top of it and patted his chest. "Any time you're ready, sweetheart."

Sarah drew a deep breath, wondering why she was suddenly nervous. It couldn't have anything to do with the way Joe had watched her as she'd talked with Logan—fists curled, dark eyes flashing fire. Could it? Was he jealous?

She gave Logan a small, tight smile and lifted her thigh, settling her knees on either side of his raised head.

"Lean forward and brace yourself," he said from between her legs. "We'll get you settled."

Sarah blew out breath and did as Logan asked. No arguments. Then she peeked at Joe from beneath her lashes. His face was tight, his eyes narrowing—and not in a nice way.

Logan's hands slid between her legs and cupped her bottom, urging her to shift to the side and then bringing her lower until his hot breath blew across her open pussy.

"Oh," she breathed. "That's nice." Another peek at Joe. His knuckles whitened.

Logan's tongue stroked her labia, long strokes that glided from the bottom of her folds to her clit.

"Don't get too comfortable," Logan said, squeezing her cheeks. "You have work to do."

His cock. She had to suck him until he came. She slid her hair over one shoulder to keep it out of the way and to give Joe a clear view of what she was doing. Then she leaned down and licked the length of Logan's shaft, closing her eyes because he tasted like sexy male—clean and musky—and because Joe couldn't drag his gaze from her tongue's slow movements.

"Like that?" she asked Logan.

"Swallow it, already," he grumbled.

She grinned, came up on her arms, centered her mouth over his cock, and then sank, groaning as she took him down her throat like he was the best thing she'd tasted all night.

"Logan, when we're through, I'm going to have to kick your ass."

5

Joe'd had enough of watching Logan and Sarah sharing smiles and teasing glances. Had enough of her groaning like she'd gone to heaven sucking another man's dick.

The tension that had gripped her lithe body earlier as she lay draped over the kneeler had dissipated. He knew Logan planned it that way—the lull before the storm—*but still*. He grunted and dragged his gaze from Sarah's talented mouth as she sucked and bobbed on Logan's cock.

His own cock needed some action, something to soothe the beast rising up to burn the back of his throat with bile. Why he was so pissed, he couldn't really have said. His mind couldn't think logically at the moment. He wanted to act, to do something that would get her attention and not let her ease back into complacency because she'd think she'd won.

Sarah couldn't win. Not if he ever wanted her to see him as her true mate. Simple as that. He had to have her firmly beneath his thumb.

He grabbed the tube of lubricant and crawled onto the bed behind her.

Her back stiffened instantly; her up-and-down glides slowed as she waited to see what he'd do next. She knew what was going to happen because he'd broadcasted his interest in her ass, prepared her little furled entrance for his cock with gentle care.

The "what" she knew good and well. Her own feelings about the matter had to be in turmoil.

He liked smelling fear on her. Loved the uneasy way she glanced at him when she didn't know what was coming next or what he was thinking.

Keeping her guessing would keep him on his toes if he could just think with his mind instead of with his tormented cock.

He still felt the sting from the strafing she'd given him with her teeth. What would surprise her?

Her ass was right in front of him, her cheeks parted by her spread legs, her skin still pinkened from the swats of the flogger. Tomorrow he wouldn't be surprised if a few welts marred those pretty pale globes.

He cupped her buttocks, spreading his fingers wide to hold as much of her ample bottom as he could. *Generous* was a word he'd read but never appreciated in the context of an ass, but right now the word felt just about perfect on his lips.

His lips . . . his tongue . . .

She wasn't going to like this, would be shocked to her pretty pink toes. But he bent over her ass and licked the seam between her buttocks, listening for the hitch of her breath as he neared her back entrance. "Don't you come. Don't you dare come until I tell you."

She rose off Logan's shaft and huffed. "As if! What the fuck are you doing anyway?"

"Getting me a taste. A forbidden taste, sweetheart. There's not anything I won't do to you. Not anything you won't let me do."

"I'm not tied up like a goddamn goose ready for the roaster pan. Do the other thing, but this is just wrong."

"There's no wrong, if you like it."

"Well, I don't."

Joe proved her a liar with the next lazy lap around her asshole. "Gawd, Joe. Stop!" she groaned.

His tongue swirled on her asshole, and then he opened her with slippery fingers and prodded the tip of his tongue inside.

"Please don't," Sarah mewled, her voice taut and tearful as she bent over Logan, mortified at Joe's intimate actions.

Only her words lacked true conviction. Logan had latched hard on to her clitoris, circling as though he and Joe had given each other secret signals, because their tonguing was escalating.

Her thighs and belly trembled. Logan's cock bumped her chin, and she opened without thinking, swallowing the crown and groaning as Joe's tongue poked deeper.

It was so nasty. So unthinkable, what he was doing, what she allowed.

Still he didn't stop, sliding inside her to flicker his tongue like a snake and then lapping around the tight, hot circle.

Logan spread her labia and tugged them down. The hood protecting her clit slid away, and his tongue touched the nubbin directly. She sank low on his cock, groaning all the way down.

Soft laughter from the man beneath her gusted hotly on her open sex. Fingers stroked into her pussy.

Joe's tongue withdrew, and something hard and narrow dipped into her ass, followed by a slide of cool, oozing gel. A finger slipped inside, and the loosened ring allowed it, clasping to hold it there.

She marveled at how quickly she'd come to accept the penetration, the intimacies they layered, one after the other until her brain was on overload, unable to complain or respond with embarrassment for the things they did without ever once seeking her compliance.

Of course, she wasn't exactly screaming. But she could already tell she would. She'd never been so overwhelmed.

Joe's finger glided out, and he shifted behind her. Jesus, he was going to do it. Going to shove his thick, hard cock inside her, *and she wanted it.*

Her mouth sank on Logan, her lips closing tight around him as she breathed through her nose and used him to still the scream rising in her throat.

Joe's blunt head pressed against her as his thumbs held her open; then he adjusted again, rising higher to arrow his cock directly inside her. He pumped against the ring and then rolled his hips, the screwing motion easing the tension gripping the ring.

He screwed until she drew a deep breath and forced her heart to calm, her muscles to relax, and then he pushed inside, the crown breaching the ring.

Joe held still behind her. "Are you okay? Can you take it?"

She liked how tight his voice was, how intense and harsh the delivery of the words. The pressure her little asshole exerted around him had to be exquisite. Yet he held himself, waiting for her to answer.

And there was pain, but not so much she wanted him to stop.

Heat flooded her face, her chest. Tremors spread from her clitoris, rippling along her thighs, belly, and buttocks.

She didn't want to come off Logan to speak. Didn't think she could without losing it and screaming hard. She rammed his cock down her throat and then undulated her hips, a shallow flex that pulled on Joe's cock and told him wordlessly that she needed him to move.

"Sweet, sweet fuck," Joe murmured, beginning a slow rocking motion that was too much and not enough. Another finger entered her, filling her pussy, while Logan's tongue toggled her clit.

Rhythmic moans began to come, one after the other, first hers, then theirs. So much sexy noise surrounded her, she felt enclosed in rapture.

Sarah admitted she didn't have their discipline. She came first, her shout muffled around Logan's cock. She bucked against Logan's mouth and fingers and Joe's stroking cock until her body hung limp, her thighs quaking. Joe's arm encircled her waist to keep her poised above his friend.

Then Logan raised his knees and thrust his cock up and down, cramming past her tongue until she felt a hunger she'd never experienced, to feel the hard, muscled men below and behind her exploding inside her.

She wrapped fingers tightly around Logan's shaft and suctioned, bobbing up and down, swallowing around him to increase the sensations she delivered.

Logan's fingers withdrew, and his tongue soothed the hot friction he'd built, lapping at her, murmuring against her to encourage her as she worked his cock.

Joe plunged relentlessly into her ass, stroking deeper, harder until the burning intensified and she thought she wouldn't be able to take it another minute.

Suddenly Joe stiffened behind her, and heat spurted inside her. Logan roared beneath her, and cum bathed the back of her throat.

As the men stroked and shuddered, Sarah felt a smile tighten the lips stretched so deliciously around the grinding cock.

Joe gripped her waist and pulled her up, leaving her impaled and sitting on his lap. Logan jackknifed up and turned, his legs spreading wide as he sat in front of her, cupped her breasts with his hands, and leaned in to kiss her.

Joe's lips skimmed her neck and shoulder. Logan sucked her lips while massaging her nipples.

Sandwiched between two heaving, sweaty chests, Sarah closed her eyes and tilted her head backward to rest against Joe's chest.

"That was fucking amazing," she breathed.

Logan's lips hardened against hers and drew back, a grin lifting one side of his mouth. "Girl's got a potty mouth."

"Girl's been fucked half to death," Sarah grumbled.

Joe bit her shoulder. "We're going to lift you off. It's probably going to hurt."

Logan's hands gripped her waist, and he picked her up, sliding her off Joe's cock.

Sarah's breath hissed between her teeth.

Logan lay back, bringing her over him. Her thighs slid to either side of his hips, and she knew what view she presented to Joe, but she couldn't muster more than a groan.

The bed rose. Footsteps padded to the bathroom. Water ran. Joe returned with a steaming cloth and washed her again.

"I can't believe I'm letting you do that," she said drowsily, her cheek nuzzling moist, satin-smooth skin.

"You're mine. To do with as I wish," Joe said softly.

"Then why am I going to sleep on top of another man?"

Logan's chest shook beneath her, and she found herself rolling to her side and Joe's long, lean body snuggling against her back. She opened her eyes.

Logan's gaze was locked with Joe's just beyond her shoulder. She didn't have the strength to do more than wonder what their looks said to one another. "No fair talking behind my back."

"Didn't say a word," Logan said.

"Sure. What would you need to say in private when you got everything you wanted from me already?"

"Stop it," Joe said softly.

"What?" she asked sleepily.

"This wasn't about me getting what I wanted from you. And it wasn't about what Logan wanted. Although, I have to admit, you were . . . amazing."

"You're a man. It was about winding me up so hard I couldn't raise a word of protest."

"What was all that cussing for earlier? And tell me that was someone else telling me what she wasn't going to do."

"You knew it was just talk. You got me to go along with every little thing you wanted."

"I was gauging your responses, what your body was telling us both about what pleased you."

Sarah huffed. "Could have listened to my mouth and not wasted so much time."

"Your mouth is the problem, kitten. You shoot it off but rarely say what you really think or want."

"You think you know better than me?"

"I'm learning," Joe murmured sexily. "That's what tonight was all about."

Sarah stifled a yawn. "What'd you two learn?"

"You're damn loud when you're pissed off," Logan groused.

"Not something you couldn't have learned from one of your spies."

"You bite your lip and get quiet when something really gets to you," Joe said and then paused. "No comeback? Nothing smart to say now?"

"I'm tired. I want to sleep."

"You're tired? But your heart's beating like a bass drum. You want me to drop the conversation because I'm making you uncomfortable. It's because I'm getting close."

"The only way you'd get closer is if you stuck that dick grinding against my bottom where it belongs for once."

"Does my dick belong inside you?"

"I'm here now. And I'm wet. Isn't that enough?"

"It's a start."

"Joe?"

"Yeah, kitten."

"I'm not so tired now."

Again, the men's glances met above her. Logan's mouth curved.

"Just to let you know," she uttered testily, "I don't think we can do that thing again."

"Your ass is strictly off limits for at least another week. I don't want to hurt you."

Logan rolled off the bed, and Joe's arms enclosed her. He turned her, coming over her. Her arms and legs opened instantly to wrap around him.

His kiss was a sweet, suctioning melding of lips that generated a warmth inside her chest she tried her damndest to ignore. But the melting, choking heat remained there anyway, growing more insistent, crowding her heart.

When his hands cupped her cheeks as though she were precious, she mewled into his mouth and closed her eyes tightly.

Again, the bed dipped, and this time she nearly growled because she didn't want the tenderness of Joe's kiss to end. However, he released her lip and rolled away.

A glance at Logan's steady gaze and the mask he dangled at the end of his index finger was all it took to set her heart thumping hard inside her chest and her body melting.

Joe thrust a hand beneath her neck and lifted her head while Logan fit the black mask over her eyes and tugged the straps at either side of her temples to make it snug.

She couldn't see a thing, but they could. The thought left her feeling very vulnerable. Hard, muscled bodies stretched out beside her, flanking her. Joe on her right. Logan on the left. A hand cupped one breast, and because of the angle of the thumb toggling her distended nipple, she knew it was Logan.

Determined to keep track of who did what because her perception was all she could control, she concentrated on every little caress, every breath that gusted against her skin.

Joe's head neared, warm breath and then lips touching her shoulder, gliding downward to mouth the top of her right breast. His tongue flicked out and traced the indention between her breasts. Fingers plumped up her breast, but it took a moment to realize it had to be Logan because her mind was honed in on what Joe was doing, and her whole body quivered, waiting for him to touch her nipple with this slippery tongue.

When his lips closed around the peak, her groan was an inelegant "uhhhnnnn." Logan squeezed her breast, forcing the tender tissue into a funnel that slid deep between Joe's widened lips. He gobbled at her breast, suckled, lapped around the areola until she realized her thighs had scissored together, building friction in her core.

Another mouth latched on to the opposite breast.

The men didn't work precisely in tandem. Joe gently laved. Logan lashed. Joe latched on to her nipple and mouthed it, his tongue rubbing the tip. Logan suctioned at the areola, biting the tip, applying just enough pressure to make her gasp and squirm.

With darkness surrounding her, touch, sound, and scent amplified.

The moist, decadent sounds the men made had her cringing at first. So much sound bombarded her, the dull, heavy throb of her own pulse, the moist clasp of her pussy as her inner muscles rippled up and down her channel, her breathy moans.

As wrung out as she'd felt when Joe had started, the realization that she had yet to experience the thrust of his cock inside her pussy ratcheted up her excitement.

Each touch of skin, lip, tongue, and rasping, calloused fingers sent darts of aching heat straight to her core.

However, it was the smells permeating the air that were the most obscene, the most erotic.

The tang of semen and male sweat, the crisp, pungent odor of aroused pussy hovered like a cloud. It embarrassed her, yet she couldn't mention it, couldn't resist what they were doing to beg them to let her bathe.

They controlled her. This time without needing restraints. They ruled her lust.

The men scooted down the bed, abandoning her breasts, and she shivered as hands and lips trailed her ribs, dipped into the hollow of her tummy, took turns swirling around her belly button until her hips rocked up and down, silently begging for attention.

But the men left her shivering alone on the mattress. The bedding above her rustled. Then hands she couldn't assign to either turned her to her stomach while another set pushed a pillow beneath her hips and then another until her ass was raised high.

Would they spank her again? Surely now they'd fuck her.

With the flash-fire heat of her first orgasm past, her body demanded a slower pace, a harder, more intense experience.

Hands swept her bottom, pausing to rub the tender welts and then scooping between her thighs to force them wider.

Sarah complied automatically, easing apart her knees, and then thought better of it.

She wasn't a goddamn doll. She closed her stance, defying the hands pressing against her inner thighs.

She'd hoped for a laugh or rumbling command, just to let her identify the man kneeling behind her.

Instead a tongue trailed the crease of her ass.

"Thought you were leaving that alone," she said tightly.

The tongue continued gliding downward, pausing to circle her anus.

Sarah whimpered and pressed hot cheeks into the cool satin coverlet; then slowly she parted her legs.

A palm cupped her pussy; two fingers slid inside and then pulled away.

A fingertip painted her lips, and she smelled her own aroma, licking around her lips to taste.

Foil ripped. Twice. Latex snapped.

Blunt thickness pushed against her opening, and Sarah nearly wept with relief. But whose cock was it?

Both men's cocks were a generous size. Joe's tip was round, the shaft thick and the girth uniform.

Logan's crown had a lovely flange around it that was pronounced when she'd sucked him off, but her pussy wasn't as discerning.

Besides, they'd both donned condoms. Was it because it made them feel more uniform? It couldn't be because they cared whether they gave her anything nasty. She'd taken them into her mouth. Taken Joe's bare cock into her ass and never once questioned the lack of protection.

She was reckless, but she wasn't stupid. Why hadn't she noticed? "We forgot something . . . before," she mumbled, embarrassed to be mentioning it now.

"What'd we forget, Sarah?" Logan said in his silky voice.

"Protection."

"You on the pill?"

"Of course."

"Then don't you worry."

The cock easing into her slowed.

"Shouldn't we be the ones worrying?" Joe asked, his voice less relaxed. "You've got quite a reputation—most of it bad."

Sarah groaned, not wanting to admit her past wasn't quite so blemished. "That was high school. Mostly."

All motion halted.

"Mostly a big act, Sarah?" Joe asked.

Her cunt squeezed around the long, thick column. "I'm fucking both of you, aren't I?"

"It's okay, you know," Logan said softly. "We've both done our homework. You're wild, but you're not easy, not like you want everyone to think. It's all right to lack a little confidence with us. We aren't judging skill. We aren't going to make fun of you if you get a little scared."

"I'm not scared."

"Should we be worried, kitten?"

Couldn't they just leave the subject alone? "No worries," she blurted, sorry she'd ever mentioned it.

"We trusted you'd tell us if there were."

Movement resumed. The cock burrowing its way into her pussy was plenty thick, slickened with a lubricant, she guessed, something that warmed with friction.

Hands gripped her ass. The cock thrusting inside her slid in and out in even, measured strokes—the motion so controlled that after a minute or two she bit her lips to halt the screech of frustration tearing at her throat to get out.

They remained silent. To trick her? To keep her guessing whose dick shafted her? They hadn't said she had to be quiet. But could she be herself and not earn a punishment if she complained about the lackluster fucking she was getting now?

"Okay, I'm bored."

6

Smack!

Sarah jerked at the stinging slap, but managed not to yelp—
barely.

The motion continued uninterrupted. Even strokes. Thick,
blunt thrusts that crammed deep but somehow managed to arrest her arousal.

She wasn't going to get off this way. Her bottom burned,
but the heat from the single blow did add an interesting kink.

"Look, I let you guys get your kicks. I got both of you off.
The least you can do is follow through."

Smack!

"That hurt," she gritted out. "But if you'd allow a little con-
structive criticism, you'd do better to slap my cunt like that
rather than spank my ass!"

Smack!

Tears prickled behind her closed eyelids. "All right, so I
know I'm a slow learner, but Jesus, gimme a hint."

She cringed, waiting for another slap, but when it didn't

come, she drew in a deep, ragged breath. "So you won't punish me for talking, but you will when I make demands."

The man behind her withdrew his cock and slipped off the bed. The mattress dipped. Thighs snuggled close to hers. A cock, this one not slick with her juices, centered on her opening and drove inside.

She groaned. "You're not going to let me come, right? You're going to fuck me raw, trading off so neither of you blows, and I can't either. That's just . . . mean."

The motion resumed, evenly paced but at a slightly different angle. Due to anatomy? She'd thought they both possessed straight cocks and were of a similar height. No downward or upward curves or sideways kinks.

She would have noticed differentiations like that, right?

This one's angle of entry ground against the nerves deep in her vagina, stroking her special spot with just enough pressure that desire coiled deep inside her womb.

Sarah fought hard to hide her excitement. If they guessed, would they change up again, just to keep her on an agonizing verge?

God, she had to keep talking, but she couldn't think. She bucked hard and screeched, "If I'd wanted to fuck a metronome I'd have hit on my old piano teacher!"

Smack!

Gawd, that felt divine. Honey oozed from deep inside her, coating the cock thrusting steadily. Could he tell through the latex? Sarah came up on her elbows and arched her back, letting her mystery man's thrusts force her forward and back and raking her nipples on satin until they were hardened pebbles, so sensitized by friction she thought she might come from cool, smooth abrasion.

A hand slipped beneath her. Fingers tweaked a nipple. Then

a shove between her shoulder blades pressed her hard into the mattress, denying her that pleasure.

A sob caught her unprepared. Then another jerked her torso. The tears that had prickled now leaked, soaking into the silk covering her eyes.

The motion stopped. Slick snaps sounded.

Her body bobbed on the mattress as movement around her unbalanced her for a moment. Then her shoulders were being lifted, and something warm nudged her chin, slid along her cheek.

Musky male scent filled her nostrils, and she stroked out her tongue and licked the bare, satiny shaft centering on her mouth.

Sarah sank, groaning, swallowing as the cock slid along her tongue and bumped the back of her throat. She sucked it, murmuring a protest when hands cupped her face and brought her up and then slowly down.

"Be careful not to bite," came a voice too strained to identify.

Sarah nodded around the cock and continued to rise and fall.

Weight redistributed on the mattress; hands closed on her hips. A cock nudged against her entrance and then thrust sharply inside.

She gasped, her pussy tightening, her mouth clamping hard around the cock, lips shielding her teeth.

Sharp thrusts tunneled deep, quickening, strengthening.

Sarah hung on the hands gripping her shoulders, accepting the shallow upward thrusts into her throat, trying to quell the palsied shudders of her own body as she was fucked deliciously, thoroughly.

She wanted to come, hovered on the very edge, but fought the urge to surrender, waiting—waiting as the man behind her pounded her pussy.

Liquid spilled from her depths, adding satisfyingly wet noises to enflame her senses as his belly and balls slammed into her buttocks and cunt.

Pleasure washed her skin in waves of heat. Sweat broke out on her back, breasts, and face. Her jaws and lips cramped, straining to remain open, but she didn't dare balk, not by action or groan.

She was close. So goddamn close.

Hands slipped around her belly and burrowed between her legs. A finger touched her clit.

A mewling, strangling cry erupted from her throat, muffled by the plunging cock. But they heard.

"Now, Sarah. Come now."

She shattered into a million pieces as salty cum bathed her throat in sweet heat, and the man behind her exploded in a flurry of short, harsh thrusts that banged her forward and back until she had to come off the cock in her mouth or risk suffocating. She screamed and fell limply, her cheek sliding along a moist shaft, cuddling it, kissing it.

Lips glided along her shoulder, pressing through her hair against her neck. Hands soothed her head, caressed her breasts, her waist, encircling her and holding her close as a body shuddered and shook with the last scalding emissions jetting against her womb.

The mask was tugged away, and she turned her face, looking up the length of the cock she'd worked to find Logan, his skin ruddy with exertion, his expression soft and pleased.

Sarah stroked out her tongue and licked him. As close to a kiss of gratitude as she could manage.

Behind her, hard abs flexed, arms drew her closer, and Joe brought her upright, still impaled on his cock—this time pinned by her pussy. "Logan, get out of here."

Logan winked and crawled off the bed, padding away to the bathroom where the water ran.

Sarah's chest heaved as she dragged in deep breaths. Joe's hands skimmed her belly, her breasts, and down again, sinking between her legs to swirl on her clit, which was still engorged, still exposed. Her breath hitched.

"Too much?"

"Just sensitive."

His hands glided up to cuddle her breasts.

"What's next?" she asked.

"How do you feel?"

Sarah wished she could summon a bit of defiance, just for pride's sake, but she sniffed. "I feel shattered."

Warm lips glided along her cheek, and she turned her head to meet his kiss. His tongue skimmed her lower lip and then stroked gently inside. A palm cupped her cheek in a touch so tender and tentative she nearly wept.

Which made her jerk away. She trained her gaze on the headboard in front of her and blinked against the moisture.

"I'll take you home."

She nodded, not trusting her voice.

Joe lifted her slowly until his cock fell from between her folds. With the connection between their bodies broken, she could finally get her emotions in control. She climbed off the bed and stood beside it, waiting as he left in search of their clothing.

But how could she dress, sticky as she was?

She went to the doorway of the bathroom and knocked softly.

"It's unlocked," Logan called out.

"I'm just going to use your sink," she said, twisting the doorknob.

Inside steam filled the room. She rubbed the glass over the sink with her hand and grimaced at her appearance. Her hair

146

was a messy riot of lank curls. Her lips and cheeks were raw and reddened.

She bent and ran cold water, rinsing her skin to cool the burn.

"You two heading out?" Logan asked from beyond the curtain.

"He's taking me home."

"Want some advice?" he asked more softly.

"From my friend or his?"

"Do I have to choose? I think I've earned bragging rights as a friend to both of you," Logan drawled.

Sarah wet a washcloth and eyed the curtain before bringing it between her legs to scrub. "Go ahead."

"Wait for his call."

Sarah closed her eyes. "Wait for his call? That's it? You really think I'm the kind of girl who waits around on any man's call?"

"You're not. That's why it's important that you do. Think about it, okay?"

"Sure."

"Sarah?"

She grimaced, recognizing the teasing note in his voice. "I'm still here."

"I wasn't lying when I said plum becomes you. So does leather and a pink ass. Joe's a lucky man."

She slung her washcloth over the top of the curtain and trounced out of the bathroom followed by Logan's laughter.

Back in the bedroom, Joe waited, his features drawn in taut relief. "Kissing Logan good-bye?"

"I forgot about that. Better go back." Joe grabbed her hand and pulled her toward the door. "My clothes. Can I at least dress before we go outside?"

"Do it in the truck."

The drive to her place was made in stony silence. She'd dressed, combed her hair with her fingers, added a swipe of lipstick to her sore mouth, and then contemplated the stick shift while Joe drove.

"Nothing happened in the bathroom, if that's what you're mad about. I just wanted to wash up. I felt sticky."

Joe exhaled loudly. "There aren't going to be any repeats of tonight. Logan's never going to have you again."

She stayed silent, not knowing how exactly to respond. "Fine," she finally managed with a shrug, only mildly disappointed. Logan was a handsome man with *mad* sexual prowess, but her interests had landed squarely on Joe. When he didn't clarify whether there would be any repeats between just the two of them, she grew anxious, which made her angry that she really cared whether the arrogant bastard wanted her or not. "So if I can't have Logan again, what about you?"

"You're mine."

"I'm yours, and I'm supposed to accept your pronouncement just because you've decided? What makes you think I'll agree?" She folded her arms across her chest and scowled. "The fact you made me come? Hate to break it to you, but I've had orgasms before."

"I didn't doubt that for a second. And maybe someday I'll be ready to hear all about your sexual exploits, but right now I'm trying to forget the sight of you swallowing Logan's cock like you couldn't get enough of him."

"You're mad because I enjoyed what you arranged?" she asked, anger heating slowly like kindling catching that first spark of fire.

"It's not your fault. It's mine. I know that. Just give me a little time."

"I'll give you lots of time. The rest of your life, in fact. Because I won't ever talk to you again. Stop the truck!"

"Sarah . . ." he said, his voice rising in warning.

"No! You're unbelievably arrogant. You think you can tell me who I can be with, yet you're not sharing what *wonders* I'm going to receive in exchange. I'm just supposed to say, 'Yes, sir,' and keep my mouth closed while you get over being mad because you made me fuck your best friend. Man, have you got the wrong girl."

The truck jerked to the right, wheels spinning in gravel, as he ground to a halt on the side of the highway.

Sarah saw the taut fury in his features, and her heart skipped a beat. She grabbed the door handle, popped it open, slid to the ground, and ran.

Only, her sexy, high-heeled sandals sank in the gravel with each step. He was on her in a minute. An arm latched around her waist, and he carried her over one hip like a bag of potatoes back to his truck. He slung her into the open door and, before she could sit up, yanked her spandex skirt down her thighs and off her feet.

The skirt flew over his shoulder into the ditch, and he stepped up on the running board, capturing the hands slapping at his shoulders and head in one fist. The other hand loosened his jeans and drew out his cock. His thickness butted once against her opening and then slammed hard and deep.

Sarah came up on her elbows to scream at him, but her breath caught at his expression. The fierce, feral fury stamped on his taut features warred with the regret glittering in his eyes.

Tears blinded her, and she relented, tilting back her head as he began to power into her. His strong thrusts shook her body, causing her breasts to shimmy.

She braced one foot against the door frame, lay back on the seat, and stretched out her arms, one hand gripping the gun rack in the window and the other the steering wheel.

"Damnit, Sarah," he ground out.

"I know, I know, baby," she whispered. "So goddamn good . . . ahhh!"

His hands gripped her hips and jerked her toward him as he thrust again and again. Tension built in her core, and her pussy clamped down on his cock. The friction he built inside her was molten hot.

She watched him, her gaze never straying. She noted the veins rising on his forearms as he gripped her hard, the sharp, strained edges of his jaw and cheekbones, the sweat gathering on his upper lip and forehead.

Mostly she watched the long, thick column of his cock as he hammered in and out of her in violent strokes.

Sarah's breaths grew jagged, her legs tensed, and all along her inner channel muscles rippled, caressing Joe's cock, clasping and releasing his shaft to draw him deeper.

Joe's thrusts quickened until he jackhammered against her pussy, short grunts gusting, his belly and balls slapping moisture where they landed.

"I can't wait . . . don't make me wait," she pleaded.

"Come, baby. *Fuck!*" he shouted, pounding harder, climbing into the cab to follow her as her hands lost their grips and she scooted deeper into the cab with each thrust.

Sarah sobbed, arching her back as a moment of perfect ecstasy pricked her nipples and sent waves of heat washing over her skin. Small convulsions vibrated up and down her channel, and, at last, she jerked, crying out as the pleasure exploded.

Joe collapsed on top of her, breathing hard.

Sarah wrapped her arms around him, gasping to fill her starved lungs.

Gradually his breaths evened, and he lifted his head from her shoulder. He wiped the tears sliding into her hair with his thumbs and then bracketed her face between his hands. "I know I don't say the right things. But I don't feel very civilized when I'm around you. It's been that way from the first time I saw you. I want to mark you like a dog, rub my smell and semen all over you so any man who passes you will know you're mine."

Sarah's mouth opened, but she didn't know how to respond. What he said, the deep, growling texture of his voice as he'd said it, answered an emotion welling deep inside her. "I never say the right things either. I think I want to be the bitch so men know not to try to get too close. I'm not any good at being a girlfriend." His lips tightened, and she smoothed her thumb over his bottom lip, watching his mouth rather than his darkly glittering eyes. "I'm scared of what you make me want."

"It's a start," he whispered, kissing her mouth in slow, suctioning circles. "Gonna wait for my call?"

Sarah punched his shoulder.

7

***

Having a possessive boyfriend had its pitfalls and perks—it was also a lot of fun.

Whenever she wanted an obedience refresher, she had only to don a flirty little skirt and head to the bar, where invariably he'd find her and haul her butt out. Sometimes they even made it home to her bed before he "punished" her.

But he'd been reasonable—he'd allowed her to select the flogger he used from an online BDSM store. She'd added a leather slapper she'd nicknamed "the cunt clapper" because that's where she liked it aimed.

When she heard his truck grind to a halt outside her house one Sunday morning, she formed her lips into a straight line before she opened the door.

She knew exactly what he was thinking when he parked behind the sleek sedan already hogging her driveway. She answered the knock, closing the door behind her to stand on the stoop.

His gaze narrowed, and his hand came up to push against the door, but she stepped close enough that her nipples, covered only by her thin nightgown and robe, beaded against his chest.

"Sarah..."

One side of her mouth quirked at the tense warning. Lordy, he was going to punish her body deliciously—after her company was gone.

She stood on tiptoe and softly brushed his lips with hers. "Come inside." Grabbing his hand, she turned and pulled him through the door, leading him into her kitchen. "Daddy, I'd like you to meet Joe."

Joe felt his face heat with embarrassment as the judge looked over the top of the paper he'd been reading and gave him a steely glare. "It's a little early for a social call, don't you think?"

"Maybe it's a little late by my standards, Daddy," Sarah said, sounding amused. "He worked last night."

"One of the new deputies . . . I know. He's appeared in traffic court a few times already." Judge Michelson set aside the paper and leaned back in his chair. "So you're dating my daughter. Have to wonder why. She's not exactly been the most obedient daughter."

Joe's lips twitched. The emphasis on the word *obedient* and the sparkle in the judge's eye said he knew something about the nature of Joe's battles with Sarah. Seemed nothing stayed private long in a small town.

"Sarah just needed a firm hand," Joe drawled, taking a seat opposite the judge and then jerking back in his chair when a coffee cup landed with a thud in front of him. Joe used a napkin to wipe up the mess, and then lifted his cup. "Perfect, sweetheart. Just enough cream to ease the bitterness."

Dishes rattled behind him, and he pursed his lips to hide a smile.

The judge arched a salt-and-pepper brow. "I should thank you for your discretion."

"My discretion?"

"The bet Sarah accepted. I understand I have you to thank for putting a stop to that nonsense."

"Daddy!"

"Now, pumpkin, are you mad because I mentioned it or because I knew all about it?"

Joe chuckled, warming up to the judge instantly. Her father knew her well and seemed appreciative of having another man take her in hand.

Judge Michelson rose from his seat and extended a hand toward Joe. "Don't be a stranger. Sarah, you bring him around the house. Maybe he'd like to come fish in the pond with me sometime soon."

"I do have some new lures I'd love to try out."

Joe glanced at Sarah, whose face turned beet red. He'd managed to fashion half a dozen new and inventive hooks lately, some of them suitable for snagging a croppy or a bass.

The judge bent and kissed Sarah's cheek, gave Joe a wink, and let himself out.

The silence that followed was filled only with puffs of indignation from Sarah. "Wouldn't you know he'd take to you right away?"

"You aren't pleased?"

"No! You two will be sharing all kinds of secrets about ways to torment me."

"I hardly think your daddy's gonna give me advice about where to crack my whip."

"No, it'll be so much worse. He'll start making plans."

Joe plucked the towel from her hands and hung it over the side of the sink. Then he turned her to face him, bringing her close to his hips and the heavy bulge the hint of her sweet perfume had mustered. "And plans are a bad thing?"

She swallowed, and her gaze dropped to his chest. "I don't want you feeling crowded. He can be a little overbearing. And as soon as he figures out you're moving in with me, he won't be subtle about expecting something more out of you."

"What will he expect?"

Her eyes met his, uncertainty causing them to glitter. "For you to marry me."

Joe raised both eyebrows, pretending surprise, when secretly he was pleased she'd mentioned the *M* word. It meant she'd been thinking about their future. "I'm a big boy. I think I can take care of myself when he starts to put the pressure on."

Her lips formed a straight line, and two spots of bright color flushed both cheeks. Joe could feel the tension stiffening her back. She'd wanted a less ambiguous answer and was mad at herself for expecting one.

He lifted a hand, grabbed a handful of her glossy, pale curls, and forced her head back until her gaze met his. "How many times do I have to tell you you're mine? When are you gonna believe it?"

Her lips relaxed. A deep sigh filled her chest. "I guess I don't have much patience."

Joe snorted, which earned him a pinch. "Did you get much sleep last night?" he murmured against her hair.

"Why? Is there some reason you need me rested?"

"Just checking." He unwrapped his arms from around her and stepped away. "I got a couple hours of sleep, but, then, I don't need much when I'm inspired. I do, however, need food. What's for breakfast?"

Sarah had just picked up the dishes from the table and poured Joe another cup of coffee when the doorbell rang again.

Her eyes rounded in alarm, but Joe's lips curled in amusement. "You gonna answer that?"

"What if it's my dad?" she asked, tugging the sides of the apron around her bottom but coming up several inches short.

"It's not. Answer the door just like you are," he said in his bedroom voice—the one that was hard-edged and surly and never failed to make her melt.

He smacked his knee once, a reminder of what he'd paddle next if she didn't hop to.

Cursing hotly under breath, she stomped out of the kitchen to the front door, closed her eyes, and opened it.

"Mornin', kitten. Joe said he might be here all day," Logan said, his voice choked with laughter. "Thought I'd stop in to say hello."

"Oh, it's just you," she said, wrinkling her nose and pretending she wasn't relieved and delighted.

Running into Logan Ross, which she did often, proved less embarrassing than she'd feared. She had a soft spot in her heart for the man and knew he cared about her, too, because he'd threatened to kick Joe's ass if he ever hurt her.

"He's in the kitchen," she said, turning to let him see her naked ass as she made her way down the short hallway.

Logan's chuckles followed her all the way back.

Once inside the kitchen, she reached for the towel and threw it at Joe's head. "What would you have done if it hadn't been him?"

Joe caught the towel and grinned. "Apologized for your naughty streak and told whoever it was I'd make damn sure you never did it again."

"And they'd believe you?"

"Do you really think they'd doubt it?" Logan interjected. "All they'd have to do is see the two of you watching each other." He slid into a seat at the table and tugged at his shirt collar. "Damn, is it hot in here, or is it just me?"

Joe patted his knee, and Sarah happily climbed on, glad the top of her apron hid her nipples because they'd sprouted like winter crocuses, and he'd know it was because Logan's glance was eating her up.

Logan's eyes fell on the bowl of fruit in the center of her kitchen table. Oranges, shiny apples, and one plump plum.

Sarah's back straightened as Logan's eyes narrowed in wicked satisfaction. She sent Joe a wild-eyed glance and felt relief at the sudden tension in his features.

No way would he allow him to do that again. . . .

"Sarah, sweetheart," Joe said softly, "why don't you show Logan how well behaved you are now?"

"Joe?" she said, her blood racing and excitement dampening her curls.

Logan plucked the plum from the bowl and held it between his fingers.

"Bend over in front of him."

"I thought you said—"

"He's not going to fuck you, baby."

She gulped against the knot lodged at the back of her throat and carefully scooted off his thigh. Coming around the table, she squared her shoulders, letting her frustration show in her face, but only for Logan to see.

His legs were spread as he sat in his chair, and he held up one hand and circled his fingers, indicating she should turn.

With her face set in an unconcerned mask, she turned and bent over, displaying her ass.

"Widen your legs. I need those pretty lips parted."

"Damn," she whispered and widened her stance, bracing her hands on her knees as fingers spread her, holding her open, and the plum was inserted. His fingers tugged at her lips, arranging them to clasp the fruit, and then a fingertip rubbed her clit briefly and drew away.

She shot him a glare over her shoulder, but he winked and turned his attention back to Joe. She straightened and walked stiffly back to Joe who patted his knee.

Afraid she'd crush the fruit when she sat on his thigh, she perched on the edge and clasped her legs tightly together to hold the plum inside her.

"That favor you owe me," Logan began. "I'm calling in my marker."

Joe swore and then wrapped an arm around Sarah's waist. "What do you have in mind?"

"I'd like to invite the two of you over for a party."

Joe's face relaxed; a smile began to curve his mouth. "As long as we lay some ground rules first. Sarah's marrying me, and I don't want anyone doubting the paternity of any baby she has."

Sarah jerked. Juice from the plum seeped from her, dripping loudly on the floor. "I'm marrying you? Says who?"

"Me. Now be quiet while we talk."

Sarah couldn't help it. Her labia began to pulse, squeezing the plum. More juice dripped to the floor. He wanted to marry her. She'd hoped for it, kind of expected it after the way he'd acted with her father, but, still, she would have liked to be asked first.

"Sarah, you're making a mess. How about cleaning up the floor?" Joe said, his voice suspiciously even.

She rose clumsily, trying to clutch her thighs together to retain the plum. She reached for the towel lying on the table.

"No, I want you to lick it up."

Her body vibrated like he'd pressed that little butterfly's remote, but it was just his voice, the sweet tension in his tone, that set her off.

Not caring what Logan saw, she slowly sank to her knees, placed both hands on the floor, and stuck her ass in the air as she licked the droplets of plum juice.

Fingers traced the edges of her furled lips and prodded the plum.

She moaned, waiting for it, knowing what he was about to do and that he was letting Logan, with his dark, compelling gaze, watch.

Joe dropped to the floor behind her. His nose nuzzled her sex. "God, I love the way this smells. Lemon and plum. Your sweet cunt." His tongue stroked over the fruit, glancing on her folds.

Sarah shivered and dropped to her elbows.

The plum burst, and she knew he'd bit into it. Tongue and teeth pulled it from inside her.

"Logan . . ." Joe spit out.

"I'm out of here. Friday night?"

"We'll be there."

Logan laughed all the way to the door, but Sarah couldn't have cared less because Joe hauled her to her feet and bent her over the edge of the table.

The rasp of a zipper and a deep, masculine groan sounded behind her, and then the tip of his glorious cock was pushing inside.

Sarah stretched out on the cool wood, enjoying the smooth forward-and-back glides that slid her nipples along the surface, but especially the steady thrust of his thick cock as it crammed into her pussy.

The apron fell open, the ties drifting toward the floor. "I like you all domestic."

"Dream on if you ever think I'm gonna be barefoot and pregnant and waiting on your ass."

Smack!

Sarah smiled and laid her hot cheek on the table. "When did you decide you wanted to marry me?"

"When I was following your pretty ass bent over your motorcycle," he said, his voice tight as he hammered into her.

"Know when I decided I wanted to marry you?"

"Tell me, baby."

"When it finally sank in why you brought me to Logan's that first night."

"Why do you think I did it?"

"Because you knew you had to shock me. Had to be the best I'd ever had. And you were . . . are." She groaned when fingers reached beneath her belly and strummed her clit.

"When are you going to say it?" he asked gruffly.

"That I love you?"

"Yeah."

"I thought I already had."

"When? I must have missed it."

"Every time I disobeyed you. I begged for you to touch me, to discipline me. Think I'd let just any man do that?"

A growl rumbled behind her, fingers plucked and squeezed her clit, his thickness punished her, stroking deep and hard.

"Don't ever expect me to be good," she murmured. "I've got no incentive to change."

"Baby," he whispered, finishing her off with a flourish, "I'll never admit this again, but I love the fact you're a bad, bad girl."

Night Watch

1

Logan Ross let his police cruiser idle past the middle of town to survey his domain. Since moving to Honkytonk from San Antonio, he had learned to appreciate the slower pace and savor small things, such as the change of seasons, even if there were only two in Texas. It was certainly different from life in the city.

Here it was on a Friday morning opening a three-day weekend, and there weren't any commuters honking horns or rat-race executives screaming into cell phones. Nope. Shopkeepers busied themselves around their white limestone stores with their brightly colored windowsills and door frames, putting up sale signs and displaying their wares on unattended tables under their equally bright awnings.

His gaze snagged on Annie's Antiques, as Annie, not to be confused with the original Annie, who happened to be her grandmother, carefully arranged an array of quilts on an out-side table. It was just the type of thing that would attract some-one who wanted to make a home. Instead of admiring the quilts, he paused to appreciate the fit of her chic sundress before allowing his gaze to move restlessly on.

Since his buddies had settled down, Logan found himself feeling more and more like he was standing on the outside looking in at happiness that continued to elude him. Both Cody and Joe seemed to thrive on their domestic arrangements, making Logan wonder what he was missing.

Still, life in Honkytonk was good. And Logan thought he might just have found the remedy to the constant lonely ache that settled in his chest at night and gripped his loins so tightly no amount of self-gratification could relieve it.

Shaking it off, his gaze went back to the town, and there *she* was.

Schoolteacher, came the primal growl rumbling up inside him. Every red corpuscle streaming through his veins rushed south.

The tall, gawky figure striding down Main Street straight toward him zeroed his attention from everything else around him.

Just a glimpse of the unfashionable denim smock she wore was enough to make him hard as rock. Schoolteachers never dressed chic. Still, it didn't matter to him. She could wear a gunny sack and push his buttons.

His reaction to her still shocked him on some level. She wasn't his usual type, which was a woman built like a brick house with curves so deep and round he could clamp his fingers on her flesh and steer her like a Porsche.

No, *Schoolteacher* was downright bony, with an angular face. Her medium-brown hair was the same soft shade as the deer he'd stalked through the woods just last weekend. Come to think of it, she resembled the creature with its slender, muscular build and darting glances, too.

Maybe that was the attraction—he equated the woman to prey.

Still, her demeanor and her wardrobe choices made him wince. Prim, buttoned up, unfashionably *homey*. While he watched, she stopped to chat with Annie as she ran a hand over the bright handmade quilts. Some were older and yellowed with time, while others showed less age and were every color of the rainbow. Even as he watched, she picked up the sign that read GOOD PRICE FOR A GOOD HOME.

Standing next to the chic and well-dressed Annie, Logan had to question his reactions to her. But, as ugly as her dress was, it couldn't hide the slender curve of her hips or the length of her coltish legs. Even her hideous brown sandals turned him on. They made her feet look like a duck's paddles until you looked closely and saw the slender beauty of her toes.

He'd caught a glimpse of them once when he'd cornered her in the Gas 'n' Go mini mart squeezing fruit. A plum, to be exact. Just the thought of it made him shift uncomfortably in his seat.

Her long fingers had engulfed it, wrapping around the plump fruit to squeeze gently.

Naturally he'd pictured her squeezing something else just about the same size and circumference. He'd been arrested in place, watching her test the fruit and vegetables for ripeness.

Hell, she'd been so intent, sniffing the stem of a cantaloupe. He had snuck right up behind her and reached over her shoulder for a honeydew before she'd seen him. Her shock had made him smile and had totally knocked her off balance.

She'd backed up, her bottom brushing the front of his denim jeans, and he'd known the exact moment she realized what she'd snuggled up against. Her cheeks had blushed a fiery red, and her soft mouth had gulped like a guppy's.

He'd mumbled an apology, embarrassed at his lack of self-control, and walked stiffly away, catching a glimpse of a sexy novel in her cart as he passed. But he couldn't help glancing over his shoulder for one more look.

She'd placed her hands on the melons as though afraid her legs would crumble, and he'd left the store still smiling.

Over the months he'd been in Honkytonk, it seemed as though he was fated to have her because something kept placing her in his path.

The one house that had suited his needs sat at the end of a quiet cul-de-sac right next to hers.

Then the sheriff had selected him as the new liaison at the high school to roam the halls, get familiar with the kids, and lead the anti-drug-use education classes.

His first class had been in the room right next to hers. Of course, she'd dropped the handouts she'd carried the moment she saw him step outside the door of his classroom.

Like a waterfall of white and black, the papers had spilled at her feet, and then she'd sloshed coffee from the cup she carried as she bent over too fast, trying to retrieve them.

He'd knelt at her feet and gathered the handouts, wiping coffee from them on his pant leg before handing them back to her.

When he'd caught the surprised pleasure in her rounded eyes, he'd felt like a hero. But she'd quickly blinked and stiffened, her mouth sliding into that firm, prim line he was beginning to know all too well.

That didn't stop him from feeling like that guy who'd whipped his cape over a mud puddle for some queen long ago. Perhaps fortunately for him, the woman who stood in front of him didn't have a clue what more he was willing to do to please her.

Somehow, someday soon, *Schoolteacher* was going to come to him for instruction.

Over the past weeks, he'd fed her tantalizing glimpses of his body and his interests.

He'd padded barefoot to the mailbox when he'd spotted her car pulling into her driveway. He'd purposely worn a thin pair of sweatpants that fell beneath the notches of his hips and molded his sex in blatant detail.

He'd invited his friends for barbecues on his back deck and left the windows open so that she might hear their rowdy shouts when they watched a game on the television.

One night after he'd spotted her standing in the field between their lots with her telescope pointing toward the sky, he'd made damn sure she had more interesting sights to train her lens on.

Perhaps he'd shared a little too much. Maybe he'd even frightened her. But it was best she understood his needs from the outset. Besides, fear was something he could twist into obsession.

In the meantime, he trailed her surreptitiously in his patrol car, pulling into a parking space when she entered a shop and then continuing to trail her when she came out.

How she could have failed to notice him, stalking her along the narrow street, mystified him. But then again, most times he saw her, her eyes seemed blurred as though staring at something in the distance. *Schoolteacher* seemed perpetually lost in a daydream.

How he wished he could slide inside her mind. Were her dreams filled with erotic images of bodies dipping and writhing toward ecstasy? Or were they more romantic?

Logan grimaced, wondering if he'd have to do some research to figure out what a woman like her would find irresistible. His gaze passed the bookstore with its blue and white awning and tables set on the sidewalk for passersby to stop and sample the books.

Logan glanced at his watch. His lunch break was coming up. He had just enough time.

A breeze tugged at the hair Amy Keating had scraped back into a ponytail to keep it out of the way, and she hoped the wind didn't continue to build, or this night's expedition would be a bust.

If the sky remained clear, and the wind didn't interfere too much with her charts and equipment, she'd be closer to her self-imposed goal.

Concentrating on the celestial bodies on Messier's list, rather than the corporal and virile specimen next door, had proven the greater challenge these past weeks.

Her neighbor commanded attention wherever he went. She wasn't the only one to notice.

The day he'd surprised her in the hallway at school, and she'd dumped the work sheets she had prepared for her class at his feet, she hadn't been the only female in the vicinity to sigh as his big, brawny body folded gracefully to the floor. When he'd dried her coffee-stained papers on his thick, muscular thigh, she hadn't been able to drag her eyes from him. Something in her chest had tightened. Sensual awareness had sharpened to an exquisitely honed edge.

As he'd lifted the papers to return them to her, his fingers had slid along her palm. A little electric current had passed from him, and she'd stiffened with shock. Heat curled deep inside her.

As she'd sputtered her thanks and then hurried through her door, she'd heard Carla Banks and Vanessa Rosas in the hallway giggling. She must have looked like a red-faced fool. But what woman wouldn't melt into a puddle at just a glimpse of his powerful frame and handsome face? That he'd been clothed in a crisply starched deputy's uniform had only added to his masculine charm.

His universal appeal had given her the strength of will to carry on as usual, despite the constant distraction of seeing him everywhere she went. If she didn't know any better, she might have thought he was stalking her, which could only be wishful thinking on her part. What on Earth did she have to offer a man like that?

While she knew she wasn't a complete bow-wow, she was honest enough with herself to admit that she was plain. Her hair was a nondescript brown, her skin colorless with a smattering of freckles that looked like droplets of mud on a pale blanket of snow. It was her height, however, that was her most notable flaw. Nearly six feet tall, she was too large to inspire a man's protective instincts—something she completely, secretly craved.

Not for the first time in her twenty-eight years, she wondered how wonderful it must be for one of *those women*, the full-figured Barbie dolls whose heads snuggled nicely against a man's chest. Hers, she imagined, would lie atop Deputy Ross's broad shoulders.

Annoyed with herself for wasting time yearning for something she'd never have, she pulled a flashlight from her bag and turned it on. The red lens was just bright enough to check her star chart for settings for her scope without destroying her night vision.

M43—the Orion Nebula—beckoned.

In the distance, the growl of a powerful engine rumbled loudly as it approached. Neighborhood dogs barked. Car doors slammed shut. Laughter pierced the air—a feminine squeal, followed by low, rumbling, masculine chuckles.

Lord, no. Not again.

She'd recognized the woman's voice. Although the last time she'd heard it, Sarah Michelson was cursing a filthy blue streak. And no wonder, after what the two of them had done to her.

Yet she was here again. Did that mean . . . ?

No, Amy wasn't going to peek. The last time had been devastating. She'd been in this same exact spot, at approximately the same time, when she'd trained her telescope on that special room of his with the window facing this very field.

Oh, the things she'd seen!

Her cheeks had burned for days. Her body had felt tight, hot, so filled with sexual frustration she'd fished out the vibrator her sister had given her one Christmas from its box underneath the bathroom sink.

For several nights afterward, she'd lain in her bed, rolling the smooth gel head over her sex, plunging it deep into her core, trying to satisfy the cravings the trio had awakened.

Light spilled across the clearing, shining from the naughty room, bleaching the dried grass a pale gray.

Amy stood in the darkness, just beyond the light, staring at the ground. *I'm not going to watch, I'm not going to . . .*

She closed her eyes briefly, calling for inner fortitude, and then lifted her tripod to reposition it, pointing the scope toward the room.

She adjusted the focus, zooming in on a patch of pink skin. A protruding nipple. *Oh. My. God.* An aroused nipple surrounded by a very round and generous breast.

A dark figure stepped in the way, blocking her view.

Her head jerked up, and she stared into the window. Logan Ross leaned against the window frame. His features, burnished by the subtle lighting in the room, were drawn and taut—and he was staring directly at her!

She whirled around, pressing a hand against her chest. He knew! Sweet Jesus, what did he think of her now?

Slowly she glanced over her shoulder, pretending to reach for her bag, and then caught his gaze again. He straightened, moving away from the window.

He strode toward Sarah, lifting her hand and bringing her forward, placing her in front of the window but not so close that Amy couldn't see most of her shape, head to knees.

Slowly he peeled away the blonde's clothing while Joe Chavez took a seat at a small wooden table and watched, his gaze never leaving Sarah's pretty body as it was bared one piece at a time.

When she was completely naked, Logan lifted her hand and twirled her under his arm as though dancing her around in slow-motion, and Amy understood.

He was letting her watch them. Inviting her to do so.

Amy swallowed, her eyes filling as the painful yearning swamped her again. Everything missing from her staid little life was there on display.

But why was he doing this? As punishment for intruding on their games? Or was he trying to tempt her? *Her*, plain Amy Keating?

While both possibilities struck a chord of fear inside her, still she couldn't drag herself away as Logan led Sarah to a wooden frame she hadn't seen in the room the last time she'd spied on the three of them.

Made of gleaming wood and shaped like an *X*, there were shackles—leather bindings with metal buckles—attached to each arm.

Sarah meekly stepped up to the frame, leaning her back against it, and lifted her arms for Logan to place the straps around one wrist and then the other and lock her into place.

Then Sarah widened her stance, her legs settling against the lower half of the wooden beams, and her ankles were restrained.

Next, Logan carried a black hood to Sarah, which he pulled over her head, completely concealing her face. He tucked her long white-blond hair beneath it, and only the curves Amy already knew so well identified the woman as Sarah.

Joe rose from his chair to join Logan. Both men ran their hands over Sarah's body, smoothing broad palms from her shoulders to her feet.

Sarah's chest rose and fell more sharply. Her skin flushed with heat that spread like warm butter over her skin.

Joe bent and captured one of Sarah's nipples, cupping her breast and holding it, squeezing it while he tugged and lashed his tongue at her dimpled areola.

Logan strode to the opposite side of the room, disappearing from her view. Amy waited anxiously for him to return, afraid for a moment that he might be coming outside to confront her, but then he returned holding one of his short whips. He flicked the tail in the air.

Sarah jerked at the sound, her head turning to follow it as he flicked it again.

Amy began to sweat, imagining what it must be like to feel the lash he used to stripe the woman's flesh.

Each stroke caused Sarah's hands to tighten above the restraints, her back to bow.

Amy wished she could hear. Wished she knew whether the woman suffered or was enthralled.

Nothing in Amy's experience could fill the lack of sound. She didn't know what the crack of the leather flanges would sound like landing on flesh. Didn't know what the men's voices would sound like—harsh and commanding, tight with sexual excitement, or low murmurs intended to soothe a woman's fears?

When Logan turned the short whip upside down and skimmed the handle up the woman's thigh, Amy's breath caught.

It disappeared inside the woman's body as his arm stroked up and down, fucking her with it.

Her own body spilled fluid onto the crotch of her cotton

panties. But the sight was too distant for her to know if the woman enjoyed it quite as much as she did. She trained the telescope again on the window and adjusted the focus, bending to the eyepiece and skimming her gaze along Sarah's voluptuous body until she found the thatch of blond hair.

The men had been careful to leave her a clear view of the woman's pussy and of the large hand gripping the handle as it was pushed up and down between Sarah Michelson's legs.

The other woman's thighs gleamed with moisture; her folds were red and swollen. Oh, she enjoyed it, all right. Her body vibrated with her pleasure. Her thighs strained wider to allow Logan to continue to fuck her.

Logan pulled the handle from her vagina while Joe unbuckled the restraints.

Sarah sagged against Joe's chest, but he held her away. Then the men walked her to the window, forcing her head down, and she raised her hands to hold the bottom of the windowsill so her body was bent, her breasts swaying.

Then Logan gripped the wet handle, raised it high, and struck her buttocks.

Sarah's head dropped lower, her knuckles whitening against the casing she clutched hard. However, she did nothing to avoid the blows that followed in quick succession, aimed at different spots.

He paused, thrust a hand downward, and then lifted his fingers to his mouth and sucked on them.

Amy quivered at his expression. Dark, intense, his gaze rising to meet hers across the yard.

From the corner of her eye, she saw Joe tug his tee over his head and shove down his pants. He walked toward Logan and held out his hand for the whip, which Logan surrendered immediately, stepping back.

Joe brushed the flanges over Sarah's trembling back and buttocks and then dropped it. His hands clasped her cheeks and massaged them, lifting them up and then releasing them. His hand raised, and he slapped her with his open palm.

Amy followed the motion, watching as he delivered another blow to the other cheek, and then realized she'd lost sight of Logan again. She searched the room, her breath releasing when he stepped back into view, only to choke when she saw that he was nude.

His cock rose straight from his groin.

Joe glanced over at him and then laughed.

Logan's expression was rueful, but he gripped his cock in one hand and stroked it, up and down. He stood to the side of Sarah, and Joe turned her to face Logan, still bent over.

Her hands reached in front of her, caught hold of Logan's cock with one, cupped his balls with the other, and tugged him toward her face.

Joe reached around her, rolling up the bottom edge of the hood until her mouth was exposed.

She licked her lips once and then stuck out her tongue and wet the tip of Logan's cock.

They were in perfect profile. Amy could see everything. Joe palming Sarah's ass and thrusting his hips toward her, his cock disappearing, sliding into Sarah's body. Sarah opening her mouth wide and swallowing Logan's cock as he fucked her mouth, his gaze intent on Sarah's motions as she licked and sucked and then swallowed him again.

Then his head turned slowly, his gaze meeting Amy's again, and Amy backed up against her folding table, grabbing the edge to steady herself.

This was all for her. Staged for her to see. Her gaze slid away from his, dropping to where Sarah greedily gobbled him up.

Impossibly the other woman swallowed his length, her mouth

stretching around his girth, her cheeks hollowing as she sucked, billowing as she drew off and breathed.

Her breasts and ass jiggled with the force of Joe's strokes.

Amy met Logan's gaze again, locking with his for a long moment, trying to read whatever message he was trying to send her over the distance.

Was he really mocking her? He needn't have gone to such extremes to make her feel unequal. She didn't possess the feminine beauty of Sarah Michelson. He didn't have to drive his cock like a stake through her heart to make that point.

Or was he telling her what she should expect, what he meant to do to her? As intimidating as this staged tableau was, more frightening to Amy was the thought that she'd eagerly let herself be used, to be mocked or pleasured, for the sheer orgasmic sensation of feeling Logan slide between her lips . . . and, dear God, her legs.

Whatever he wanted, she would willingly give for just one night with Logan Ross.

2

"Is she still watching?" Joe asked, his voice tight.

"Don't you have more self-control than that?" Logan muttered.

Sarah giggled around Logan's cock.

"Just asking," Joe said between tightly clenched jaws. "You sure this is the way to woo this girl?"

"I'm not sure of a damn thing. But I don't want her painting rosy pictures about what being with me will be like."

"Shock therapy?"

"Just letting her see the truth."

"Sounds serious. Didn't think you'd ever be bit by the bug."

"I'm not sure what this is. But I'm damn tired of following her around like a lovesick pup. She'll either go for it or call the cops on me."

"Which could be a little embarrassing. Sarah could wind up sitting in her daddy's docket after all."

Sarah slurped and came off Logan's cock.

Logan gritted his teeth, ready to fist his hand in her hair to keep her where he needed her.

"You two are so completely clueless," Sarah said, rolling her eyes. "If she's still watching you watching her, she's plenty into you, Logan. Although I have to say you could have started her out with something a little less intimidating than flogging me within an inch of orgasm."

"She wasn't intimidated," Logan muttered.

"You could tell what she was thinking from across a dark yard?"

"She didn't grab the edge of the table until I faced her. She's curious."

"Why don't you just invite her in?" Joe said tightly, still pounding at Sarah's pussy.

"And expose her to your two kinky selves? I don't want her running screaming for her door."

"But you'd let her see us?"

"This isn't the first time she's watched," he reminded them.

"So what's next? Do I get to come sometime soon?" Joe growled.

"Me, too," Sarah chirped. "I'm just a little worked up here."

"Baby," Joe crooned, "there's no 'little worked up' to you. You're so fucking wet my dick's swimming in your cunt."

"Gawd, I love it when you talk dirty."

Logan stepped back. "You two finish up."

"You kicking us out?" Joe asked, his eyebrows rising.

"Yeah." He knelt and pushed up Sarah's torso and latched on to a nipple, nipping the tight bud with his teeth.

Her body vibrated and then jerked as Joe hammered her to orgasm. Sarah's cries, tight yet throaty, and Joe's heavy grunts made him smile.

Sure, his cock was still aching, but as soon as these two were out of the door, he was going to move into the next stage of his plan to seduce *Schoolteacher*.

* * *

Amy stuffed her chart and flashlight into her bag and folded up her table, ready to escape, the trio having left the room just moments before.

With the three of them apparently finished, she didn't want to risk having her neighbor confront her.

She raised the lens cap dangling on a string to cover the end of the telescope and then glanced back inside the room.

Logan had returned.

Her hand paused midair, the lens cap falling from numb fingertips. He was still completely nude and pacing the room like a caged tiger.

Everything about him oozed frustration. From the jerky, heavy movements of his naturally graceful body to the erection that hadn't waned.

He disappeared for a moment and then stepped into her view again, straps dangling from his fingers.

She lowered her face to the eyepiece again. The straps were leather with Velcro tabs and metal slides. Their purpose became clear when he dropped one strap beneath his balls and laid another on top and cinched them. The next strap encircled his engorged cock. He pulled the tabs, tightening the harness.

If possible, his erection seemed to thicken and lengthen, or was his massive size just emphasized by the framing of the taut leather?

It didn't matter; she knew he used it to arrest his arousal, maintaining it at its fullest to prolong his pleasure.

He picked up one of those short whips with the leather flanges and stood directly in front of the window again.

His gaze didn't meet hers. It remained on his swollen sex. Widening his stance, he draped the flanges over his shaft and pulled the handle, letting them caress his length.

Over and over again, he slowly dragged it up and across his length and then dropped his arm at his side. With his free hand he cupped his balls, lifting them, drawing her gaze to their smooth, hairless surface. Reddened, bulging, he caressed them gently and tugged, then let them go. Next he lifted his shaft straight up and struck his balls with the whip.

Amy gasped. She'd always assumed the most sensitive and vulnerable part of a man could never take a blow, but there he stood, striking his balls with the whip, resetting his feet to widen his legs and then striking again.

Fascinated, she had to force herself to raise the scope to his face to see how he took his self-flagellation.

His face was tight, deep lines bracketing his mouth, his eyebrows drawn into a dark, forbidding frown. A shiver crawled up her spine at his expression, and then another shuddered through her when his gaze lifted.

He struck himself again, and she watched his mouth fall open around a groan she couldn't hear. His eyes closed, and the hand on his cock stroked up and down his shaft.

Why did he do this? Why did he seek pain when he could so easily pleasure himself?

Or was the pain part of the pleasure?

She remembered tweaking her own nipples when she'd masturbated and thought she might understand, in a very small way, what drove him now.

He tossed the whip to the side and picked up a plastic bottle he'd placed on the windowsill. Something she'd missed when she'd been staring so intently at his body.

He squirted it into his palm and then smoothed the liquid over his cock, his hands skimming his length until his shaft gleamed as though oiled. And perhaps it was. She couldn't really tell from where she stood. She wondered whether it was scented. Whether it warmed with friction. She wished she could wrap her fingers around his satiny flesh and find out for herself.

With a tightening of his jaw, he slowly wrapped the fingers

of one hand around himself and began to pump his hand up and down his shaft while loosening the straps encasing him.

As if she were in the room with him, encouraging him, she felt relief that at last he was going to end his torture. Evenly paced strokes smoothed up and down the thick column, and she watched the arm delivering the strokes flex, veins rising on his biceps as he labored.

His chest gleamed with a light sheen of sweat that darkened the thick, curling fur clothing his skin. His breaths deepened, the heavy slabs of muscle lifting and falling more rapidly now.

Her own breaths quickened, growing shallow and ragged. Her hand gripped the plastic cylinder of the telescope, and she compared its hard metal surface to the view of his rigid, veined staff and tried to imagine the skin moving beneath her hand as she fisted him.

His belly jumped and quivered, his thighs tensed, and suddenly his strokes shortened, growing more frantic, less controlled.

She held her breath.

Thin stripes of pearlescent cum spurted from the tip of his cock, falling back to his hand, coating it, mixing with the oily liquid moistening his shaft until his hand glided in wetness.

The wet heat between her own legs shocked her. She'd felt outside herself watching him, but all along her own body had grown aroused. She shifted her stance, the friction of her cotton shorts rubbing between her thighs not nearly enough to ease the ache centered on her hardening clitoris.

Her hand sank between her legs, delving beneath the edge of her shorts and between her legs. She withdrew her fingers and rubbed the creamy fluid with her thumb and then lifted her face.

He'd watched. His hand left his cock, and he licked the back of it.

Amy didn't know where she found the courage, but she raised her fingers to her lips and stuffed them into her mouth.

Logan's face relaxed, warmth seeping into his expression.

Encouraged by his approval, she withdrew her fingers and then slid them back into her mouth, her lips closing around them to suck the flavor of her arousal, just as she wanted to do with his cock.

She pulled them from her mouth again and stood in the darkness. This odd communion between them felt real, felt as though they were somehow engaged in a mutual seduction, but she wasn't sure she was brave enough to continue.

He raised his hand, fingers spread.

Five fingers. *Five minutes?* Did he mean for her to wait? He turned and strode naked from the room while she quivered in the darkness and contemplated making a mad dash for her back door.

But her equipment. She couldn't leave it. And she couldn't lug it back quickly enough.

A door opened and slammed shut. A dark figure emerged from the shadows engulfing the side of his home, striding straight for her, and she groaned.

She wasn't ready for this. What would she say?

His long strides ate up the distance between them, and then he stepped into the light spilling from his window. She saw that he'd donned blue jeans and sandals. And she felt disappointment that he wasn't still nude.

He reached her, his hands coming up to cup her cheeks, and then he was bending toward her.

Logan's lips touched hers, and Amy gasped, opening beneath the gentle pressure. His tongue swept into her mouth, and she got her first taste of Logan's cum.

Another stroke, and she realized he tasted her arousal, and

then he was dragging up her hand, bringing her two fingers to their joined mouths. His tongue licked her fingers and her lips, and she was encouraged to do the same, sharing her arousal with him just as she might share food with a lover.

It was the most erotic experience of her life, that kiss. Warm, wet . . . messy.

When he drew back, they both breathed heavily, and she swayed toward him, her knees weakening.

His arms surrounded her, supporting her weight, and he pushed her head to his shoulder. Her cheek did indeed rest there naturally. Her head fit in the corner of his neck, and it was more pleasurable then she could ever have imagined.

His skin was hot, bathed in sweat. She struck out her tongue and tasted it, and his soft chuckle warmed the side of her face. "Are you okay?" he asked, his deep voice thick and gravelly.

She shivered at the visceral sensation of his voice scraping across her skin. "I'm not sure."

"That's all right. This is enough for now." He held her away from him and reached a hand behind him, returning with a single dark rose.

She took it from him, closing her eyes as she inhaled the fragrance permeating the soft petals. "I didn't mean to spy on you."

"I know. But you couldn't resist staying either, could you?"

She shook her head, glad of the darkness hiding her blush.

"You did it on purpose. Was it because you knew I'd be here?"

"Of course."

"But why?"

His lips curved slowly. "I don't know how most men set out to get your attention, schoolteacher, but I wanted to make an impression."

A smile tugged at her lips, and she ducked her head. "A simple hello would have worked just as well. As a matter of fact, picking up those papers made me—"

"Wet?"

She groaned softly. "God, how can you be so casual saying that to me? You don't even know me."

"I know more than you think. I'm going to ask you to go to dinner with me tomorrow night, and you're going to say yes."

Amy shivered at the razor intensity of his tone, imagining how he'd sound whispering in her ear when they made love. A silly thought. "But why? Why me?"

"You've been driving me crazy. For weeks. I wanted to ask before, but you needed to know some things about me first."

"That's why you staged this?"

He didn't respond, but she knew it was true.

His lips tightened. "Let me help you take your equipment back."

A frisson of alarm bit her spine. Did he expect her to invite him in? Her house was a mess, and she was wearing her oldest pair of panties.

"Don't worry. Only to the door. We can take this at your pace. Whatever you're comfortable with."

"You're willing to do that for me?"

"For as long as it takes. And if you ask me why again, I'll kiss you again."

She had to think about that. Another kiss would be nice.

"Maybe you want another anyway?" he asked, amusement softening his rugged voice.

"Please," she said softly.

"I like the way you say that."

This time, his kiss was more restrained. Sweeter. His lips rubbed against hers, and she lifted her hands timidly to embrace his shoulders, filling the need to measure their breadth and steely mettle.

His soft groan swept away her reticence, and she leaned into him, letting her breasts mash against his chest and rising on her toes to meet his kiss directly. For once her height pleased her. She opened her eyes to find him staring back and broke the kiss.

"I don't mind that you're a little shy," he said, his strong hands gently cupping her hips.

"I do."

"Do you feel at a disadvantage?"

"I feel unequal. Completely overwhelmed."

His head canted to the side, his gaze thoughtful. "Because you don't think you're attractive to me?"

He'd nailed the problem mercilessly. And because his instinct had been so dead-on, she thought it was probably true.

He grabbed her hand and pulled it to his groin, flattening her palm against him. "I just came, and I'm not Superman, but you make me this way."

Her hand cupped his burgeoning erection, and she couldn't help but trace the length of him through his clothing. "I don't care why you want me," she said simply.

One dark brow rose. "Are you willing to settle for less than love because you don't think that can happen between us?"

"I don't have any expectations. I promise."

"How convenient," he said, a nasty edge entering his voice.

"I hope so."

He shook his head, his expression clearing and becoming slightly bemused. "Uh . . . let's get this gear inside."

She started to lift the pack, but he took the straps from her and shouldered it. Then he lifted the card table and leaned down to grab the tripod and hefted it over the other shoulder.

"I guess I'll just lead the way," she said, feeling a little flustered at how easily he'd taken over.

It was nice having a man acting the gentleman. But then she

had to remind herself that just half an hour ago, he'd been tonguing another woman's breast. She lifted the rose to idly draw on its scent.

They made it the porch, and she opened her door, taking a deep breath before turning to invite him in.

Logan shook his head. "Don't invite me in."

Only partly relieved, her eyebrows rose. "You don't want to come inside?"

"It's too soon."

Her mouth opened, wanting to deny it, but she knew if he stepped over the threshold he wouldn't be leaving until morning. And he was right. She had a lot to think about—and panties to consign to the trash can.

He leaned the tripod against the wall, set down the card table and the bag, and stepped off the porch before meeting her gaze again.

"Tomorrow night, then? Wear a dress. Something midthigh. Do you have something like that?"

"Sure," she said vaguely.

With a nod, he turned and blended into the darkness, leaving her wilting against her front door.

3

The next afternoon Amy was on her knees sliding out the shallow plastic box from beneath the bed, eager for a little dress-up. She'd already spent the day cleaning the house. Now she wanted to do everything she could to give herself a little boost in self-confidence before her date with Logan.

She'd pulled a dress from her closet, still wrapped in plastic from the store. The short, navy sheath with tiny sprigs of pale gray and pink flowers had been bought on a whim and never worn. Too short for school, and with no man around to inspire in her the courage to actually wear it in public, it had stayed at the back of her closet. But not tonight. A pair of silver sandals, also never worn, would complete the ensemble.

The choice of dress and shoes had been the easy part. She hoped what was stored in the bin would solve the rest of her problem. She pulled the black thong panties and corset from the bin and bit her lip, wondering if the corset was too much.

It was another gift from her happily married sister whose answer to all dating woes was the right underwear.

Amy dropped her robe on the bed and slid into the panties,

enjoying the thrill of the narrow strip of fabric sliding between her buttocks.

She felt naughty and a little braver when she turned in front of the mirror to assure herself her butt didn't look like a sumo wrestler's.

The corset wasn't as easy to don. The slender cords cinching the waist laced up the back. Before attempting to put it on, she fed the strings through the eyelets, leaving them loose, and then shimmied the silk garment up her long legs and tugged it over her hips. That was the easy part. Reaching behind her to draw the ends of the strings up and tighten them took a contortionist's skill, but, then, it wasn't designed for a woman to put on, or remove, by herself.

The thought of Logan seeing her in this drove her to persevere. She wanted to impress him. Let him think she was less of a mouse than she really was.

The thought of what he'd done last night, how he'd kissed her, what he'd said, had left her warm and pink-cheeked all day long.

Last night had been only the beginning.

This morning when she'd pulled into the teacher's parking lot, his squad car was already there. He'd unfolded his large frame from his seat when she brought her Honda to a halt and walked to her door.

She'd been breathless, caught off guard, seeing him so soon. Dressed in his khaki uniform shirt, dark pants, and a cream cowboy hat, she'd melted into a gooey puddle. She'd sat stunned until he opened the door and leaned inside to brush her lips with a swift, chaste kiss.

"Let me get your things," he'd said.

He'd shouldered her bag and carried her books like any other high school male trying to make a good impression on a girl, and she'd been plenty impressed.

So had Carla and Vanessa, whose jaws dropped as he strode by, walking at Amy's side.

After he'd laid his burden on her desk, she'd noticed the bulge in his pants pocket, but she'd been too polite to comment. He'd reached into his pocket and pulled out a small apple, rubbed it on his shirtsleeve, and left it in the center of her desk without another word.

Then he'd turned, walking past the girls and winking at them before leaving.

The girls had rushed forward, swarming her.

"Oh, my God, Miss Keating! Is he crushin' on you?"

She'd laughed as they'd squealed, feeling almost as giddy as they had, and then assured them he wasn't "crushing" on her but letting slip that he had asked her on a date.

They'd made her swear to tell them every detail, and she'd crossed her fingers behind her back because if things went as she hoped, there was no way on God's green Earth she'd ever tell a soul.

"Damnit." The ties behind her back defied her. She'd gotten them almost tight enough to cinch her waist and then dropped the strings. Rather than loosen them and start over, she hurried to the kitchen and drew a set of tongs from the drawer beside the sink.

But as she was turning she caught a glimpse of Logan pulling into his drive. Her attention snagged, and the tongs brushed the wall, hitting the garbage-disposal switch.

The dry, grating noise from the disposal as it ground to life startled her, and she dropped the tongs on the floor, bent to pick them up, and started turning back to the sink to switch off the disposal.

That was when she felt the corset cinch tighter. Amy tried to pull away from the sink, wondering what she'd caught the ties on, but couldn't budge. In fact, the corset continued to constrict around her waist, drawing her backward toward the counter. Then the disposal began to make a horrible, garbled noise and cut off.

With a fateful certainty, Amy knew exactly where the ends of the slender cords were stuck.

Panicked, she reached for the knife drawer, determined to cut the cord, but her long arms couldn't quite reach.

With her back to the counter and her body pulled tight against it, she stood helpless for several minutes wondering what she could do.

Her house was too far from Logan's to shout for help. Besides, how embarrassing would that be?

Her gaze landed on the phone on the opposite counter. If she could just reach the phone and hit one of her speed-dial numbers . . .

Lord, she couldn't see the digits from here. Whomever she reached, whoever came to help, it was going to be a long damn time before she lived down the humiliation.

Tears welled in her eyes. She'd so looked forward to tonight, but this was the pinprick to burst her euphoric bubble and return her feet to solid ground.

Logan Ross was willing to take her out. Probably willing to fuck her. But he wasn't going to stay in her life. However much she longed for it happen.

Logan answered the phone on the fourth ring, having rushed straight from the shower. Water ran off his skin and hair in rivulets, dripping on the carpet. "Ross here," he barked, irritated because he'd recognized the number on his Caller ID.

"I know you're off duty," the dispatcher, Nancy Sessions, said, "but we're sending you on a call."

Logan heard snickering in the background and nearly hung up the phone in her ear. He'd been teased mercilessly when he'd let slip about his date that day at work. Seemed his buddies thought the match a bit odd.

"You know I have plans for tonight," he gritted out, "So why the hell are you calling me?"

"Um . . ." She broke off, and more muffled snickers sounded on the line. "We're shorthanded. Besides we knew you'd want to handle this one . . . *p-personally*." The last word sounded as though it had been squeezed through an accordion, she was laughing so hard.

Logan never liked to let anyone get to him, proving a lack of self-discipline, so he took a quick breath and tightened the towel he had wrapped around his hips before he responded. "Okay, I'll bite," he said evenly. "What's the emergency?"

"Seems your pretty little neighbor . . . has gotten herself into a p-predicament. . . ." she said, her voice tight, laughter edging every word.

Amy? His heart stopped. He dropped the phone and rushed to the door, pausing only long enough to slip on a pair of flip-flops before running across the grass separating their houses.

Moments later, he pounded on Amy's door. "Amy? Are you all right? Open the door!"

"Oh, my freaking God," came a faint, mournful voice. She sounded near to tears.

"Amy!" he shouted. "Open the door if you can."

"I can't," she groaned.

He backed up, preparing to kick it in.

"It's open. Don't bust it down, for God's sake!"

He turned the handle and entered, his gaze panning a living room and then narrowing on the opening into the kitchen where the sounds of soft, shuddering sobs emanated.

Jesus, had she injured herself? Was she bleeding out? He rushed through the doorway and then skidded to a halt on the tile floor when he saw her. She was backed up to the kitchen sink, her body bent unnaturally. Her hands clutched the edge of the counter beside her hips—her narrow but nicely rounded hips.

"You're not hurt?" he asked softly, noting the tears welling in her eyes.

"Just stuck," she said, her voice sounding thick and raw.

Relief poured through him, and he nearly smiled at her predicament, but he knew she already felt humiliated. Her face and the tops of her tiny breasts were flushed a deep rose.

His gaze snapped back up to hers. "I'm here to help."

"I called nine-one-one," she said softly and then sniffed. "Wasn't sure who I reached when I called. Had to hit speed dial with my toes."

His gaze dropped to the phone on the floor, and he realized she must have had to stretch those long, long legs up to the opposite counter to reach it, toppling it down before she nudged the button with her toes.

"They called me because I'm right next door." And because they knew darn well he was excited about his date. He strode toward the telephone, picked it up, and set it on the counter, hanging up the handset to cut the connection, knowing he'd just spoiled the rest of Nancy's fun.

"I couldn't reach a knife or scissors," she said, sniffing. "The strings got caught up in the garbage disposal."

"I see," he said softly, turning back to her. No wonder her back was arched so sharply. And beautifully. Her body was bowed; the bottom edge of the corset had risen to bare a pale ribbon of flesh above the silky material of her thong panties.

Logan slammed the door on the arousal creeping into his dick. As much as he was tempted to take advantage of the situation any man would enjoy, he had another agenda to advance.

She needed him.

"There are scissors over there," she said, lifting a hand from the counter to point to a cup filled with pens.

Logan shook himself, knowing he could get lost staring. He retrieved the scissors and walked slowly toward her. He had to stand close to see around her. Black silk cords, stretched taut, disappeared into the garbage disposal.

He snipped them and then caught the ends as she pulled away from the sink. "Let me," he said. "You still have plenty left to tie a bow."

"I feel so foolish. I never wear anything like this. . . ."

"I never would have pictured it either," he murmured.

"Should have stuck to white panties and bra."

He finished the bow and cupped her shoulders from behind; then he leaned forward to breathe in the scent of the soft brown hair she'd twisted into a messy knot at the back of her head. "I think you're lovely."

Her head angled sharply toward him, and he drew back. "Really?"

"To tell you the truth, I've been picturing you in granny panties. That image in my head has kept me hard for weeks."

Her eyes widened. Her teeth nibbled at her bottom lip. "I can change."

"Don't. I think it's sweet you wanted to make an impression. But did you really expect me to see this tonight?"

Her blush deepened, and her glance slid away. "I shouldn't have assumed you wanted me . . . that way."

His hands tightened. "Oh, I want you, all right. But not before you're ready. I don't want to rush you. We've got plenty of time to get to know each other."

Her gaze slid away. "What if I don't want to wait?" she whispered.

Logan's plans to woo her slowly crumbled at the hint of

longing in her tone. He cupped her cheek with his palm and turned her face back toward his. The stark hunger he saw in her hazel eyes was all he'd hoped for. "Because we both know you're going to need help getting out of this thing," he said softly, squeezing her shoulders, "keep it on and go finish dressing."

She nodded; her tongue swept out to lick her lower lip, and he knew what she was asking for, even if she didn't.

He bent and pressed his lips to hers. Just a quick brush of lips was all he planned, but her tongue stroked his lip, and he groaned, leaning closer. The tips of their tongues met and then slid sinuously together.

He tamped down his growing desire and broke the kiss. "I better get out of here before I embarrass myself."

Her gaze dropped to the towel and then darted back up to his chest. "Not anything I haven't already seen," she said, a smile crimping a corner of her wide mouth.

He smiled. "Or tasted."

Her blush deepened as she met his glance.

"Get dressed. I'll be back in an hour." He strode away, adjusting his towel. As he crossed the yard, he heard an engine.

"Hey, Ross!" came a shout from a squad car parked on the street between the two houses. Deputy Kramer raised a cell phone he held in his hand.

Logan shot him the finger and started cussing. No doubt his picture would be passed around the station house and posted to the bulletin board. Him in his tented towel.

But he couldn't be too irritated. Not with the picture firmly burnished in his mind of Amy standing with her back arched like an exotic bird, the tops of her small breasts quivering with each ragged exhalation.

Her body was long and slender like a willow switch. *Flexible.*

What he'd seen of her narrow hips and buttocks aroused a predatory hunger. He'd wanted to keep her there, strip the panties down her long legs, and devour her sweet heat.

The expression she'd worn was the only thing that had held him back. She'd been embarrassed to the point of tears, her modest nature compromised. He'd bet anything she would have preferred a stranger seeing her like that over him.

She'd wanted to make an impression. Prove she was willing to try to match his appetites.

Damn, he couldn't get the image of her out of his mind or the scent of her light floral perfume and heavier feminine musk.

Already he was imagining her strapped to the St. Andrew's cross. He'd bet her limbs would stretch the length of the crossed ties. He also knew her long legs would wrap nicely around his hips, locking him to her body.

4

Amy opened the door as soon as she heard the heavy tread of Logan's feet crossing her porch.

"Don't you know you're supposed to keep me waiting?" he said, the corners of his firm mouth rising.

"Is that a rule?" she asked without thinking and then lost her train of thought. Her first sight of him, standing in the fading sunlight, took her breath away.

He'd dressed in black slacks that hugged his muscled thighs and a gray, button-down dress shirt with the neck opened. Dark hairs brushed the open edges of the fabric, reminding her of just how well furred, how primitive the man beneath the clothes really was.

He held a bouquet of roses in his hand and offered them to her.

She took a moment to close her eyes and inhale the softly scented petals, anything to break her hungry stare and gather her shattered poise.

When she lifted her gaze to his, she found him sweeping her body with a possessive glance. "When I said midthigh . . ." he took a deep breath and shook his head, "I didn't have a clue how much skin you'd leave bare."

"Is it a problem? Is it too much?"

"No. It's just me. And don't pay any attention if I start growling to warn any other men away tonight."

She smiled. As though that would ever happen. "Let me put these in water."

"Wait. I have something else."

She paused, catching on the muted intensity of his expression as he dug a hand into his pocket and fished out a metal oval object. Recognizing what it was, because her sister had sent her a link to an online sex-toy shop, she drew in a sharp breath. "I thought you were going to take this slowly. You said . . ."

"It's up to you, Amy. You set the pace."

She raised a shaking hand and took the egg. "Now?" she asked.

"Yes."

She turned away, ready to head to the privacy of her bedroom to insert the little vibrator, but his fingers closed around her hand. "Here."

She blinked. "We're facing the street."

"No one's here. Just slip your hand under your skirt, slide that sexy little thong to the side, and slip it in."

The tone of his voice had changed from his signature rumble to a sexy purr. Knowing her face was glowing with embarrassment, she passed him the roses and raised her skirt just enough to get her hand beneath it. She nudged aside the crotch of her underwear and slid the egg into her pussy. "What if it falls out?"

"Push it deeper. But you're going to have to hold it inside all night."

With him watching her face, she tried to keep her expression blank, but the egg began to vibrate, and her mouth rounded as she gasped.

She closed her eyes like a child might. *If I can't see him, he can't see me.*

As the gentle hum continued, she shoved the vibrator deeper and then quickly pulled away her hand.

His hand lifted her chin. A kiss feathered her lips.

She sighed into his mouth. "Can you hear it?" she whispered.

"Only because I'm close to you like now. No one else will. I promise."

She opened her eyes, surprised to find him still so close, his lips hovering over hers. "I'm going to walk funny, trying to keep it there."

"Then everyone will know," he said, amusement lightening the deep purr.

He didn't seem to care about that fact, almost as though he wished other men would guess and know he'd been the one responsible. The idea grew to a certainty with the slight curl of his lip and dark, glittering stare. She drew back. "The roses?" she said, her voice choking.

Shaken but secretly thrilled, she left them in a vase on the counter, gathered her silver clutch, and followed him outside, placing her trust in his ability to keep her from making a complete fool out of herself tonight.

The night couldn't have been more perfect—or more frustrating. Over thick steaks at the Steers 'n' Steaks, they shared stories from their past and talked about work, pretending everything was normal—just a date between two people who were getting to know each other.

Beneath the innocuous chatter, sensual tension built, fueled by their mutual attraction and the wicked little secret they shared.

When the egg was quiet, she had long moments to collect her composure, sip slowly at a glass of wine, and gather her scattered thoughts to keep up her end of the long conversation.

When it hummed into life, she sat with her jaw slowly sagging, her eyelids dipping, and her hands clamping on the edge of the table as her libido rocketed.

He knew just how far to take her before relenting, knew just when to jack up her desire to keep her hovering on that jagged edge of arousal.

By the time he pulled his truck into his driveway, Amy's excitement had her whole body quivering, her silky panties drenched, and a nasty spot soaking through the back of her short skirt.

Her hand went to the door handle.

"Wait for me. I'll get that," he said, tension adding a bit of rasp to his quiet tone.

She watched him walk around the front of the truck, her gaze catching on the sexy curve of his mouth, the dark intent in his watchful eyes. Her body shivered so violently she doubted she could walk to the front door.

Logan opened her door and waited while she slid sideways to climb down, but his hands cupped her knees, halting her in place. Slowly he pressed them open until her skirt stopped the movement. "Lie back."

His tone held such a note of command that before she even gave a thought about what he asked and why, she found herself reclining, allowing him to shove up her skirt to her hips and helping him bare her by lifting her bottom for the fabric to bunch at her waist.

"The scent of you in the cab . . ." A deep inhalation was followed by a soft sigh of air she felt through the thin material covering her sex.

Sweet Jesus. His head was between her legs, looking at her, smelling her. Fingers traced the length of her pussy through her panties, and then one dipped into her entrance like a small penis sheathed in silk.

Her thighs tensed at the intrusion. Her hand swept her belly, trying to still the little tremors that rippled across it.

The finger withdrew and dragged upward, rubbing on her cloaked clit, sparking another wave of shivering arousal. Her thighs were lifted over strong shoulders, and he dragged her bottom to the edge of the seat. Fingers gently pushed aside the fabric, and his tongue stroked her.

"I can feel the vibrations on my tongue. I can hear them."

She could, too, as well as the moist clasp of her labia around her entrance. She moaned and then bit her lip to still her cries.

"No one can hear you but me," he growled. "Let me hear what I do to you. Let me know if I please you."

"If you please me?" she said, her voice rising in disbelief. "You're killing me."

Soft chuckles accompanied short gusts of air that warmed her moist sex. Then his lips took her, suckling on her folds, and his tongue slid along the quivering edges.

Fingers stretched her sex upward, and cool air touched her swollen clit. Then warm, wet, suctioning lips surrounded it, and she couldn't hold back the high-pitched keening that tore at her throat.

With her vagina filled with strengthening vibrations and his mouth and tongue nipping and circling on her clit, Amy couldn't halt her headlong flight into ecstasy. Her head thrashed on the seat; her fingers threaded through his warm, thick hair and held him there until she slowly fell back down to earth.

Her panties slid back over her sex. Her legs slid off his shoulders, and Logan pulled her upright.

With her skirt around her waist, and her heart beating madly, Amy's hand went to her hair to smooth it down, just to stall him for a moment while she gulped deep breaths of air. It was almost embarrassing how quickly she'd come.

"Come inside?" he asked, extending his open palm.

Again she didn't hesitate, and she let him pull her from the truck.

He led her inside his home. She glanced around, but the living room was darkened. With a similar layout as her own house, she knew he was leading her to his bedroom. Not the naughty room that faced the field.

Inside the bedroom, lamps at each side of the bed cast a golden glow over a brown satin coverlet covering a massive king-size bed.

And although this would be their first time to make love completely, Logan left her standing at the end of the bed while he pulled his wallet from his pocket and dropped it and his keys on a wooden tray on the dresser. Things he probably did every day without thinking. He unbuttoned his cuffs, opened his shirt, and shrugged it off.

Feeling a little forgotten, she asked, "Should I undress?"

His head turned, his gaze narrowing, but not in an intimidating way. He seemed to be studying her. "Are you waiting for me to tell you?"

Because she didn't know what he expected, she shrugged. Logan wasn't like any other man she'd ever dated. His needs, his tastes were beyond her comprehension. So were his expectations. "Should I?"

His smile, although warm, sent shivers along her skin and raised goose bumps along her arms. His features were taut, his eyebrows slightly drawn, darkening his eyes. "Do you know what I am?"

"A deputy?"

He shook his head. "Have you heard the term BDSM?"

She nodded slowly. She'd seen the Web sites, the ones her sister sent her to. "The things you did with them, Joe Chavez and Sarah . . . that's what you're talking about." At his slow nod, she continued. "Do you want to do that with me?" she asked, although not exactly sure she was ready for the answer.

Sure, her curiosity had been whetted by her voyeuristic introduction, but it had been so long since she'd been with a man. She wanted tenderness. Comfort.

"You're afraid, but you're willing, aren't you?"

She nodded quickly before her courage deserted her.

His chest lifted, and his features softened. "Someday. Maybe sooner than I think. For now, let's go slowly. I want you undressed."

Because she didn't want to extend this conversation, she reached to the zipper at the back of her dress.

"I'd do that for you, but I want to watch. Do you understand?"

"I know you can be a gentleman. But I understand. I watched you, after all." She started the zipper down behind her neck and then dropped her hands and reached behind again to lower it the length of her back. The fabric parted, cool air slipping beneath to lick at the perspiration beginning to gather between her shoulder blades.

The dress slithered to the floor, and she stepped out of the dark silken pool and then bent to take off the sandals and straightened.

Standing in her corset and panties, she should have felt more at ease. He'd seen her like this before.

But his unrelenting stare didn't give her a clue about what he really thought. Did he think her torso was too long? Too lacking in curves?

"Turn around."

Again, without a moment's thought, she did as he commanded, turning slowly. Now, this was a view she hadn't offered him before, and she closed her eyes. She knew her ass was small.

When her back was to him, he said, "Bend at the waist."

God, no. But she hesitated for only a moment and then bent, bracing her hands on her knees.

His footsteps drew close. The strap that bisected her buttocks was tugged, tightening it against her, and then dropped. Fingers slid beneath the crotch of her panties and tunneled into her. The egg and his fingers withdrew.

He walked away, but still she remained bent. Some instinct told her she'd pleased him before with her obedience. His pleasure warmed her. However embarrassing presenting her ass for him to watch might be, she wanted to please him more than any woman ever had.

He approached again. A palm cupped one cheek and squeezed and then cupped the other and patted it.

"Your skin's beautiful. Soft."

She'd loofahed until her whole body was reddened and then smoothed on moisturizer lightly scented with mango and rose. She was damn glad she'd gone to the extra effort.

Fingers plucked the ties of her corset, and it gradually loosened. She drew a deep breath.

"Straighten and turn around."

Her hand clutched the sagging garment to her chest as she turned.

One dark eyebrow arched.

Amy firmed her mouth and dropped her hands. The corset slipped just beneath her breasts, catching on the slim curves of her hips.

His gaze dropped immediately to her breasts, which she knew were small with proportionately small nipples. There was barely enough curve for a man to cup inside his palm.

"Are you sensitive there?" he asked.

She nodded. Wasn't every woman?

"Very?"

"I don't know."

"We'll see." His fingers curved around the dainty tips and pinched.

Her breath hitched as pleasure arced, sending darts of heat toward her core.

"Too much?" he asked.

"Please . . . don't stop."

He came closer, his fingers tugging and squeezing her tender tips. "I could suck all of you into my mouth," he said in that deepening tone that made her shiver.

"I know I'm small."

"You're perfect."

She snorted. Her first act of dissension.

"You don't think so?"

Amy kept her gaze on a point on the wall beyond his shoulder as he continued to tease her nipples with alternating strong tugs and gentle rubs.

"See?" he said, dropping his hands. "Perfect. They look as though they're begging to be sipped."

The tips of her nipples were elongated and a deep, rosy brown. The areolae were slightly dimpled. Staring at herself and knowing he was watching her face for her reaction and not her chest seemed somehow more erotic than his touches had been.

"Take the rest of your clothes off and meet me in the bathroom." Without a backward glance, he left her standing in the middle of his bedroom floor.

The sound of water filling a tub galvanized her. She shimmied the corset over her hips and let it drop, kicking it away. Then she pushed her panties down.

She was hurrying to the bathroom door before she thought that maybe she shouldn't act so eager. He liked her obedience, but he'd also enjoyed Sarah's defiance. Would he become bored if she succumbed too quickly, if she surrendered herself completely to his whims?

But she couldn't think about that now. He might have made her come with his mouth and a shiny little egg, but her body still ached to be filled. If tonight was all she had, she wasn't going to waste a moment on flashes of self-doubt.

He was bent over the tub, fingers beneath the fall of water from the tap as he adjusted the temperature.

"Shall I get into the tub?" she asked, waiting for him to turn, but she caught his reflection in the mirror and saw the way he gazed back at her, his nostrils flaring, his body tightening. She'd never felt sexier.

"Not yet," he finally replied, leaving the water running. He strode toward the counter, pulled a towel from the rack beside it, and placed it on the counter beside the sink. "Come over here."

She approached him just as he pulled open a drawer and pulled out an electric shaver. "Um . . . what's that for?"

"I'm going to shave your pussy before I bathe you."

Before he bathes me . . . ? Wait—she rolled the conversation back. "You're going to shave me. But why?"

"Because it's my preference. Do you have a problem with that?"

"No . . . no problem. But . . . Sarah wasn't shaved."

"She isn't mine."

Amy liked the sound of that. But for how long did he want that to be true? "And I am? But we're just getting to know each other."

"Sweetheart, we've been getting to know each other for weeks." He opened the towel on top of the countertop. "To catch the hairs."

"I don't know. Maybe if you let me do this myself."

"You'd deny me the pleasure?"

She didn't understand how a man could derive pleasure from such an intimate task. Something in her expression must have told him so because he folded his arms over his chest, and his expression grew set and watchful.

He was firm on this point. Or was he testing her to see if she would obey? "I feel like I don't know the rules here. I want to please you. I want this to be . . . perfect, but this . . ." she said, waving her hand at the razor. "It's embarrassing."

"How can this be more intimate, more embarrassing, than you letting me eat your pussy out?"

Her face burned with the memory. Yeah, that had been her on the front seat of his truck, letting him have her in full view of anyone who might have driven by. "Fine," she said, the word clipped. She strode toward him, heat in her cheeks.

He gripped her waist, and before she could protest that she was too heavy, he'd lifted her easily to the countertop. "Oh," she gasped.

"Open your legs and lean back. Then scoot your ass forward. I need room. And I need to see."

Lord, she wished her thighs didn't spread like butter over the edge of the counter, but she eased back, bracing a hand behind her for support, and then slowly parted her legs.

But he wasn't satisfied, pressing against her inner thighs to widen them farther. Then he trailed his fingertips over her still moist folds, combing through her short curls. "Same color as the hair on your head," he said, smiling slightly. "And thick."

Was it an unusual amount? She hadn't thought so, but then again she hadn't seen many other pussies, not since gym class in high school anyway. "Would you just start?" she asked, agonized with humiliation.

His gaze lifted from her sex. "I don't like that you're embarrassed."

And how am I supposed to be casual with this?

Taking a deep breath, she struggled to relax. She had promised herself she would do anything for one night with him. If letting him shave her was the cost, so be it. Mustering up her courage, she went for boldness and tried to keep the tremor out of her voice.

"Isn't it your job to put me at ease?"

A brow lifted, but he withheld further comment and picked up the electric shaver. "I'll use this to clear away the bulk of it, but I'll have to use a double-edged razor to make you smooth."

Self-doubt threatened to cripple her new adventure.

Sure, his body was to die for. But so far, he hadn't shown any interest in putting his amazing cock into action. She wondered if he'd changed his mind, or if he had more "improvement projects" to complete before he'd be satisfied she was good enough for him.

The razor hummed louder than the egg, but her body seemed conditioned to respond to the sound. Her blood raced faster, heating her up, causing perspiration to gather on her forehead and upper lip. Her embarrassment faded as she worried about hiding her arousal, which seeped steadily toward the lips he shaved.

His thumb brushed over one side of her folds, and the razor followed, the teeth of the razor gliding across her skin and lifting tufts of her brown hair, which he efficiently plucked away and dropped into the trash can beside his feet.

She wondered at the thought and preparation that had gone into this task and felt confused by the emotions roiling inside her. Besides the waning mortification, she also felt oddly cherished.

A tall, handsome man was shaving her pussy, changing something about her appearance—that no one else would ever see or know about—to suit his own desires.

How could she argue with that? Why would she even want to try? If permitting this oddly endearing intimacy pleased him, who was she to complain?

The razor continued its monotonous hum, and she relaxed, wondering idly if it was possible to come from the vibrations. Would he be surprised?

5

The razor chuffed upward, smoothing over her mons, denuding her of hair, and then delved into the crevice between her thigh and lips.

She opened wider before he asked, and she kept staring at his hands, fascinated with the care he took. When he completed the process with the other fold, he turned off the razor and set it aside. "Into the tub with you now."

He helped her off the counter, and she slid past him, sighing as her skin brushed his.

The water was deep, and he emptied a bottle of white liquid into the tub. With a swirl of his fingers, the scent of roses filled the air in the steamy room.

She stepped over the edge of the tall tub and sank until the milky water reached her shoulders. "This smells divine."

"A milk bath with rosewater."

She bit back the question she wanted to ask. Was this part of an established routine, another of his preferences with "his" women? If so, she really didn't want to know. Instead she asked, "Will you be joining me?"

"No, thanks. I just needed the bristles softened. You can stand up now."

She accepted the hand he held out and stood in the tub while he sat along the curved edge. He shook a can of lady's shaving cream and then blew foam into his palm, which he used to coat her sex. The double-bladed razor he wielded next didn't give her a moment's worry. He'd done this before, after all.

At his urging, she placed one foot on the edge of the tub, opening herself to him, and he slowly, deftly shaved the rest of the tiny hairs away, wiping the blade with a cloth to remove the hair and keep the water clean.

When he'd finished, he swiped away the excess foam. His fingers smoothed over her folds. "Feel this," he said, glancing up at her.

She cupped herself. It felt foreign, not like part of her body at all, that baby smoothness on her mound and pussy. Her skin was soft and so sensitive she shivered at the touch of her own fingers.

He was smiling when she lifted her gaze again to him. "Now get into the bath."

She slid down, sighing. The temptation to keep touching herself there was so strong she placed her hands on the rim and gripped it. But soon enough, Logan gave her something else to obsess about. He stripped, seeming unaware of her staring.

This close, with all that burnished skin and his thick red-brown cock exposed, she couldn't help but feast her eyes on his body. "Thought you weren't going to join me," she murmured.

"I'm not, but why get my clothes wet? Remember, I'm bathing you." He grabbed a washcloth and sat on the tub edge again. "Where do you want me to start?"

Because her body was completely concealed beneath the milky water, some of her confidence returned. She gave him a little smile. "Can I choose the interesting bits first?"

"Things might be over pretty quick."

"I'm getting a little anxious. I wouldn't mind."

He trailed a finger down her cheek. "This isn't a race, Amy. And every part of you interests me. Will you let me explore?"

Again she swallowed, this time because her mouth had gone dry. "Then start with my toes. I'm really ticklish there, and if you get that over with first, the rest won't be spoiled with a fit of giggles."

With a smile, he scooted down and held out his palm. She hated giving him her foot. It was really large. She would have had to lop off her toes and half of her foot to fit it into Cinder-alla's tiny slipper.

But she relented, lifting her size eleven. "They're kind of big," she said, hating how unsure she felt.

Logan shrugged, beginning to rub the soapy cloth over the top of her foot. "You're a tall girl. Besides, they're pretty. No monkey toes. No piggy toes."

She smiled. "You're a strange man. I've watched you do some pretty nasty things, and yet you're so nice."

Without taking his gaze from her foot, he raised an eyebrow. "Nasty and nice can't coexist?"

"It's unexpected."

"Ready?" he asked, holding up the cloth in front of the bottom of her foot.

"Oh, God. I'm going to squeal like a piglet. Had a pedicure once, and you would have sworn the woman was trying to kill me from the amount of noise I made."

"I'll be quick. Brace yourself."

She closed her eyes and wrinkled her nose. Her hands clamped hard on the tub as he began to rub the terry cloth in circles on her feet. Air hissed between her clenched teeth.

"Not so bad, huh?"

"Torture," she gritted out.

"Really?"

"Hell, yeah," she grumbled. "Besides, I thought I was going to be delightfully debauched tonight, not tickled to death."

"Debauched? Does anyone even use that word anymore?"

"Depends on what you read, I guess."

"Romances?" he asked, rooting in the water for her other foot.

"Don't make fun of me," she said and then gasped as he began to rub the cloth along her instep.

"I wouldn't dream of it. I thought I did a pretty good job of keeping a straight face earlier today."

She pried her eyes open. "That's just mean. You know I want to forget that ever happened."

"How did it happen anyway?" he asked, sliding the soapy cloth up her calf. "I'll admit it was the most unusual rescue I've ever made."

"It was all your fault, you know," she said, paying close attention to where he stopped—at her knee. Then he dropped the cloth into the water, soaped his hands, and began to knead her thigh with his bare hands.

"How's that? My fault, I mean," he said, continuing like he didn't know she was on the edge here, hoping he'd rub closer to what ached. "Was I there in your kitchen when it happened?"

"No!" She groaned when his fingers dipped below the water to skim the crease between her inner thigh and labia. "But you were pulling into your driveway. I got a little distracted." Just like she was now.

"You were spying on me again," he said, squirting more soap into his palms and working a lather into her other calf, smoothing his hands in broad caresses up and down her leg.

God, what were they talking about? Spying? "I can't help myself," she gasped, gripping the edge of the tub again.

"I don't mind you watching. But I like this better." Both hands skimming her thighs disappeared into the milky water and slid up the insides to slide along the twin creases and then caress her labia.

Amy closed her eyes. Her mouth pursed to blow deep breaths between her lips. As he massaged her sex, she swallowed hard, trying to concentrate. "I like this better, too. I wondered what it would be like. Just didn't think you'd be so persnickety."

"Persnickety?"

He glided his fingers down, past her lips, entering new territory. The sensation—slippery soap, thick, water-softened fingers—was amazing, while his direction rang alarm bells. But she couldn't manage a protest. It felt too divine.

"Is that even a word?" he asked softly. "Don't tell me, another one of those romance-novel words."

She shook her head. "No! One of my grandma's words. Means I didn't know you'd be so worried about cleanliness."

"Baby, this isn't about cleaning you up. It's about getting you accustomed to me handling you. However I want. Touching you wherever I please."

And it pleased him to glide his fingers over her puckered hole? Jesus.

"Did you do this with Sarah?" she blurted.

"Why are we talking about her?"

"I just wondered."

"Sarah's my friend. She's Joe's woman. His problem. I don't think I'll be intimate with her again."

"Because you're done with her? Or just because she's Joe's? Don't get angry, I just don't understand. You had sex with her. Just the other night."

"And you can't comprehend having sex just because it's fun? Or because there's a need?"

"I guess I can understand the need." Yes, she could because his intimate ministrations were unleashing a maelstrom of need. Who knew she'd love everything he did, even this?

"I guess you do understand," he crooned. His hands withdrew. "Put your legs over the side of the tub."

She gripped the tub harder because she knew if she didn't do this right she'd slide right under the water, and she didn't want to give him a reason to laugh, didn't want his expression to lose its heated tension.

She lifted one leg and placed it over the edge; then she lifted the other, opening herself. Her ass floated up from the bottom of the tub. Her nipples peeked from beneath the milky surface like cherries floating on a bowl of cream.

Again his arms descended, and his hands clasped her buttocks, delivering a gentle squeeze that did nothing to ease the anxiety and arousal growing inside her.

Then, with one hand supporting her bottom, fingers traced the crevice dividing her bottom. They drew downward, touching her tender, puckered hole and then circled on it.

She closed her eyes tightly. Again, because she didn't want him to see the emotion sure to be swirling in her eyes—and because his expression had grown too intense, too frightening for her to handle.

A finger pressed against her tiny opening, the blunt tip pushing relentlessly until she breathed deeply and forced herself to relax. He wanted this. She wouldn't deny she wanted it, too.

His finger eased inside her, and a tiny mewling cry broke between her lips.

"It's okay," he said, his voice tight. "This is all I'm going to do there for now. You're tight. I won't hurt you. But, baby, I'm so hard thinking about what it's going to be like when you are ready for me to play there I don't think I can wait another minute to be inside you."

She opened her eyes and met his gaze. His skin was reddening, his cheekbones and jaw etched with straining arousal.

His finger withdrew from her ass, and he lifted her thighs back into the tub. He offered her his hand and helped her up—help she needed because her legs felt like rubber bands.

She stepped out of the tub. He already had a thick towel waiting. He wrapped her in it and then bent and picked her up.

"I'm too heavy for this," she gasped, flinging her arms around his shoulders because she was sure he'd drop her.

"Don't worry about me," he said, his voice grating.

"You're straining something. Put me down."

"You're straining my patience. Let me do this right," he muttered, turning and walking through the door to his bed. He stood her beside it and pulled back the coverlet.

Her gaze snagged on the sheet he uncovered. Rose petals were sprinkled on the deep cream satin.

Her gaze came back up to his. "You did that for me?"

"You don't like it?" he said, his expression revealing a moment of uncertain confusion.

"They're going to stick to everything."

A frown drew his brows together. "Let me shake them off."

"Don't," she said, grabbing the arm he'd already raised. "I like it. It was just . . . unexpected. I would have thought . . ." She shook her head, afraid to say more and insult him.

"I told you. The other things I'd like to do will come later."

To stop him from frowning and worrying about her less-than-thrilled reaction, she raised a knee and climbed onto the bed. She rolled to her back and then grabbed up some of the rose petals and placed them on her breasts, her belly, her inner thighs, where they stuck to the moisture still clinging to her skin. "I can't believe you went to this much bother . . . for me."

"You keep saying that like you don't think you deserve it."

"It's so romantic. I've never had a man want so badly to please me."

"I'm glad I'm the first." His gaze raked her body, and his

214

tense expression didn't ease a bit. If anything, it grew darker. His eyelids grew lambent, his nostrils flared, his chest filled with a deeply drawn breath.

"Why don't you join me?" she asked, adding a little smile. "Unless you think you'll look foolish wearing petals, too."

His eyes narrowed, and he climbed onto the bed, "walking" toward her on his fists and knees like a hungry predator scenting a very tasty meal.

Amy's heart thudded in her chest, and she opened her legs and her arms, inviting him closer, begging him silently to end the torment swelling her sex and her heart.

He came over her, his knees roughly shoving her thighs wider, his hands landing on either side of her shoulders. Poised above her, he gazed down between their bodies.

She followed his slow glance, watched the tremors shivering across her belly and the telltale jerks of his cock each time her shivers touched him.

"We should talk."

She dragged her gaze upward reluctantly. "About?" she asked, trying not to wail. She was within moments of easing the ache he'd built inside her, and he wanted a conversation?

"How many lovers have you had?" he growled.

What was the right answer? Given his handsome looks, she guessed she'd hate his answer, but hers was dismally unimpressive. He'd know how unattractive she was. Would he rethink what he ever saw in her?

"Have there been so many you have to think about it?" he asked, his voice roughening.

"No!" she said, fighting for composure that was rapidly deserting her. "Three. One in high school. Two in college. None since I graduated and started teaching here," she admitted in a rush.

"How long ago?"

"Since I've slept with anyone?" she asked, her voice rising. He nodded sharply.

"Four years. Why?"

"You should be asking me some questions now."

But she didn't want to know. She wanted to get *busy*! "How many?" she asked.

"Can't count."

"And I already know about your last. So we're done, right?"

"I didn't always use a condom with her. With Sarah."

"Do you have one? Do we need it? I'm on the pill. Periods."

His eyes squeezed shut, and his cock rubbed against her belly; then he jerked it back. "I'm a fucking selfish prick."

"Because you don't want to use one? I get that. And I don't care."

"No. I told you I wouldn't hurt you. Fuck!" He reached to the nightstand and jerked open the drawer, drawing out a packet, which he ripped open with his teeth. The rubber fell onto her chest among the petals still sticking to her skin.

She grabbed it and then thrust her hand between them, wrapped her long fingers around his cock, and rolled it down his shaft.

Then she waited for his gaze to lock with hers and pushed him between her legs, centering his blunt head against her entrance. She smoothed both palms up his chest, reveling in the rippling muscle and crisp hair that made him male as much as the thick shaft beginning to push inside her body.

But he'd only drilled the head of his cock inside her. Again he paused, his jaw clamping tight.

"Do I have to ask any more questions? We both know you didn't need to protect yourself from me."

"I didn't really think that'd be an issue. Not for either of us. There's been only Sarah since I came here. I'm trying to get a grip. Gimme a second."

His confession gave her a sense of empowerment. She wrapped

her hands around the back of his neck and lifted her head to whisper in his ear. "Please don't hold back on account of me. Fuck me, Logan Ross. Wild and hard."

A groan ripped from his tightly drawn lips, and his cock pushed through her folds, rushing inside.

She was wet, ready, but still not prepared for his girth. *GodohGodohGod.* She raised her knees to cup his hips and give him a better, straighter angle to drive deep, eager and anxious to take more.

"Should have let me do this right," he gritted out. "I would have gone slow. You're so goddamn tight."

"Just don't stop. Please," she said, digging her fingernails deep into his skin, raking them down his back, tempting the harsh, commanding predator to unleash.

His cock withdrew a couple inches and then rammed deeper, withdrew and tunneled harder, gliding through her moist, hot walls, churning her arousal like butter with his rapid thrusts.

"*Sssoooo* good, Logan," she said, squeezing shut her eyes and rolling her head on the mattress beneath her.

His hips bucked, buttocks flexing, hardening to steel as he stroked deeper. His glides entered a rhythm that matched her heart beating faster and faster. He hammered her pussy so powerfully, so relentlessly, all she could do was wrap her arms and legs around him and hold on for the ride. She knew now that she'd fucked only boys, not a full-grown, masterful man. The difference was electrifying.

Her whole body felt pummeled, stroked, charged with an electrical arcing heat that gripped her core, tightened her thighs and belly, clamped her inner muscles around him, adding to the friction he built with each deeply potent thrust.

Her nipples raked his furred chest, her fingers clung, nails gripping rippling muscle. When his torso came down on top of hers, and his body continued to rut hard, she bit his shoulder.

"Jesus! Fuck! Amy . . ."

"Don't stop . . . please, oh, please . . ." She kissed the mark she'd left on his skin, licked his neck, nipped his chin, and clawed, reaching for the climax he was delivering in steady, jerking thrusts.

His breaths rasped, turning to grunts as he hammered harder, pushing air from her body in equally animalistic gusts.

She didn't care how she sounded, couldn't stop her frenzied kisses and scratches. She was there. *There.* "Logan!" she shouted.

Her whole face tightened. She forgot to breathe. The moment the wave crashed over her, he swept her away, right out of herself, hurling her toward heaven.

When she came back, her head was thrashing, and his face was buried in her neck, his body rocking with hers and trembling.

A sob shook her, and she hugged him closer. Her fingers loosened, and she stroked his back, up and down as his movements slowed and then stopped.

He sagged against her, still locked inside her body as her pussy caressed his long shaft with convulsions that gradually faded.

Both of them breathing hard, they lay locked together. Amy wiped her wet cheek on his sweaty shoulder. He mumbled something unintelligible, and his arms dug beneath her to cradle her against him.

She must have zoned for a moment. When she opened her eyes, she found him staring down at her, a satisfied smirk curving one side of his mouth. "Damn," he breathed.

Amy blinked and then stared at the dark pink teeth marks she'd left in his shoulder. "Oh, my God. I'm so sorry."

He let loose a sound that was a perfect morph between a grunt and a laugh. "Damn."

"Was it all right for you?" she asked, cringing at how sophomoric that had to sound to a man like him.

He blew a deep breath between his lips and then reached behind him to unlatch her legs from his back. He pushed them down, lifting slightly to allow them to stretch straight on either side of his. "Am I crushing you?"

She shook her head. "I'm a big girl, remember? I like this, too." She didn't miss the fact he hadn't answered her. Part of her atom-bomb afterglow faded to a pale, glimmering night-light.

Logan groaned, and his back arched. He slid a hand between them and caught the end of his condom before he slipped out of her.

Then he rolled to his back.

Amy lay beside him, listening to his labored breaths, feeling abandoned and afraid she might start to cry. Why she felt so deeply, she couldn't have explained, least of all to herself. The sex had been amazing. She'd gotten so much more than she'd hoped for.

But she was greedy. She wanted his approval. Wanted a sign of affection from him. She knew she'd probably scare him half to death if she put her feelings to words.

His arm landed just above her head. "Come here."

Amy sighed and rolled toward him, happier the instant his arm brought her against his body. She lifted her leg over his hips and slid her arm across his chest. Snuggling her cheek against the damp hair on his chest, she could at last enjoy the feeling of connection she so badly needed.

His chest rose and then slowly fell. He took her hand, threaded his fingers through hers, and raised their joined embrace to his mouth, kissing the back of her hand. "It was good for me, too, baby."

6

Logan woke feeling chilled. Amy had left his bed. For a moment, he froze, wondering if she'd left without saying a word, and if he'd blown it.

He'd wanted to romance her. Bring her along slowly. Build her need for his touch in gradual levels until she was ready for him to begin to introduce her to the lifestyle he felt instinctively she was made for.

Instead he'd pounded her like a high school kid who'd gotten his first taste of pussy and couldn't control the hormones raging through him.

He should have known he'd run into trouble. The last night he'd brought Sarah and Joe here, Joe had taken one look at his cock and laughed. His cock had hardened fast, leaving him breathless and trembling with excitement as soon as he'd chucked his pants in front of the window . . . because he knew Amy was watching.

Control had always been important to him. Not only because he liked to think his brain was the one in charge, but also because at critical moments in his relations with a woman, he needed restraint to prevent harm. He was a big guy and in top shape. Restraint wasn't a choice but an imperative. He'd left bruises on Amy; he'd known it when he cupped her buttocks and slammed into her. He'd crammed himself into her so fast and so hard he knew she'd be sore today.

The thought should have shamed him, but instead he felt only a primal satisfaction as his unruly cock thickened and lengthened, rising again despite his conscience's urgings for a little self-control.

He knew he was a long way from being ready to train Amy when he couldn't manage his own raging hard-on.

But where the hell was she?

He rolled out of bed, his feet hitting the floor, and he stalked toward the open bathroom door. The room was empty now but filled with steam. Another towel lay on top of the laundry basket. So she'd showered.

Logan strode out of the bedroom and cocked his ear. He heard faint stirrings in the playroom. A smile tugged at his lips. Though he'd been arguing with himself about putting the brakes on that aspect of his sexuality, Amy was plainly curious. He slowly turned the doorknob and cracked the door.

What he saw made his cock pulse. So much for his vaunted control.

Amy was gloriously naked and standing on the metal footings of the St. Andrew's cross. Her ankles were strapped into the buckles. She'd also moved the arm shackles up the wooden structure, refastening bolts and lug nuts behind the frame to move them up to suit her height. She had one hand resting in the padded leather manacle.

She'd also found the black hood he'd used on Sarah. She'd rolled it down her face, keeping her lips and mouth free.

He padded quietly across the floor to stand in front of her. Her head turned. Maybe she'd heard a slight sound, but the way she nibbled on her bottom lip said she wasn't sure.

He lifted a hand and ran a fingertip around one rosy areola.

"Logan?" she asked, uncertainty shaking her voice.

"Worried it might be someone else?"

"I wasn't sure if it was Logan or . . . Master."

Logan stood still, his chest expanding, his cock growing steely. "What's your preference, baby?"

"I don't want you thinking I'm some lightweight."

"I don't."

"I don't want you thinking of me as only a vanilla kind of girl."

"You aren't?" he murmured, reaching up to close the last shackle. The crisp rasp of Velcro closing and the jangle of the buckle acted like the fiercest aphrodisiac on his libido. If Amy could see his face tightening, his muscles flexing now, she might have had cause to rethink her naive plan to seduce him.

"Maybe I don't want what I've had before," she said, her voice sounding a little forlorn.

"I didn't frighten you before? I wasn't very gentle."

"I loved it. But I frightened myself. I bit you. And you have ugly scratches all over your back."

"I can feel them now. Every time I flex. I love it. Means you lost control. That makes a man feel . . . powerful."

Her lips twisted into a smile. "Funny, that's just the adjective I associate with you."

Logan stepped close enough that his cock pressed against her mons. "See what you do to me? That's powerful. I usually have more control. I pride myself on it. Are you sure about putting yourself in my care?"

"Can I be a little afraid?"

"Fear is healthy. It can also be sexy as hell."

Her chest expanded slowly. "I want this. Please."

"Do you think this is all whips and crosses?"

"No. I did a little research. After I watched you. I wanted to understand."

"Research?" He smiled. Well, so had he. The romance novel he'd bought had given him a blueprint to follow—flowers, dinner, a rose-petals-strewn bed—but he hadn't counted on his own impatience or, more surprisingly, hers.

He cleared his throat. "When I'm 'Master,' " he said, removing any trace of amusement from his voice, "you can't speak unless I allow it."

Her lips firmed. Seemed she was ready to start right now.

"This is a process. Not one that can be accomplished in just one night."

"It will take longer?" She didn't sound the least bit sorry to hear that.

"A long process," he purred. "I can guide you, if you like."

Her lips crimped. Suppressing a smile, perhaps? "Please, Master," she replied in her prim, schoolteacher voice.

"You're still talking," he said, reaching up to pinch a nipple.

"Oh! Then we've already started?"

"Sure you want to?"

She swallowed and wet her bottom lip with her tongue and then nodded. Logan couldn't help himself. Her mouth was still slightly swollen from his earlier kisses. It pouted. Already he knew how much a kiss went toward soothing her. He leaned forward and brushed her lips.

Her sigh was soft, warm, entering his mouth a moment before her tongue did the same. He sucked on it and then slid his own inside her mouth to taste her sweet breath again as it sighed into him.

When he pulled away, his erection was painfully hard. His balls drew up against his groin.

"May I pull this hood the rest of the way down?" he asked, not waiting for an answer, wanting to stave off the temptation to kiss her again, but missing her expressive mouth as soon as he'd covered it.

He walked to the wall where his floggers, whips, and other wanded implements were mounted. He chose a flogger with supple suede flanges and a tickler with soft, silken bristles. From a drawer beneath the display, he pulled a small narrow plug and a tube of lubricant. He brought them to her, along with a folding table, and set it beside her, laying down the tools for her pleasure carefully and silently.

He glanced at Amy, standing so still, her body tense, poised to accept anything he wished to do. From the start she'd been eager to be led.

Schoolteacher was a dream come true. Better than he'd imagined. Malleable, passionate. Eager to serve and to be pleasured.

Tonight he'd give her a very gentle introduction, but he didn't doubt she wouldn't think so. She hadn't a clue, no matter how much research she'd done. She couldn't comprehend the trust between a dominant and his submissive. She might understand some of the practices and think she wanted to learn the intricacies of the perversions, but he was learning that she did have limits. And she had defied him. In her way.

She'd balked at being shaved.

In the end, her soft mons had delighted her. But because he'd been in a hurry to bury his cock inside her, he really hadn't given her a reward for her obedience or shown her how much more sensation she would feel without that silky cloak of hair.

He'd remedy that shortly.

"I know I told you I wouldn't play with one tiny entrance. But because you seem so eager to begin training . . ."

Amy's chest quivered on a shallow breath.

"I'm going to insert a plug. Something very small to begin

stretching you, readying you for my cock. Don't worry that I'll get too eager and try to rush you. I promised not to hurt you, and I know I didn't keep that promise very well, but in this you can trust me."

He picked up the soft, plastic plug and lubed it with his fingers. Then he knelt between her legs. Her sex was moist but not nearly as wet as he would have liked. He needed her deeply aroused.

He rubbed his fingers over her mound, enjoying the softness and the appearance of her pale creamy skin and reddened pussy. Then he slid his fingers between her raw folds and rubbed her clit.

Again her pretty little tits quivered, the stems beginning to draw into taut points. He trailed along her damp folds, dipping inside to swirl in her honeyed depths, penetrating as far as his fingers could reach and drawing more fluid down.

He needed a taste. Just a quick one. He rose slightly and opened his mouth to suckle her smooth labia, teasing the edges with lazy drifts of his tongue and then thrusting into her and lapping upward to glaze her clit.

Her body trembled, and her thighs hardened.

Tracing his fingers lower, he rubbed along her sensitive perineum, ignoring her gulping breaths and, at last, arriving at his destination.

He parted her buttocks, widening them to stroke two fingers around and around her tight entrance. He dipped inside, just one fingertip, and her anus closed hard around him, trying to eject it.

Logan brought the narrow tip of the plug to her entrance and inserted it, twisting it to deposit some of the lubricant on her tight ring. Then he pushed it slowly inward.

Her breaths came faster, shallower.

Carefully he pulled it out and then pressed it a little deeper, still twisting, and then rolled it in a widening circle to ease her tight grasp.

Logan gritted his teeth against the strength of his own arousal, rising hard, tensing his thighs and filling his cock to the point of pain. He could already imagine how he'd feel sliding into her ass, the ring gripping him tighter than any cock ring he'd ever cinched around the base of his shaft.

But she was a long way from being ready for that. He'd promised.

He withdrew the device and slipped the metal tip of the tube into her opening and squeezed more lube directly inside her.

Amy moaned. It was a tiny, wounded, desperate sound, but still she held her words.

"I know this is uncomfortable. A tight fit. I'm going to push it back inside, and I won't stop, but you have to do something to make it easier. You have to trust me. You have to relax and allow me to do it. You have to take charge of your body. Overrule the natural urge to resist the intrusion. Can you do that? Nod if you can."

It didn't come quickly. Several quivering breaths moved the hood over her mouth, but then it came. A slow, definite nod.

Logan kissed her thigh and bent closer again, gently placing the plug at her entrance and pushing inward.

The first couple of inches entered easier than before, but as its shape broadened, he could feel resistance again. "Easy," he whispered. "Let me in, baby. Don't fight. You're mine to do with as I please. This pleases me very much."

As the broadest part of the plug slid past the ring, he exhaled, relieved he'd gotten her this far. The narrowing at the base would keep it in place while he played. "All done," he said, straightening. "That will stay there until I take it out."

Logan stood, returning the lube to the tray, and then took a long drink of the sight of Amy Keating.

Her body was taut, her hands fisted above the shackles.

He didn't like that she was nervous. He slicked his hand over her smooth mound and thrust two fingers inside her, curving them upward as he toggled her clit with his thumb.

A tiny, thready moan seeped from her, and he continued to finger her, watching closely to catch the subtle changes in her breathing and deepening flush of color that painted her chest.

"Have I told you how beautiful your body is?"

Her breath caught, but she held her tongue.

"Your length is a perfect match for mine. I like that I don't have to bend very far to kiss you. I like that when I pull your hips into mine, my cock ruts against your sex."

He came closer and glided his lips along the top of her shoulder. "You're so tall, I can fuck you standing without lifting you. Want me to prove it to you now?"

Her nod was swift, her breaths faster, rasping, billowing against the black fabric.

"I will. But not quite yet. You wanted to know what it was like to taste the flick of one of my floggers. I've chosen the softest I own because I don't want you alarmed. Has anyone ever used one on you? No? Has anyone spanked you?"

A sideways jerk of her head was all she could manage. His fingers, soaked in her arousal, were a more convincing answer.

Her body tensed, her hips flexing forward and back in the tiniest pulses to draw on the fingers fucking into her.

He withdrew his fingers and slid his cock along her folds, gliding forward and back. "I'm hard. If I wasn't, I would have wanted you to suck on it, to unfurl it with your mouth."

He drew back, picked up the flogger, draped the leather strands over her shoulder, and pulled it downward, gliding it over her pebbled nipples. Then he pulled it away and gave her nipple a light slap. Not even enough to leave her skin pink, and yet she jerked against the bindings.

He flicked the tail against the other nipple, just a little sharper, and she grunted.

He slapped her belly and then her hips, flicked the tail at her thighs and brought it between her legs to lash upward, stinging her pussy.

Amy's back bowed; her belly undulated, curving upward, her thighs straining to widen, inviting another lash, which landed at the center of her pussy.

Logan reached between her legs, soothing the stinging flesh with his fingers swirling over her lips. While she'd been wet before, now honey trickled along the inside of one thigh.

Laying down the flogger, he picked up the silky tickler and worked it like a painter's brush, stroking her breasts, her belly, and then brushing lightly over her mound.

He parted her with his thumb and forefinger and twisted the soft bristles over her clit.

Amy's thighs shivered, and her hips rocked, stroking toward the wand.

"While I'm sure your research was extensive, I'm wondering if you understand what motivates a person to choose to be the way I am, or to choose to serve a man like me. It's not about the kink. Not really. I'm a man, and smelling your arousal, feeling the slick moisture building in your sex, that's enough to make me hard. Sliding inside your tight little cunt is enough to make me come."

He tossed down the wand and undid her restraints, catching her when she sagged toward him. He carried her to the floor, pressing her down until she leaned on her hands, her knees braced apart.

His whisked off the hood and waited while she blinked her eyes to adjust to the light; then he dug his fingers into her hair and tilted her head back.

Her mouth opened naturally as he drew her back. "What motivates me is feeding a need inside you that desires to be led, craves to serve. I'm not looking for a doormat and would never expect you to cater to me anytime except within the confines of this room. Are you willing to serve me, Amy?"

Amy licked her lips. Everything he'd done and said was so foreign, so far removed from her experience. The free-thinking woman she was, the woman who'd excelled at school and carved out a career and a home for herself, should have felt more resistance to his invitation.

Instead she melted at the heat and need reflected in his dark gaze. Her heart trembled, her pussy flooded, her limbs shook, threatening to collapse beneath her.

The tension his body radiated told her this was a crossing point, and that if she balked, even for a second, she could expect more of what he'd given her before, which had been amazing. But she wanted to take the deeper journey. Learn the secrets to his soul, as corny as that sounded.

"How can I serve you?" she whispered.

A swallow worked the muscles of his throat. His eyes glowed with warmth and approval. "You may have my cock. To play with as you please. My reward for your obedience."

She almost smiled. Her reward would be his as well, only she guessed that when he was in "master mode," his pleasure wouldn't always be so straightforward. But hadn't she dreamed of taking him with her mouth? "May I speak?"

He nodded, his jaw grinding taut.

Amy rubbed her cheek along his heated shaft, drinking in the scent of his musk, and then raised her gaze. "I thought I knew what I wanted. What any woman wants. A man who loves me. A man who will be a partner. What you're offering— what it sounds like to me—is more than that, not less. I do this because I want you. All of you. But not because I could have been this way with any other man. Do you understand?"

"I didn't think you would ever have walked into a club and offered yourself as a sub to any other man."

She nodded. "I would never do that."

"Is that because this is abhorrent to you?"

Her smile slowly stretched her trembling lips. "No, it's because I never wanted a man so badly. The things you want from me are things I want to give. I crave serving you because I know the pleasure I bring you will be returned. Is that enough?"

Logan's face suffused with lust, triggering a jolt of heat that released a steady flow of excitement.

His half-lidded gaze swept her face, landing on her lips. "It's more than I could have hoped. But right now I'm afraid I have to demand that you take my cock between your lovely pouting lips and suck me."

She canted her head and gave him as close to a sultry look as she could manage, given she was fighting a grin. "Do you expect me to always be obedient?"

His rueful smile was everything she'd desired. "Hell, no," he growled.

"Do I have to like everything?"

"No, but experimenting will be part of the fun."

"Do you know that the idea of becoming slave to your master feels kind of liberating?"

"I think you do understand," he crooned.

Right now, Amy wanted his satiny cock sliding into her mouth. But the act wasn't the one of submission he had in mind, because she intended to enslave him.

As he pushed his cock downward toward her lips, she stroked her tongue over the tip, licking up a gleaming drop of pre-cum. Salty, musky flavor exploded on her tongue, and she eagerly opened her lips to suckle the spongy cap.

As she suctioned and swirled her tongue over him, she lost herself in the pleasure of his taste and the varying textures of his manhood. The soft head gave way to steely, satiny smooth shaft. Her sex and sphincter began to pulse as she remembered how his girth and length had stretched her. The tenderness of the tissues lining her channel, of the ring gripping the plug, were sexy reminders of the power of her attraction over him.

That Logan found her long, supple body lovely fueled her love for him, an acknowledgment she'd keep to herself because she didn't want to rush him.

He was a man, and even in her limited experience, she understood his need to lead her on this journey.

So she moaned around him to tell him how much she honored his masculinity, how much she desired him. As she knelt and wrapped her hands around him, she gripped him firmly, twisting her hands around his shaft as she rocked forward to engulf him in her wet heat.

She'd let him think about another moist place as she swallowed and her throat clasped around his head. When one hand cupped his smooth, velvety sac and rolled his balls in her palm, she hoped he remembered the pleasure of banging them against her soft, moist flesh.

She didn't have to wait long. The hand digging into her hair pulled her head back, and he slid his cock from her mouth, stuck his hands beneath her arms, and forced her to her feet.

His powerful arms enclosed her, and his cock rutted against her belly as his lips slammed into hers.

Their tongues dueled while he walked her backward until her back met a wall. His hips pulled back, his hand thrust between their bodies and dragged down the tip until he slid between her folds and stroked along her slit.

She was drenched, her excitement coating him. He dipped, and suddenly his cock was at her entrance and driving upward.

Logan grabbed her hands, laced his fingers through hers, and pressed them to the wall while he began to fuck in and out of her, each stroke ending with a grinding motion that rubbed his pubic bone into her clitoris.

Their gazes met, her head tilting only slightly. His mouth was curved into a feral smile that fanned the fire building in her core into a gusting, flaring flame.

Amy wanted to wrap her arms and legs around him, wanted to feel his arms squeeze the breath from her, but he rutted into her, banging her body into the wall.

Her frustration built, and she began to writhe against him, shoving her hips against him to meet his fierce strokes despite the uncomfortable pull on the device still lodged in her ass.

Gradually the violent, desperate nature of his passion overwhelmed her, and she stood on her tiptoes, pressing hard against the wall to curve her belly upward to receive his thrusts.

He dropped her hands and gripped her hips, sliding her up the wall, off her toes, curling his torso and resting his head against her shoulder while he hammered her.

Amy left her legs dangling, but her arms encircled him, fingers pulling at his hair, digging into his skin, inciting him to greater urgency that caused them both to grunt like animals as they mated.

When her orgasm exploded through her, she drew up her knees, flattening her heels on the wall, and trusted him to hold her.

He came a second before she did, flooding her with cum. His shout, guttural and triumphant, was followed with her own keening cry. When he slumped against her, she wrapped her body around him, and they both sank clumsily to the floor.

Amy was gasping for air, her body still convulsing, when his hands cupped her face; his lips trailed her cheek and jaw, and, at last, closed over her mouth.

She bit his bottom lip, released it, and then stroked her tongue into his mouth.

When his lips left hers, she opened her eyes. His laugh, a deep, rumbling gust, jerked the chest still smashed against hers.

His face was reddened and sweating. His eyes narrowed. "Who mastered whom?" he asked, the corners of his lips curling in a smug smile.

"I think I need a few more lessons," she said, her voice every bit as ragged as her breaths while she struggled to calm her erratic heartbeats. "I haven't quite grasped the concept of submission."

His dark lashes flickered over coffee eyes. "It'll be my pleasure to teach you."

She smiled and nuzzled his skin with her nose, breathing in the scent of sex and his heavy, male musk.

"Amy . . ."

Her eyelids scraped lazily upward. His expression made her breath catch.

His large, rugged palms bracketed her face as a hint of some dark emotion swept away his usual swagger. "I want more."

Her lips parted. She sensed what he wanted to say but understood he couldn't quite put his feelings to words. How she knew, she couldn't have said, but that warm, melting heat that seemed to accompany every thought she'd ever had of him built inside her.

She could be brave and stalwart for them both. "I love you, Logan Ross."

His lips slammed into hers, and she had his answer in the shudder that racked his large, powerful frame.

Amy gripped his shoulders and pushed him to his back. Her pussy clasped around him, her inner muscles sucking at his cock, drawing him deeper until slowly he grew, nudging along her channel, filling her body as his desperate hands climbed her back and brought her down against his chest.

She snuggled her face into the corner of his neck and sighed as his lips pressed fevered kisses to her cheek and ear. She had never felt so cherished, so feminine.

As Amy shoved off his chest and began to rock gracefully, relentlessly on his thickening cock, she didn't think she'd have to wait very long for him to find the words.

For now, she basked in the approval in his glittering gaze and the tenderness of the calloused hands that molded her small breasts.

Logan was hers—her lover, her other half, her heart's master.

Turn the page
for a tantalizing preview
of HITTIN' IT
by Amie Stuart!

On sale now!

1

"Hey! What's your name?"

To his friends and family, he was Will; to everyone else, he was God, as in "Please God, don't kill me."

To his ex-girlfriend, he was, "You impotent bastard."

Whatever.

His driver's license said he was William Tanner Collier of Oklahoma City. But to this man, he was, "Roy . . . Roy Rogers."

"Hey, Roy." Not surprisingly, the man didn't even blink at Will's fake name. Never mind that Roy Rogers was an American legend. Most people saw and heard what they wanted—no more; no less.

Instead, he smiled, a red, wet-lipped smile that might have scared a lesser man than Will. "Buy me a drink?"

Under that few day's growth of beard, Will's new friend looked like he could stand to skip a few drinks.

"Sorry." Will shrugged and turned away, signaling his lack of interest and silently praying the man would move on. He was blocking Will's view.

Instead of leaving, the other man settled on the stool and lit a cigarette, adding to the cloud of smoke that hung thick as LA smog over the bar. Will narrowed his burning eyes and sighed, hoping like hell he wouldn't have to move. The only other good vantage point was across the bar where a guy who looked big and intimidating enough to be one of Tommy "Lupo" Brown's thugs raised a beer to Will. He lowered his eyes, focusing on the glass of Guinness in front of him as the thump of the bass vibrated his eardrums. He wasn't exactly sure he wanted to sit next to a gay man who might actually stand a chance of beating him up.

Not that he *would* beat Will up, but if he tried, Will would have to shoot him. He really didn't need that sort of attention. And besides, hiding a body that big would take a lot of work.

He much preferred the precision and perfect execution of a well-thought-out job to a random kill. The unpredictable was destined to be messy and could land his ass in places he didn't want to be.

Like prison.

He'd had a few close calls. When you killed people for a living, they came with the territory. He brushed it off, trying to focus on the job at hand.

> *Derek Frost: Dark blond hair, 5'10", 180 lbs, brown eyes, pierced nipples (not that anyone but Will's current employer and Derek's lovers knew that), heavy drinker, and a predilection for gay bars even though he swears up and down he likes women better than men—but not by much.*

For reasons that were of no interest to Will, Derek's business partner wanted him dead. Which explained why Will was currently sitting in a rundown gay bar in Phoenix, Arizona. Derek was quite the social butterfly, though he had abysmal taste in bars—gay or otherwise.

Will's new friend finally gave up and left, and now Will had a bird's-eye view of Derek and Loverboy ensconced in a booth about ten feet away. Satisfied they weren't going anywhere for a while, he turned away before someone, anyone, noticed him staring at the couple. Once again he caught the eye of the man across the bar—the *big* one. Despite the dive status of the Oil Spout, flirty seemed as out of place as Will felt. He shrugged, hoping the other man wouldn't take it as an invitation, and took a deep drink of his beer, letting the cool, dark brew slide across his tongue, savoring the thick, yeasty flavor while he turned his attention elsewhere. Like the two girly men there in the corner, having a bitch-fest complete with claws and pouty, scowling faces. Will waited to see if someone would throw a punch, rolling his eyes when all that happened was a slap.

So much for entertainment.

He took another small sip of his beer, not wanting his head clouded for the job in front of him. For the most part, Will could have passed any of these men on the street and they never would've known he'd spent the better part of his life as a professional hit man. Not that they probably cared one way or the other. He didn't bother sparing much brainpower on them either. Will cared about the job, his family, himself. And once upon a time, he'd cared about Tilly Acuna. Until Tilly had informed him he was as warm and passionate as a brick wall and suggested maybe he find a man to snuggle with from now on. He'd packed up his things and moved out, storing his stuff at his parents' place in Oklahoma City and taking this job. He'd thought that time and distance would help. They had, to a point.

Sadly, Tilly wasn't the first woman to point out his failings when it came to the fairer sex, and it wasn't just in the bedroom.

It was everything.

The flowers, the talking, the movies—how did women watch that shit? Anniversaries and her friends and his friends, and friends' weddings and babies and . . . in the end he'd decided maybe

Tilly was onto something. Maybe he was gay. God knows he'd yet to find a woman he couldn't live without let alone a woman he could make happy.

And surely a relationship with a man would be . . . easier. *Much easier.* There'd be football and beer, tortilla chips and queso dip, belching and no bitching about missed anniversaries or ditched dinner parties. Across the way, the two queens had devolved into a full-out slap-fest. The bartender opened the lift and stepped through, bat in hand, shouting at the top of his lungs. At that point, Will decided he wanted a real man. Then he accidentally caught the eye of the thug on the other side of the bar. He had a fresh beer. Now that was a man. A real man. Someone you could play softball and football with and . . . just then, Will's ass puckered.

He hadn't quite worked out the sex issue.

If given the choice, Will preferred killing from a distance. Times like these, he didn't always get his wish. Not that he was squeamish, but distance negated problems like fibers, witnesses, and DNA. Unfortunately, his quarry lived in a low-slung, one-story house smack in the middle of one of Scottsdale's nicer neighborhoods. That combined with Derek's crazy work schedule made a long-distance kill impossible. Too many unknowns: the neighbor out walking his dog late at night, the couple out for a midnight swim, a sick baby . . . all of them could bring Will attention he didn't need. And as close as he was to retirement, he wasn't about to risk spending the rest of his life in a ten-by-ten cell.

He slipped out of the bar shortly after Derek and Loverboy and followed them at a discreet distance in the black, '76 Monte Carlo he'd picked up in Flagstaff for a song. He'd chosen the older model car because it was heavy and fairly non-descript. If Derek ran true to form, and Will was counting on him to, he'd spend approximately ninety minutes with his new friend, then leave for home, stopping once to get cigarettes and a Dr. Pepper. Will followed them into the condo complex, cruising past as Derek and his companion stepped into a nondescript condo. He circled around to make sure Derek's car was still there, then pulled into a fast-food place across the road to eat—and kill some time.

As meticulous as he was, he could only plan things up to a certain point. The rest was left to the foibles of his fellow man, and if there was one thing he'd learned, man could fuck things up royally.

Luckily, tonight was not one of those nights. Eighty-seven minutes later, Derek's car pulled out onto the deserted streets. Will leisurely wadded up the burger he'd barely touched, and threw it into the trash before starting the car. It roared to life as only a 405 could—with a predatory growl that would have scared off the fiercest jungle cats—and he backed out, his power steering squealing slightly as he turned hard on the wheel. He was in no hurry; he knew exactly where his quarry was going.

Home.

He followed at a leisurely pace, letting Derek get far enough ahead that he'd never dream he was being followed. After a while, the city lights disappeared and the darkness was occasionally punctuated by a porch light. Will slowed down as he came around a curve only ten minutes from Derek's home. The other man's elegant Cadillac was sitting on the side of the road thanks to an "untimely" flat tire. The car was an older model, pre-OnStar, and out here, cell-phone reception was spotty, thanks to the hills.

Derek was too drunk to change the tire, and yes, so drunk he shouldn't even have been driving in the first place. And he was *far* too drunk to do something as simple as call AAA, when he could walk the quarter mile home.

Will rolled down the windows, slowing the car to a crawl and killing the lights. The late-night air was cool and damp as if weighted down by the quiet. He eased to a stop at the top of the hill, watching Derek get out of the car and slowly weave his way down the asphalt. Thanks to Will's slightly clammy hands, the steering wheel was a little slippery in his grip as he checked the rearview mirror for headlights. His oh-so-familiar case of nerves didn't come from a fear of getting caught so much as a fear of pesky human variables.

This was where weeks and sometimes months of planning and patience came in handy. Once he worked the execution of the job out in his head, Will didn't think too much about the actual person. He'd learned a long time ago it was better (read *easier*) if he kept things all nice and businesslike. His job wasn't just about killing. Any fool could kill. But a pro could make it look good, look like an accident, fate, the luck of the draw, not murder. And Will *was* a pro.

Will's pulse picked up pace, his heart beating a rough tattoo in his chest as he glanced in the rearview one more time. Inky blackness greeted him.

And he had to get to Derek before he got much closer to the turnoff for his subdivision. The houses nearest the corner were quiet and dark as was everything for as far as Will could see. He sucked in a deep breath, blew it out, and pressed down on the gas, steadily accelerating, weaving down the two-lane road like a roller coaster picking up speed. The engine sang under the hood as he careened toward Derek, who didn't even realize he'd seen his last sunset.

And his last sunrise.

Will never slowed down as the car ate the road between them, never slowed down as the bumper kissed Derek, plowing him down, and the car rolled over him. He didn't slam on the brakes afterward, but slowed gradually so as to not alert any-one. The car finally rocked to a stop and he backed up, parking short of where Derek's body was.

Will snapped on some gloves, climbed out, and jogged to

where the other man's body lay. His rubber-soled shoes were whisper quiet on the asphalt. His quarry didn't move; the moonlight glimmered off the dark pool growing around his head. Careful to avoid the rapidly growing puddle of blood, Will reached down, checked for a pulse, then smiled in satisfaction when he found none. He stood for a moment longer, waiting to see if the man's chest would rise or fall, but it remained still.

Around him the night was so quiet not even a cricket dared to chirp.

Washing a car at two in the morning was out of the question, so Will parked (far *far* away from the body) and wiped down the bumper and hood with some bleach water and paper towels. Crude maybe, but his cleanup job should, at the least, fool a cop in the dark. Back in the car, Will buckled up and pulled out a disposable cell phone. He sent a quick text message, slipped the SIM card out, and pulled back onto the highway. Once he felt safe enough, he tossed the card out the window, anxious to get to Tucson.

By tomorrow night he'd receive the last half of his fee, putting him that much closer to his retirement goal of ten million dollars (give or take, thanks to the costs associated with shuffling and hiding the money from Uncle Sam).

He was so tired that, by the time he hit the outskirts of Tucson, he could barely see straight, but his work was far from done. He turned off the highway and drove deep into the desert, heading for an old abandoned gas station he'd found while doing recon. He'd left a second car there—a beat-up Ford Escort. A flashlight clutched between his teeth, Will once again went to work scrubbing minute traces of evidence off the Monte Carlo's grill, then wiped down the inside of the car. He was counting on Mother Nature to obliterate his tire tracks as he headed toward Tucson in the Escort.

He parked the poor battered Ford workhorse on the top

level of the parking garage attached to the hotel he'd checked into a week ago. He grabbed the black bag containing his favorite gun and a pair of gloves and crossed to the elevator just as the purple sky was growing streaked with sherbet orange.

Once Will dropped his bag in the Tahoe he'd left parked a few stories down, he headed for the hotel and a well-deserved rest.

He scrubbed at his face, his hands heavy with fatigue. A nice hot shower and couple hours sleep and he'd be back on the road.

Will had just veered south onto the home stretch to El Paso when he spotted the ugly yellow van sitting on the side of the road ahead. At first he thought it was a trick of the sunlight, a figment of his fatigued brain, but as his Tahoe clicked off each tenth of a mile, he realized there was a woman standing next to the van, her skirt blowing in the breeze. He took his foot off the gas, tapping the brake and slowing to sixty.

He didn't trust anyone, not even a woman who *appeared* to be alone, but the manners his mom had instilled in him from a very early age made him pull off the road and back up. He jotted down the plate number, stowed the pen and paper under the arm rest, then shoved a Glock into the back of his pants.

Climbing out, he adjusted his shirt over the gun and assessed the situation. "Need some help?"

With her long skirt and the scarf wrapped around a mass of curly, dark brown hair, she looked like one of those Traveling Irish: modern-day gypsies. They didn't usually travel alone, so he took another long, hard look at the landscape, wondering if it was a trick. Nothing but cactus and sand and shimmering heat in every direction for miles and miles.

"It's just overheated," she said.

"Want me to call a tow truck?" They were roughly thirty minutes outside of El Paso. Definitely close enough for one to come and pick her up (and he'd have done his good deed for the month).

"No." She had her hands tucked in the folds of her skirt, and her white blouse clung to her large breasts. She was pretty but sweaty and so hot her shoulders were bowed by the oppressive heat. She'd been out here a while.

"How about I take a look for you?" he offered, slowly moving closer.

"That's not necessary." The expression on her freckled face seemed wary and guarded as she shuffled from foot to foot. She backed up a bit, and he wondered what she was hiding. Just then a smallish mutt barked from the front seat. Despite his loud mouth, he looked and sounded about as ferocious as Odie from the Garfield cartoon.

"Shut up, Scamp!" She swiped a hand across her forehead and swayed on her feet, grabbing the van for support.

"How long have you been out here?"

"A while." She gave him a limp smile. "You're the first person to stop."

"I've got some water." He slowly moved toward the Tahoe. "Be right back." He got her a bottle of water from the cooler he kept in the back of the SUV, slammed the window shut, and headed toward her, only to find her on the ground.

Still clutching the water bottle, he rushed over, kneeling down on the asphalt, glad he'd worn jeans. He smoothed her hair away from her face, conscious of the constant barking of her dog and the bitter pungent aroma of coolant seeping from the bottom of the van.

He carried her to the air-conditioned comfort of the Tahoe and laid her across the empty back seat. She was pale under her tan, and thick lashes caressed her red cheeks. He dabbed at her face and neck with condensation from the water bottle, breathing a sigh of relief as she finally came around.

"What's your name?" His tongue felt thick and clumsy in his mouth.

"Sabrina . . . Walker." She wet her lips with the tip of her pink tongue and struggled to sit up as the confusion that clouded her eyes dissipated. "What happened?"

"You fainted."

"Oh," she said softly. As if she'd just realized she was alone with him in the back of his Tahoe, miles from anywhere, she drew away and licked her lips. Her eyes were busy searching for a means of escape.

"It's okay." He pressed the open bottle into her hand, then slowly backed away, taking a spot on the edge of the seat so she'd have more room.

"You? What's your name?"

He stuck with what he knew, his brain distracted by her soft, puffy-looking lips. "Roy. Now, how about that ride?"

She sipped at her water, glancing around the SUV again. She finally nodded, slowly and with obvious reservations. "I need my stuff, and my dog."

Sabrina Walker fell somewhere between milk chocolate and café au lait. Her nose was small and puglike in a cute way, her eyes a hazel green rimmed with brown. Her lush lips formed a cupid's bow. He could thank his sister for that obscure bit of description. Sabrina's long dark curly hair was shot through with red and gold—the better to make things interesting. Some might call her plump, but no one would ever call her plain.

Her van was probably shot. He couldn't leave her sitting there on the side of the road to pass out again while waiting for help that might never come. Luckily, she hadn't argued; just grabbed her dog and purse.

He did the only thing he could. He'd loaded her and her

damn dog up in his SUV. He figured he could find a garage in El Paso and buy her a meal while they waited on the tow.

"Why do you keep staring at me?" Her voice was husky, rough and unrefined like her.

He forced his attention back to the road. If he didn't stop staring, she'd jump out, moving vehicle or not. "Just wondering what you were doing out here in the middle of nowhere."

"Driving. You?"

Will laughed as much at her sarcasm as her smarts. She'd definitely been around the block a time or two. "Where you headed?"

"A Ren fair in San Antonio." The dog on her lap pawed at the console that separated them. He wasn't near as cute as she was, so Will frowned at him, hoping he'd stop before he marked up the leather.

"What the hell is a Ren fair?"

"You know, people dress up like knights and barmaids and drink mead and eat turkey legs. I tell fortunes."

"Fortunes." He snorted, thinking he told fortunes, too, but his were probably nowhere near as fun as hers.

"I'm actually pretty good."

"That's why you live in your van?" The words were out of his mouth before he could stop them, proving once again what an insensitive ass he was.

Surprisingly, she didn't rise to his unintentional bait. Just sighed, her fingers curling in her mutt's short hair as she glanced out the window. The Tahoe quickly carried them closer and closer to El Paso. In her lap, the dog whimpered briefly, raised his head, then settled back down as Sabrina stroked him. Her short, utilitarian fingers continued to gently knead as outside the SUV, the desert slowly, finally gave way to humanity.

All the while her silence dug at him, like a knife in his gut. "I'm sorry," he finally blurted out.

"Sorry for what?" She turned to look at him, her big green-ish eyes curious.

"For what I said."

"Huh?" A slight frown puckered her brow. "What did you say?"

Here they went: the passive-aggressive, dog and pony show was on. Sorry was *never* enough. They always wanted more—blood, sweat, tears, your American Express card. Whatever . . . "My comment about living in your van. I'm sorry." *There! He'd said it.*

"Oh, sure." She shrugged in a way that made him want to hit her. Though as a rule he didn't hit women, with any other woman he would have gone three rounds by now. "No problem."

Of course there was a problem. There was always a problem. And *problem* was spelled C-O-O-C-H-I-E. To get a little you had to give—*a lot*. Women were the scorekeepers, the referees, *and* the opponents, and men were expected to know all the rules; except they never let you see the rule book. Maybe he should just drop it for now.

"So what were *you* doing out here in the middle of no-where?" she asked.

"I'm a salesman."

"Wow! Your company must love you." She patted the console, indicating the SUV's luxury package.

"I'm on vacation." Jesus, surely he could lie better than this! He had to get rid of her, and soon.

She was irritating him, getting under his skin with those big eyes and full lips. And those tits . . . He turned the air conditioner on high and shifted in his seat, willing himself to not think about his cock—and her lips. Sabrina was off limits.

All women were.

He had to get rid of her and get back to Oklahoma and find a new place to live. Maybe a monastery. Did they even have monasteries in Oklahoma?